Something to Hide

By

Sheniqua Waters

Something to Hide by Sheniqua Waters

Reissued by TheWorldsBestBook.com

ISBN: 978-0615927350

Thank you for purchasing this book.

This book is dedicated to

George L. Smith

for being a faithful friend

Prologue

Virginia, United States of America – May 1842 A.D.

Lily stepped into the alleyway behind the hotel. Yellow light from the open door illuminated her path. She closed the door behind her then paused briefly unnerved by the darkness that replaced the placid light. Unwilling to risk being late, she headed toward the flurry of noise that wafted to her ears.

At the end of the alleyway, Lily rounded the hotel and viewed the activity along the main street. She took a moment to look at the gray clouds that blanketed the night sky. Then, pulling the edges of her frock together, she lowered her head and began to walk along the boarded walkway. Maneuvering around two people, she set a brisk pace.

As she walked, an image of her husband's blue eyes, thick blonde hair and chiseled chin flashed in her memory. The sound of his deep voice echoed in her mind even as her thoughts turned to the encounter she had with his mother earlier that day. By now, Brock knew her secret. In a few minutes, she would find out if he loved her enough to continue their marriage.

Lily prayed that he would.

A frown creased Lily's lips when she realized the wooden boards beneath her shoes had dissipated and dry leaves now crunched under her feet. Lifting her head, Lily came to a hesitant stop and looked around. Warily, she noticed the collection of white washed buildings had given way to ill-kept structures, the streets had emptied and all noise had ceased. Solicitously, she contemplated returning to the hotel, an eerie foreboding tempting her there.

"Lily!"

Pivoting sharply at the sound of her name, Lily looked at the person who called out to her then let out a relieved sigh. "Syrus! What are you doing here?" she questioned.

"You going to meet Brock?" Syrus asked.

Lily nodded her head as she quickly thought about the note that had been slipped under the door of her hotel room. "Brock sent me a note. He wants to meet at the warehouse down by the river. I'm not sure why he wants to meet there but—"

Without warning, Syrus pushed Lily into the darkened threshold of a nearby door cutting off her words. An instant later, he pulled her against his frame, leaned down and ran his lips possessively over her mouth.

"Sy...Syrus! What...What on earth are you doing?" Lily stammered.

"It's not too late for you to change your mind," he muttered.

"I will never change my mind!" Lily responded and pushed against his chest.

Syrus tightened his hold on her. "You think Brock is better than me, don't you?" he asked irritably.

"I don't have time for this!" Lily asserted and twisted from his grasp.

Hastily, Syrus reached out and seized her arm again. "You shouldn't have married Brock yesterday. Now, you'll live to regret what you've done."

"Let me go!"

"It's not too late to agree to my offer," he insisted.

"Never! Now, for the last time, let me go!" Lily snapped testily.

Syrus' eyes narrowed. He gritted his teeth. "As you wish," he remarked sullenly then dropped his hands to his side.

Turning quickly, Lily sprinted from Syrus and darted across the dirt street. Upon reaching the other side, she glanced over her shoulder and looked back at the darkened doorway.

Syrus was gone.

She was alone.

Telling herself to remain calm, Lily put one foot in front of the other and continued toward the river. As one block turned into another, she willed herself to ignore the murky shadows that distorted into blurs and dissolved under her feet.

The James River came into view.

Lily strained to view the large warehouse by the water. When she spotted it, she broke into a sprint.

The sound of water lapping against the bank met her ears as she neared the warehouse.

She slackened her pace a bit.

Recalling the instructions in the note, Lily rounded the corner of the warehouse and headed down the alley toward the rear entrance.

Her heart exploded in her chest when the caterwaul of a cat pierced the darkness. The shrill screech was immediately followed by the blistering clank of a tin can crashing to the ground.

"Brock!" Lily called into the darkness.

There was no answer.

Eager to find safety in Brock's strong arms, Lily focused on the back door several yards in front of her.

A few more steps.

She was almost there.

Suddenly, a shroud came out of the dark and clamped over her mouth. In a flash, she was yanked into the shadows and hauled against a wall.

Stunned by disbelief, Lily lost her ability to move.

Discerning a man's hand over her mouth, she managed to gather her wits. With a savage grunt, she lifted her foot and kicked the stranger in the groin.

The stranger released her with a calamitous yelp and crumpled forward.

Swiftly, Lily stretched out her legs and leapt forward. However, the stranger recovered quickly and grasped the hem of her frock. The material constricted around her mobilized legs pitching her forward. A panicked groan rived from her throat the moment she hit the ground with a painful thud.

Stripping a long rope from around his waist, the stranger fell to his knees next to her and grappled with her flailing arms. He seized her right arm then managed to grasp her left arm. Swiftly, he looped the rope around her wrists twice then tugged the dangling rope tight.

"Damn mongrel!" he snarled.

Lily jerked her head backward and struck the assailant in the nose.

Instantly, the man released her and reeled backward with a furious curse.

Though her arms were bound, Lily managed to scramble to her feet and began to race down the alley.

"Brock!"

The panicked yell died on her lips as she was tackled from behind and rammed back to the iron hard earth.

Lily wheezed in anguish and unleashed a deafening scream as she was flipped onto her back. Hurriedly, the assailant clasped his large dirty hand over her mouth muffling the sound. When he did, the poignant smell of sweat and musk filled her nose causing her stomach to turn violently. Suddenly, a beam of moonlight seeped from behind a gray cloud oozing dim light into the dark alley. Terror splintered in Lily stifling the scream in her throat the moment the assailant's ghoulish face was revealed.

"Got her!" the loathsome man rasped triumphantly.

Lily gulped down anxiety that rose like bile in her throat when she saw a second man rise out of the dark. The second man, careful to keep his face shrouded in darkness, slowly advanced toward her. As the man neared, he stepped into a patch of moonlight and Lily glimpsed a splotch of crimson colored hair before he melded back into the shadows.

Spurred by the quest for self-preservation, Lily swung her shackled arms wildly and kicked her feet with all her might.

Pressing his oppressive girth on her, the assailant reached in his pocket and a moment later brandished a silver bladed knife. The sharp edge of the weapon caught the moon and glistened with its light.

"This is where the road ends for you wench!" the man hissed and raised the knife above his head.

Lily blinked with trepidation unable to vanquish the fear that threatened to paralyze her. She lifted her head in horrified protest as the knife plunged downward. Tormented by overwhelming terror, Lily's limbs went limp and everything went black.

Chapter One

Four days earlier

Water droplets glistened on Lily's sun-kissed skin as she rose out of the river's pristine blue water and took the towel Brock held out to her.

"Did you enjoy the swim?" Brock asked, leading her to a blanket a few feet away.

"Yes. It was very refreshing," Lily answered as she dried her limbs. "Miss Marla would never approve of me being alone with you like this. If she finds out we didn't stay with the others at the picnic, she'll order me to never see you again," Lily stated then lowered herself onto the blanket.

"Do you always do what Miss Marla orders you to do?" Brock asked after he settled on the blanket next to her.

"Seeing as how she's been like a mother to me, I don't feel I have a choice. Besides, she's the one who taught me how to be a good girl, obviously not like the girls you're used to," Lily retorted as she ran the towel over her chestnut colored hair.

"I must admit, you aren't like any girl I've ever known," Brock chuckled.

Lily smiled and began to blot the water that soaked her clothing.

Brock watched her rub the towel across her chest.

"You enjoy doing it, don't you?" he questioned a moment later.

"Doing what?" Lily inquired.

"Being a tease."

"Wouldn't you like to know," Lily remarked coyly then tossed the towel to the ground.

Suddenly, Brock reached out and placed his hands on her hips.

"What are you doing, Brock Cunningham?" she inquired.

"What does it look like I'm doing, Lily Frasier?" Brock asked.

Before Lily could reply, Brock pulled her against his chest and tightened his arms around her frame. Welding her body to his, he lowered her to the blanket and stretched over her, burying her petite body beneath his brawny one.

The moment Brock's body touched hers, a stinging warmth scorched Lily's cool flesh. When his lips pressed against hers, the warmth flared into a ravenous spark. Audaciously, Brock searched her mouth with his igniting the igneous spark into a captivating flame. Roused into compliance by his touch, Lily parted her lips to his tongue as a wave of intense pleasure coursed through her body.

Daunted by the electrifying sensation, Lily pushed against Brock's chest and peeled her lips from his. "Brock, we shouldn't," she murmured, trying desperately to clear the euphoric haze that clouded her mind.

Brock's response was to place his fingers on her chin and look into her eyes.

"I want you," he whispered then pressed his lips to hers once again.

When Brock's lips touched hers, just as before, a wave of intoxicating pleasure coursed through Lily's veins. Propelled by an unseen force, she entwined her fingers through the golden strands of his hair and moved her lips ardently against his.

When their lips parted, Brock rose onto his elbow. Running his hand over her damp hair, he said, "I don't own a huge plantation with lots of slaves like your father, Philip. But, I've done pretty well managing the horse ranch since my father died. The ranch is starting to make a profit and I've been saving money to buy a pair of thoroughbreds to breed. I was hoping that, and the fact I love you, would be good enough for you to consider allowing me to speak to your father about courting you. What do you say?"

Lily lifted her amber colored eyes to Brock's blue ones and shook her head negatively.

"And why not?" Brock questioned.

"It would do no good since Miss Marla has arranged for me to spend the summer in Boston. I do not want to go. But, Miss Marla says—"

"Miss Marla Jane is your mammy. Not your mother. You don't have to listen to everything she says," Brock cut in.

"She thinks it's a good idea I spend the summer with my aunt," Lily replied.

"Why do you and your father listen to her?"

"Why shouldn't we? My father thinks it's a good idea for me to spend time with his sister."

"The only reason Miss Marla wants you to go to Boston to see your aunt is to keep us apart. Why can't you see that?" Brock inquired.

Lily shook her head. "It's not to keep us apart."

Brock let out a ragged sigh. "I don't understand why you're so blind when it comes to Miss Marla," he remarked.

"I'm not blind to Miss Marla!" Lily hedged and extracting herself from Brock's embrace, sat up.

"Yes you are. And, so is your father. I don't know why your father is so lenient on that woman," Brock grumbled then rose to a sitting position as well.

"Why shouldn't he be?"

"Because she's black and she's a slave."

"I don't see what that has to do with anything!"

"Don't be so naïve, Lily. It has everything to do with it," Brock insisted as a pained expression engulfed his face.

"What's wrong? Talk to me," she prodded.

"My father was betrayed by a black. He was part of a system called The Underground Railroad. He insisted on helping runaway slaves escape North. Some slaves he hid were captured by a group well known for their hatred of blacks called The Klan. One of the slaves told the Klansmen that my father helped them. The Klan came to our cabin one night. Those Klansmen, they beat my father in front of my mother and me. They made us watch as they hung him from a tree. I watched my father die..." As Brock's voice faded, his eyes clouded as if he could see an image of his father's bruised body, bloodied face and twisted neck.

Lily placed her hand over Brock's. "I'm so sorry you and your mother had to see that. I'm sorry that happened to your father," she said sorrowfully.

Brock gritted his teeth. "I learned the hard way blacks are no good and can't be trusted. That includes your precious Miss Marla," he insisted in a low voice. Then, shifting his gaze back to her, he said, "Let's not talk about it anymore. We best get back to the picnic before your father sends Syrus looking for you."

Without further words, Brock rose to his feet and held out his hand.

Lily picked up the dress she had discarded earlier then took Brock's hand.

After he helped her to her feet, she slipped on the dress while Brock picked up his white shirt from the ground and slid it over his broad shoulders. After they redressed, Brock's strong arms circled around her waist and he swept her against the solid wall of his chest. Instinctively, Lily wrapped her arms around his broad shoulders and looked up at him

"No one's going to keep us apart," he stated resolutely.

"But Brock I'm not sure—"

"Don't say anything. Just say you'll be ready when I come by Paradise Plantation to pick you up tomorrow," he commanded gently.

Lily nodded in surrender. "I'll be ready," she said softly.

Brock smiled before picking up the blanket. The couple then began their trek to join the others at the town's picnic.

Amused sounds of gleeful laughter met the couple's ears as they approached the clearing. When they stepped out of the patch of trees, the sight of children frolicking along the bank of the river came into view followed by the sight of young females sitting atop brightly colored blankets diligently watching the youngsters. Several yards away, women sat in the shade of billowing trees eating as they watched the men play sports in the blazing sun. Laughter erupted from the women when a horseshoe whizzed by the feet of two teenagers too deep in conversation to be aware of their surroundings.

"What is going on here?" a stern voice sounded.

Lily looked toward the owner of the voice and saw Brock's mother, Sylvia Cunningham, advancing toward them.

"Hello mother dear," Brock smiled at the blonde haired woman and hugged her when she came to a stop in front of him.

"Hello Mrs. Cunningham," Lily said in greeting.

Ignoring Lily's words, Sylvia looked at her son. "Where have you been?" she queried.

"Lily and I wanted to spend some time alone," Brock replied.

"*She* spent time alone with a male without a chaperone? Why doesn't that come as a surprise to me?" Sylvia questioned and cast a caustic glare at Lily.

Too stunned to retaliate, Lily lowered her eyes. After a moment, she stammered, "I...I think I see Syrus," before retreating from Sylvia's scathing stare.

§

The next evening, as promised, Brock arrived at Paradise Plantation to pick up Lily and the pair headed into town. When the couple arrived at The River Room, a popular tavern in town, it was already crowded. Several friends called out a greeting to Brock and Lily as they made their way to order drinks.

"Brock Cunningham," a sultry voice sounded.

From their places at the counter, Brock and Lily turned in unison to view the owner of the sensuous voice.

Angela Allen, a buxom blonde dressed in a dazzling gold dress, created a stunning vision as she approached the pair.

"Hello, Angela," Brock said in greeting after she came to a graceful stop next to him.

"Hello, Brock," Angela purred as she ran her fingers through her shimmering curls.

"I was just about to order drinks. Do you want something?" Brock inquired.

Angela's lips curved with a seductive smile. "What I want, I can't get behind a counter," she replied as her green eyes longingly roamed Brock's brawny physique.

Brock chuckled lightly. "What *drink* do you want?" he asked.

Angela shrugged her shoulders. "Surprise me," she answered.

Brock turned to Lily. "What do you want?"

"Something I can't get behind a counter either," Lily chimed in.

"What you want, you can get anytime," Brock assured with a wink.

"In that case, I'll take what I always take...tea," Lily smiled.

When Brock turned to order the drinks, Angela looked at Lily and said, "So Lily, I heard you're spending the summer in Boston."

"Yes. I'm going to spend the summer there."

"When do you leave?"

"In a week."

"How long will you be gone?"

"Three months."

"Three months? That's a long time to be away from a good looking man like Brock," Angela ventured and shifting her gaze took a ravenous look at Brock's taut frame.

Brock turned and handed Angela a drink.

"Save me a dance," she purred sweetly before walking away.

After collecting their drinks, Brock led Lily through the knot of patrons until he found two empty chairs.

"I hope you don't mind coming here so often," he said once they were seated.

"I know you like coming here so I don't mind. I like it except for Angela..."

"Flirting with me. She likes me, I know."

"Didn't you used to court her?"

"I did."

"What happened?"

"We got together right after my father died and it didn't work. I was angry and afraid to love. Angela, for her part, tried to make it work. But, it fell apart because I found her to be too manipulative. All of that business is over now. Since I've met you, I've learned to love again. I love your beauty, your innocence and the fact I can trust you. You don't have a cunning bone in your body. You're the perfect woman for me. That's why I'm going to do whatever I can to keep you from leaving for the summer."

Lily lowered her eyes and sipped her drink as she contemplated Brock's words.

The noise in the tavern slackened as musicians meandered onto the stage in the corner of the room.

"Wanna dance?" Brock asked when the musicians began to play a resonant piece of music.

Lily nodded her head, placed her hand in his strong one and let him lead her through the veil of cigar smoke to the dance floor. When she turned to face him, Brock circled his arms around her waist and they began to sway to the music.

Several moments later, Lily lifted her eyes to look at Brock and found him looking down at her with a loving expression on his face. An uncontrollable tingle slithered down her spine.

"Do you have any idea what you do to me?" Brock asked tenderly as he took in the powdery scent of Lily's perfume. "I've come to a conclusion," he declared.

"What conclusion is that?" Lily asked.

"I've come to the conclusion I want to make you mine in every way that counts."

"Brock, you shouldn't say such things. I leave in three days. My father won't go against Miss Marla and Miss Marla will not allow me to—"

Brock placed a finger over her lips silencing her words.

"I don't want to hear about Miss Marla. Just tell me you love me," he prompted.

"I do love you Brock. You are the man of my dreams," Lily admitted.

Upon hearing Lily's words, Brock took Lily's hands in his once again and led her out of the crowded building.

When they stood beside his wagon, he turned to her and said, "There's something I've wanted to do all night."

"What's that?" she asked.

Brock's answer was to sweep her against his chest and passionately cover her lips with his.

Enticed by Brock's hypnotic beckoning, Lily returned his kiss.

When their lips parted, she murmured his name, wrapped her arms around his neck and gazed at him through sultry eyes.

"Don't look at me that way sweetheart or I just might forget I'm a gentleman," Brock warned.

Lily's eyes sparkled with a playful glint and slipping her hands under his shirt she slid the palm of her hand across the taut muscles of his stomach.

"Lily…" Brock's next words drowned into a moan when she lowered her hands to his waist. "You touch me any lower and you may be surprised at what you find," he explained.

Lily smiled and moved her hand lower.

"Temptress!" Brock growled when her hand brushed the front of his trousers.

Lily laughed lightly.

Brock placed his hand on her bottom and fitted her snuggly against his middle. "I want to make love to you. Tell me you want to make love to me," he instructed.

"I do want to make love to you, Brock. I just want to make sure what we have will last. On one hand, I feel our love will last. On the other, Miss Marla and your mother are against us and I wonder if it's possible for us to make it."

"No matter what anyone does or says our love will last. Our love is strong and it will overcome any obstacle that gets in our way. I want you to believe that," Brock whispered.

Lily lifted her hand and touched Brock's cheek. "I will believe it," she promised.

§

A short time later, Brock guided his horse through the iron gates of Paradise Plantation toward the magnificent two story mansion that was Lily's home. The mansion's pristine white brick gleamed in the moonlight as did the giant ivy laden columns spaced at intervals along the massive veranda encircling the house.

As the wagon rolled along the dirt path, Lily lay her head on Brock's shoulder and looked at the tobacco plants undulating in the breeze from the river that flowed behind the mansion.

"I enjoyed being with you tonight. Just as I do every night," Brock said after he stopped the wagon.

"I wish our time together didn't have to end," Lily replied softly as they made their way up the stone steps of the mansion.

"It doesn't have to end. Not if you change your mind about leaving."

"Leaving you is not going to be easy," Lily admitted after they came to stand on the veranda by the front door.

Brock turned to Lily and placing the palm of his hand on the back of her neck he leaned down to kiss her.

Suddenly, the door to the mansion opened and Marla Jane, an attractive woman with brown eyes and chocolate colored skin, appeared in the doorway. Before Brock's lips met Lily's, the woman reached out, grabbed Lily's arm and yanked her into the house.

"Miss Marla!" Lily exclaimed in astonishment as she stumbled over the threshold.

Marla speared Brock with a sharp glare then slammed the door shut before he could speak.

Chapter Two

Syrus' gray eyes focused on Marla and he wrinkled his brow. He shook his head then slammed the palm of his hand on top of the dinner table. "Damn it, Marla! I've had enough of you!" he hissed.

"That's enough!" Philip Frasier snarled.

"No Father! I'm tired of her sticking her nose where it doesn't belong! You can't listen to her! You can't let another one of those buggers purchase their freedom! This is a plantation not a charity!"

"Listen to me, son. We should let the slave do it. After all, we have an obligation to affect people's lives in a positive way," Philip explained from his place across the table.

"People? Don't be ridiculous. They're Africans. Slaves. They're property. Our property. You'd do well to remember that!" Syrus barked.

"That's enough! We must change our ways and do what is right," Philip countered then took a puff on his cigar.

Syrus shook his head. "No! This is not you talking! It's what Marla wants so you're going along with it! Why do you give into the demands of your trouble making—?"

"Syrus!" Philip bit out in an angry tone. "Get a hold of yourself! You know I want Paradise Plantation to be an inheritance for you and Lily to share. But, that does not mean we can't show some compassion to others when it is needed."

"You're too soft-hearted for your own good, Father. You can't let our way of life disappear one slave at a time. You used to listen to me. Now, you listen to Marla as if she were our equal," Syrus complained.

"I do listen to you, Syrus," Philip said then turning to Marla asked, "Isn't that true?"

"Oh forget it!" Syrus bellowed casting a caustic glance at Marla who sat at the end of the table next to Lily.

With an irritated huff, Syrus pushed away from the table and stomped out of the dinning room. He walked to a table in the foyer and picked up the whip he had placed next to a vase filled with wild flowers. He secured the whip to a hook on his belt. Then, taking the stairs two at a time, he marched to his bedroom and strode out onto the second story veranda. Sullenly, he stomped to the rocking chair outside his bedroom door and sank into it.

Pausing a moment, Syrus looked out over the acres of land within his view and saw a smattering of slaves still in the fields. He noted that their dark forms created dull splotches against the pre-dusk light. Shifting his gaze, he looked at two female slaves as they walked toward the track of cold frames located a few yards from the house. Glancing toward the river, he saw a few male slaves idling by the sheds that held the hogsheads.

Settling back in the rocking chair, Syrus began to move the chair back and forth. He closed his eyes and waited while, as they did every evening he sat alone, the tentacles of loneliness spread through him.

Recollecting memories of his past, his thoughts drifted to the day he came to live at Paradise Plantation. After his mother abandoned him, the local minister had persuaded Philip Frasier to take him in to work on the tobacco plantation. Philip had been kind and accepting which helped ease the rejection he felt by his mother's abandonment.

Syrus thought about the many happy days he'd spent working alongside Philip in the fields. Philip had patiently taught him how to plant, weed, tassel and harvest the tobacco. A smile creased Syrus' lips as he remembered the day Philip adopted him. He recalled the feeling of overwhelming pride that had consumed him when he realized he finally had a home and a father to call his own.

Syrus rubbed the handle of the whip latched to his belt as he recalled the day Philip made him overseer of the plantation. It was the whip he had used to keep the slaves in line. The beatings he doled out had been often and harsh, designed to keep the slaves disciplined and the plantation running like a well-oiled machine.

The smile faded from Syrus' face as he recalled the day his dominion over the slaves had been bridled. It had been the evening he whipped a rebellious slave to death. He had rushed to the mansion to inform Philip of the slave's demise. He had charged into Philip's bedroom then abruptly halted when he saw two sweaty bodies drenched in candlelight.

It had been then that he realized the true nature of Philip's relationship with the female slave, Marla Jane. He had confronted Philip about consorting with a Negro. Philip's response had been to explain that since his wife left him and returned to her family in England, he needed companionship.

A short time later, Philip moved Marla into the mansion and gave her run of the place. Almost overnight things changed. Instead of accompanying Syrus in the fields, Philip spent hours behind the closed door of his bedroom with Marla. Once Marla heard of the slave's death, she asked Philip to forbid further beatings. Philip conceded and now, thanks to Marla, the slaves could no longer be whipped. But, despite the mandate, Syrus still wore the whip on his belt because the sight of it still caused the slaves to tremble with fear that he might one day return to using it.

Syrus opened his eyes banishing the weighty memories from his mind. He watched as the last of the sun's ray slipped behind the horizon. Leaning forward, he plucked a half smoked cigar from a tin box on the window sill and placed it between his lips. Then, rearing back, he dug in his pocket and fumbled for a match. Finding a match, he struck it against the arm of the rocking chair.

A sizzle sounded a second before a small flame burst on the end of the thin stick.

A rustling noise followed by Lily's voice met Syrus' ears. He turned his head toward the sound. It was then he noticed the door leading from Lily's bedroom was ajar. Gazing intently, he noticed that the floor length mirror within the well lit room cast a reflection onto the windowpane of the open door. The curtain on the door provided the back drop which allowed him a clear view of the contents in the room. Tilting his head, Syrus focused on the reflection displayed on the windowpane. The reflection was that of

Lily as she walked into her room and began to unbutton her blouse.

Fire burned his fingertips.

Syrus shook his hand and extinguished the flame. He extracted the cigar from his lips and turned his attention back to the open door in time to see Lily peel her blouse from her tanned shoulders.

Syrus looked away afraid he might be seen. A moment later, he realized he was shrouded in darkness. He could see in but she could not see out.

Cautiously, he peered back at the windowpane and watched as Lily nudged the top of her undergarment until her small breasts with their peach centers popped free. Enraptured, Syrus watched as Lily pushed the garment lower. Feasting his gaze on her, Syrus watched as Lily's tiny tapered-to-perfection waist, round bottom and shapely legs were revealed.

Rubbing his chin thoughtfully, Syrus thought back to the day Philip had announced he had a daughter. He remembered Philip explaining that during one of his trips to Europe, he had visited his former wife who had become pregnant and had given birth to his child. Philip explained his former wife wanted the child to be raised in America. So, he sent Marla to England to get the baby girl. When Marla returned to the plantation with the baby, she had been given the job as wet nurse due to the fact she had recently lost her own baby.

As Syrus looked at Lily, he realized he had never thought of her as anything but a scrawny kid...his little sister. Now, however, as he looked at her, he could see she was no longer a little girl. Somehow, over the years, she had grown into a woman...a beautiful woman who was not his biological sibling.

Syrus' eyes widen as oblivious of his presence, Lily turned to face him. As his gaze leisurely roamed her curves his manhood awoke, hardened and strained against his trousers. His gaze followed her graceful movements as she walked to the tub that had been prepared for her bath and lowered herself into it.

Syrus listened to the water rustling as she began to bathe herself.

Quietly...ever so quietly, he raised himself from the rocking chair and like a stealth panther marking its prey, noiselessly crept to Lily's bedroom door. As he drew closer, he saw his reflection in the glass. His tall frame, ruffled red hair, gray eyes and freckled face shown back to him. He ignored the sight of himself and peeked through the crack in the door.

Surrounded by complete darkness, Syrus watched water cascade over Lily's shoulders, slither down her tiny breasts then dangle from her nipples before dripping back into the tub.

Far too soon for his liking, Lily stepped out of the tub, dried herself and picked up a dress lying on her bed. As she slid into the dress, Marla entered the room.

As quick as a flash, Syrus pressed his back against the brick wall of the mansion and held his breath. A second later, he remembered he was shrouded by darkness and could not be seen. Pensively, he peered back into the room and saw Lily pick up a bottle of perfume.

"Brock'll be here any minute," he heard Marla say.

"I'm almost ready," Lily replied after she sat the bottle of perfume next to the lantern on the nightstand by her bed.

"Things are gettin' far too serious between you and Brock. You being with him ain't good. It'll only lead to you gettin' hurt," Marla stated in a crisp tone.

"Why do you keep saying that?" Lily bristled.

"I'm only statin' the truth. You being with Brock is impossible." Marla folded her arms. "You know his mother don't like you. You'll be miserable with her as a part of your life."

"You're just like Sylvia! You're against me and Brock and you'll do whatever you can to keep us apart! That's why you're sending me to Boston for the summer!" Lily accused.

Marla walked to Lily and placed a hand on her arm. "I only want what's best for you. You know that, don't you?" she asked.

Lily did not say a word.

Marla responded by wrapping her arms around Lily in a loving embrace. "Your father and I love you. Listen to me, we only want to protect you," she insisted.

A creak from a wagon wheel sounded drawing Syrus' attention away from the scene in Lily's room. He looked over his shoulder and saw a wagon heading toward the mansion. Upon closer inspection, Syrus realized it was Brock's wagon. He crept to a nearby column and stood behind it.

Noiselessly, he watched the wagon come to a stop in front of the mansion. A second later, he saw Brock jump out of the wagon and jaunt up the steps. Syrus leaned over the edge of the balcony and listened as Brock knocked on the front door. A few seconds later, he heard the door open and Philip's voice bid a hearty greeting. Then, the door closed suppressing further sound.

Syrus trod back to his place outside of Lily's room and looked inside. It was empty. Restlessly, he returned to his place at the edge of the balcony, leaned against a massive column and crossing his legs at the ankle, waited.

Several minutes later, the front door reopened and Brock's voice sounded. "I promise to take good care of your daughter, Mister Frasier. I'll have her back home at a decent hour," he stated.

"Don't be late!" Marla's voice called out a moment before the door clicked shut.

A second later, Brock and Lily appeared beneath the balcony. Suddenly the couple came to a stop and Brock leaned down and placed his lips on Lily's lips. Syrus shifted on his feet and moved to grip the railing. Jealousy oozed through him as he watched Lily surrender to Brock's kiss.

From his place in the shadows, Syrus watched the couple end their kiss and walk hand in hand to Brock's wagon then climb inside. He watched the couple as they drove toward the gates of Paradise. He watched until the lovers were swallowed up by the night.

Chapter Three

Lily slowly traced the outline of her lips as she recalled the feel of Brock's lips touching hers. She thought about the feel of his fingers earlier that night as he conquered the buttons of her blouse. Closing her eyes, she remembered him sliding her blouse off her shoulders and placing his lips where the silk had been.

"Make love to me," he had whispered.

Lily recalled wanting to succumb to the tantalizing torment Brock's kiss aroused in her. But, in the end, Marla's words had echoed in her mind and she pushed away from him.

Lily opened her eyes as she remembered the betrayed look that surfaced in Brock's eyes when she insisted she had to go to Boston. She thought about the months she would be away from him and her heart ached at the thought. In that moment, she couldn't imagine leaving him even for a night.

Despondently, she turned down the flame that flickered in the lantern on the nightstand beside her bed and climbed under the covers. As she settled on her back, she glanced toward the door that led to the veranda. She gasped with fright when she saw a man standing in the threshold.

The male, drenched in shadows, stepped into her room. When he did, moonlight illuminated his face and his crimson colored hair glimmered in the silver light.

"Syrus! What are you doing standing there? You scared me!" Lily scolded when she recognized it was he who stood in the doorway.

"How was your evening with Brock?" Syrus asked after he came to stand by her bed.

Lily rose to a sitting position. "He wants me to stay in town for the summer. He's upset that I can't."

"Marla won't let you stay."

"Brock doesn't understand."

"You don't need Brock."

"Brock is a wonderful man who—"

"Who will forget about you once you're gone."

"Brock will not forget about me," Lily contended.

"Marla thinks he will. That's why she wants to get you away from him," Syrus persisted.

Seeing the disgruntled look on Lily's face, Syrus sucked in a ragged breath and said, "You females are all the same. You go for a man like Brock with rugged good looks and you refuse to give a second thought to a man like me who may not be handsome or eloquently spoken."

"Syrus, I know you want to protect me. I know that as my brother—"

"I'm not your brother!" Syrus bit out in a strident tone.

Upon hearing Syrus' tone, confusion wrinkled Lily's brow.

Noting Lily's reaction, Syrus softened his voice. "What I'm trying to say is, I'm not your brother, Lily. I'm a man with feelings just like any other man."

Syrus let his eyes scan Lily's delicate frame.

Apprehensively, Lily pulled the covers to her chest. "What...What do you mean?" she stammered.

Reaching out, Syrus placed his hand over hers. In a low voice, he said, "This may come as a surprise to you. But, since you and I are not really related, I can tell you, I find you very attractive. I'm not your brother and there's no reason we can't—"

"What are you talking about?"

Syrus clutched her shoulders. "You are a beautiful woman, Lily. A woman who I could easily love."

"Syrus!" Lily jerked away from him. "I don't know what's come over you! You're my brother! There's no way anything can ever happen between us!"

"I'm not your brother!" Syrus snapped then tightening his grip he leaned inward and pressed his lips to hers.

Lily groaned in protest and pushed against his chest.

"Your kisses are warm and inviting for Brock. Why can't they be that way for me?" Syrus rasped.

"Let me go, Syrus!" Lily shrieked.

"Just think about what I've said."

"Get out of my room!" Lily screeched, slapping his hands from her skin.

Syrus moved to touch her again.

She cringed.

Syrus' eyes filled with hurt. Slowly, he stood to his feet.

"Get out now!" Lily ordered tersely.

For several moments, Syrus did not move from where he stood. Then, suddenly, without uttering another word, he spun on his heels and disappeared from the room as mysteriously as he had come.

§

Everyone would be sleep now. Marla Jane was sure of it. She sat up in her bed and breathed deeply taking in the fresh breeze that wafted into the room and ruffled the curtains. She peered toward the open door that led to the veranda and gazed at the moon stained river, illuminated like a bed of liquid gold.

Purposefully, she swung her legs over the side of her bed and inhaled sharply when the cold wood floor met her feet. After a moment's hesitation, she stood, walked to her bedroom door and opened it. Pausing a moment, she listened to the serene silence that saturated the house.

Peering down the hall, Marla confirmed that no lights showed beneath any of the bedroom doors. Quickly, she stepped into the hallway and looked toward Lily's room. She had to ensure Lily was asleep before she made it to Philip's room.

Pausing outside Lily's bedroom, Marla thought about how she had come to be standing where she was. It was because of the proposal she'd made to Philip. A necessary proposal made to secure a better life for her child.

Marla thought back to the time she had worked as a slave in the field just beyond the mansion's walls. A few months after Philip's wife left him to return to her homeland of England, he showed up at her cabin drunk demanding she share his bed. However, he had passed out before he could act upon his demand.

The next morning, after he sobered, a contrite Philip had been apologetic for his actions. However, she had not accepted his apology. Instead, she spurned his advances.

27

He pursued her until finally, one balmy summer night, when she realized she loved him, she relented and they made love.

Shortly afterward, Philip moved her into the mansion to work as the housekeeper. She had enjoyed taking care of him and tried unsuccessfully to befriend his adopted son Syrus.

When she realized she was going to have a baby, she had not been sure how Philip would react. But, to her relief, he had been overjoyed and they both anxiously awaited the birth of their child.

The baby was born. When the midwife placed the baby in her arms and she viewed the tiny girl's glowing white skin, she cried. Though Philip was the baby's father, never had she expected her baby to be anything but black. She never expected to be confronted with the fact her child could pass for a white person.

Marla recalled her experience prior to being sold to Philip. She had experienced extreme prejudice, irrational hatred and had been treated as less than human all because she was black. Marla knew if anyone found out she was her baby's mother, her baby would be stigmatized and branded an outcast. She did not want that and knew, no matter what the cost, she had to protect her child from such torment.

After anguished consideration, one solution became clear.

She made her proposal to Philip. He had protested at first. But, after Marla reminded him of her own painful experiences, he had relented. Marla lowered her eyes as she recalled Philip saying he loved her and would agree to her plan.

That had been years ago and somehow the lie she concocted had been believed. As she'd wished, her daughter had grown up ignorant of the truth. Because of her proposal, her daughter had been treated with all of the advantages of living in society as a white...of being Philip's legitimate daughter.

A bitter smile curled across Marla's lips. Due to her difficult choice all those years ago, her child had never known the degradation of bigotry. Her child had never experienced prejudice. No. Never had Lily known the heartache of hatred.

And for that, Marla was truly grateful.

§

Lily sat in her large four poster bed staring in shock at the door that led to the veranda. Rattled by Syrus' appearance and deciding to demand an apology, Lily kicked the covers from her, climbed out of her bed and traipsed to the open door. She took one step onto the veranda and a hand clasped over her mouth. A scream died in her throat when a comforting arm circled her waist and a kiss grazed her neck. Instinctively knowing who it was, she relaxed and the hand was removed from her mouth. She turned to see Brock smiling down at her.

Forgetting about Syrus, Lily rose to the tips of her toes and wrapped her arms around his neck. "Brock, how'd you get up here?" she questioned.

"I climbed up a column via some vines," he answered, placing his hands on her hips.

"What are you doing here?"

"I didn't like the way things ended between us tonight. I had to see you again."

"Oh baby..."

"Don't go to Boston, sweetheart. Stay," Brock pleaded gently. "I want you here with me. I love you." Brock leaned down and tenderly kissed her lips.

"Brock, why do you insist on making this hard?"

"I don't want it to be an easy choice for you to step out of my life. I want you to stay."

"Oh darling..."

"Say you won't leave."

"I wish I could. But, the ticket has already been bought. I have to leave."

"You don't have to do anything you don't want to do, Lily, and I'll do everything I can to convince you of that. Let me show you how much I love you," Brock stated and fitted her firmly against his middle.

As Lily looked into Brock's blue eyes a prurient shiver trickled down her spine. She remembered the wanton look Angela had given Brock and thought about Angela's remark that three months was a long time to be away from him. Suddenly, the thought of being apart from him seemed too much to bear and the reasons she had for leaving him seemed unimportant. At that moment, all she wanted to do was show him just how much she loved and cared for him.

"I love you, Brock," she whispered. Then, taking his hand, she guided him into her room and to her bed.

A twinge of shyness fluttered in Lily when she turned to face him. But, the moment her eyes reconnected with his smoldering stare, her confidence soared and she hurriedly unclasped all of the buttons on her nightgown.

Lily pulled her gown over her head and tossed it to the ground.

A groan rumbled in Brock's throat as he viewed her supple breasts. He reached out and let his broad hands graze them before he rubbed his hand over her waist and along the length of her thighs. Never taking his eyes from hers, Brock freed himself of his shirt and trousers.

Lily's eyes widened at the sight of his hardened member jutting out like a flesh colored monument. Her amazement grew when Brock clasped her waist and swept her against his rigid member.

In the next moment, their lips met in a passionate kiss and they fell on the bed.

When Brock's shaft burned the inside of her thigh with its heat, Lily knew she should put a stop to it. When his tongue captured her nipple, she knew she should protest. And, when Brock's fingers found their way between her silken folds, she knew she was going against all of Marla's well laid plans. But, at the moment, she didn't care. All that mattered was Brock and the fact she wanted to be with him. To confirm this, she pressed her thighs against his and he responded by stroking her maidenhead.

"Don't stop. Please don't stop," Lily implored breathlessly when he pulled his hand away.

Brock complied with Lily's request by replacing his hand with his tongue. Zealously, he lapped the dew of her essence causing her maiden head to throb with want. With each stroke of his tongue, Brock intensified the amorous yearning within Lily until her moans evaporated into a blissful cry. She closed her eyes as her insides exploded into a cascade of delirious sensation.

Slowly, the sensation subsided and Lily managed to raise her eyes to look at Brock. When she did, she saw him gazing at her with a pleased smile on his face. He moved to lie on his back then motioned for her to straddle him. Lily's eyes widened when she realized what he wanted.

"Are you sure?" she inquired.

"My love, I've never been more sure of anything in my life," he stated.

Rising to her knees, Lily positioned herself over him. Brock's massive hands clasped her waist and he guided her hips downward. Lily inhaled sharply as she felt herself being filled by his magnificent girth. When she was completely engulfed by him, to her wonderment, he began to move his massive hands causing her hips to glide back and forth.

"That's it," he affirmed once she found a rhythm of her own.

With her still connected to him, he flipped her so she lay on her back. Lily let out a gasp as he brazenly thrust himself into her. Instinctively, she arched her hips to him. He grunted and drove his shaft deep into her depths again. Over and over again, he seared her insides with his rigid member.

Lily fought to keep quiet in response to the scorching onslaught. But her efforts were futile as a wave of pleasure began to ravage her body. Brock's mouth covered hers muffling her scream and she felt him shutter in release as her insides erupted in ecstasy once again.

Suddenly, a noise reverberated from the hallway.

Lily realized it was the sound of Marla's bedroom door opening and closing. A moment later, footsteps sounded in the hallway and stopped outside her door.

Lily arched her eyebrow and looked at Brock.

Brock extracted himself from her and lay beside her on the bed. Quickly, Lily pulled the bed covering over him and brought it to her throat.

The door creaked as it started to open.

Lily closed her eyes and lay still as the bedroom door swung open. Instinctively, she knew it was Marla in the doorway and prayed the housekeeper would not look too closely at the bulge in the bed beside her. She also prayed Brock would stay completely still.

After a few moments, she heard Marla step back into the hallway and close the door. The sound of Marla's fading footsteps echoed through the walls as hot liquid began to trickle between Lily's thighs.

Brock pushed back the covers, picked up his shirt off of the floor and began to wipe between Lily's legs.

"You're amazing." He smiled.

"That was Miss Marla! That was a close call!"

"But it was worth it baby."

"I can't wait until the summer is over because I'm going to miss this when I'm gone," Lily uttered wistfully.

To that, Brock didn't say a word. Instead, he nestled his chin in her hair and breathe in her powdery scent.

There was silence between them.

Finally, Brock spoke. "Your leaving is not something I want to think about. Too much can happen if we are apart," he added after a moment.

"But Marla won't change her mind," Lily affirmed.

"Marry me," Brock responded.

"What?" Lily gasped.

"You heard me. I said marry me. I want you to be my wife. I want to wake up every morning with you in my bed."

"Brock! I can't believe this!"

"I know you're worried about there being so much going against us. But, our love is strong. It can withstand anything. If we stay together we can overcome any obstacle. Say you don't mind being married to a rancher. Say you'll be my wife."

"Brock! You know I don't mind being the wife of a rancher! And, I do want to be your wife!" Lily squealed delightedly and placed her hands on either side of Brock's cheek.

Brock nuzzled his nose against hers and she kissed his lips.

"I want to build a life with you, Lily. I love you more than words can say. Say you love me. Promise me you'll never leave me."

Lily gazed lovingly at Brock. "I love you Brock and I'll never leave you," she promised with a smile.

§

Standing on the veranda, Syrus placed his hand on the window pane and peered into Lily's room. He had heard Brock's voice and had come to investigate. He had observed the couple make love the first time and even saw Marla look in the room. After she walked away, Syrus remained standing where he was and watched for the second time that night as Lily straddled Brock and began to move her hips. He watched Brock reach out and cup Lily's breasts in his hand. He saw Lily respond by tossing her head back and moving her hips faster.

As Syrus stared at the couple, his imagination ignited and for a few toxic minutes it was he not Brock who caressed Lily's skin. He not Brock who ran his hands through her chestnut colored hair. He who lay her on the bed and nudged her knees apart. He who settled between her thighs. He not Brock who mounted her and explored her treasure.

Syrus clutched his hand into a fist as he viewed Brock's virile form splayed atop Lily. Succumbing to the animus within, he vowed to find a way to take Brock's place.

No matter what it took, Syrus pledged, it would be he not Brock who kissed Lily's luscious lips. He not Brock who caressed Lily's soft skin. He not Brock in Lily's bed.

§

"You look beautiful," Brock told Lily when he arrived to see her the next day. "Is anyone else here?" he asked after he stepped into the house.

"No one's here," Lily replied.

"What about Miss Marla?"

"No. She's not here. I'm alone," Lily informed him.

"That's good Mrs. Brock Cunningham." Brock grinned then reached down and scooped her into his massive arms.

Lily wrapped her arms around his neck. "We're not married yet," she giggled playfully.

"But we will be."

"We have to tell my father and Miss Marla."

"We will tell them. However, since she's alone, I thought it fitting we tell my mother first," Brock revealed.

"Tell your mother?" Suddenly, Lily wasn't feeling so playful.

"I know you're worried about my mother. She can be a bit protective, I know. But she's a good woman and I love her."

"A bit protective? Is that what you call it?" Lily questioned.

"I talked to her and I think she's going to try and accept our relationship. After I told her I proposed to you, she asked me to bring you to her house for dinner."

"Really?" Lily wondered aloud as she quickly thought about the animosity Sylvia had shown her. She wasn't sure why Brock's mother disliked her. But, there was no mistaking that fact.

"One dinner is not going to change the way your mother feels about me," Lily proclaimed as Brock carried her up the stairs to her room.

"Don't worry. Mother will love you once she gets to know you," Brock assured. "How could she not see you're perfect for me?" he added after seeing the skeptical look on Lily's face.

Lily frowned.

"I think I can find a way to help you relax before dinner," Brock said after he entered her room and dumped her onto the fluffy white covering on her bed.

"How?" Lily questioned.

Brock reached out and gave her breast a playful squeeze.

Lily swatted his hand away. "Put your hands to use and go get me a glass of water," she ordered.

"All right my love," Brock consented then headed for the door. "Don't have anything on when I get back," he called over his shoulder before he stepped out of the room and closed the door behind him.

After exiting Lily's room, Brock made his way down the quiet hallway and down the stairs. After he poured a glass of water for Lily, he headed back up the stairs. As he retraced his steps down the hall, he came upon an open door and glanced inside the room. The bedroom was a large room filled with masculine furnishings. Instinctively, Brock knew the room belonged to Lily's father.

Continuing down the hall, he came to another bedroom and noticed the door ajar. Brock halted his steps and looked inside. The room was slightly smaller than the first and contained a huge bed that had a dress lying across it. Two large doors were opened on the opposite side of the room allowing a cool breeze from the river to waft into the room.

"What do you think you're doing?" a caustic voice rumbled.

Brock turned to the speaker of the voice and saw Syrus standing at the top of the stairs.

"I'm here to see—"

"Lily," Syrus finished the sentence for him.

"I was under the impression the house was empty," Brock responded as Syrus walked to him.

"Well it's not empty anymore. And, it's not appropriate for you to be in this house alone with Lily," Syrus retorted and came to a stop next to Brock.

"I love your sister. I've asked her to marry me," Brock revealed, hoping to ease the unexplained tension in the air.

"You what!" Syrus bellowed angrily.

"Syrus, I thought you'd be happy about Lily and I? Your father has been kind to me ever since I lost my father. Once Lily and I are married, I was hoping it could be like we're both Philip's sons."

"I'm Philip's son! He doesn't need another one!" Syrus snapped.

Brock arched his eyebrows in response to the venom in Syrus' tone. "I have no intention of coming between you and Philip. I just thought that since you're Lily's brother—"

"Lily and I are not related by blood," Syrus cut in hastily.

"What I'm trying to say is, I'm happy I'm going to become a part of your family and I want you to know I plan on spending the rest of my life loving Lily."

Syrus shifted on his feet. "We shall see," he mumbled cryptically.

Brock frowned. "Is something wrong?" he asked.

Syrus waved his hands dismissively then drawled, "Nothing's wrong."

Brock nodded curtly then presenting his back to Syrus continued down the hallway.

Taking a pertinacious stance, Syrus watched Brock walk to Lily's bedroom door and open it. Instantaneously, Brock's frame became a dark silhouette against the incandescent light emanating from the bedroom. A second later, Brock swung the door wide to step into the room.

It was then that the contents of the room became visible to Syrus. Looking into the room, he saw Lily lying completely nude atop her bed. Her tawny skin a striking vision splayed amongst the bedding.

Drawn by an enticement he couldn't ignore, Syrus let his eyes roam Lily's curvy figure. Leisurely, he took in the sight of her succulent breasts, rounded hips and firm bottom. Tantalized by what he saw, his member stretched against his trousers.

As if feeling his gaze on her, Lily looked over Brock's shoulder and into the hallway. Her eyes locked with his and instantly flooded with horror. Syrus opened his mouth to utter a response. But, unaware of what had taken place, Brock stepped into the room and shut the door cutting off Syrus' view and leaving him alone in the hallway.

Chapter Four

Lily shot straight up in bed.

"Oh my God!" she shrieked and swept the bedding around her.

"What's wrong?" Brock questioned as he sat the cup of water on the nightstand by her bed.

Lily leapt to her feet. "We can't do this!" she screeched. Reeling from the sight of Syrus leering at her, but not wanting to tell Brock, she busied herself by collecting her discarded clothing.

Brock clutched Lily's wrist to stop her movement. "What's wrong?"

"We can't make love…not in this house." Lily pulled away from his grasp.

"Why not?" Brock frowned.

"Because it's not honorable until we're married. I don't want what we have to be cheap and sordid," Lily replied as she began to redress.

"Cheap and sordid? With us, that could never be," Brock assured and pulled her back to him. His large hand touched her throat and his fingers caressed the nape of her neck.

Summoning her strength, Lily managed to push away from him again.

"Damn it girl," Brock grumbled and dragged her back into his embrace.

"Brock!" she exclaimed in dissent when he began to unbutton the buttons on her blouse.

"Ssshh…" he ordered and slid the blouse off Lily's shoulder. Reaching out, he tenderly fondled her right breast then popped it into his mouth.

The feel of Brock's lips on her skin sent exotic chills rolling like hot waves through Lily's body. "No Brock…no…" she managed to mumble, amazed to realize her hands, as if controlled by a mind of their own, were running up and down his broad back.

"I can't help myself. You have that affect on me," Brock whispered.

"Brock we can't…We have to stop or my reputation will be ruined." Lily's words slurred into a gulp and somehow didn't sound as forceful as she planned.

"Your reputation is safe with me," Brock assured and flicked the point of her nipple with his tongue.

Unable to resist Brock's touch, Lily tossed her head back. Banishing thoughts about the look she had seen in Syrus' eyes, she sighed. "I'm so happy I'm going to be your wife," she mumbled.

§

The sun shone warmly and a cool breeze caressed Brock and Lily's faces as they rode to Sylvia Cunningham's home late that afternoon.

"Are you sure she wants to see me?" Lily asked again.

"Yes. Mother'll love you. Don't worry." Brock smiled encouragingly.

"Why doesn't your mother live in the cabin with you?" Lily asked after they came to a stop in front of Sylvia's cabin which was some distance from the cabin where Brock lived.

"After Father died, Mother didn't want to live in our cabin. She said it had too many painful memories. So, I built her a cabin on the edge of our property so she has her own place. It's worked out well because I have my space yet she's not far away." Shifting his gaze, Brock said, "Look, there's Mother over there!"

Lily followed Brock's gaze to see Sylvia standing over a fire pit. Delicious smelling smoke drifted toward them as they walked to where she stood.

"You're late," she said to Brock as he hugged her.

"We got involved in something."

"I'm sure I can guess what that something was," Sylvia ventured after she broke from Brock's embrace.

"Mother, have you forgotten your manners?" Brock asked.

"Nice to see you again Lily," Sylvia managed a greeting then added, "I don't see my son much since he started courting you."

"The meat looks good," Brock noted, ignoring his mother's complaint.

"It smells good," Lily stated, deciding she would be on her best behavior for Brock's sake.

"I sat a table on the porch. Go have a seat," Sylvia instructed.

Following Sylvia's instructions, Brock and Lily walked to the porch and took a seat at the table. A short time later, Sylvia brought a platter of meat and sat it before them. After which, Brock took charge of carving the meat while Sylvia served the mashed potatoes, candied yams and garden grown greens.

After the food was served, the trio began to eat.

Brock and his mother talked easily to one another. Not wanting Lily to feel left out, Brock asked questions to include her in the conversation. Encouraged by Brock's effort, Lily chimed in as much as possible.

As the trio finished their meal, the conversation turned to Brock's father and then to stories they'd heard about the activities in neighboring towns by The Klan.

"The Klan is a god forsaken bunch who can be very brutal," Brock stated with a frown.

"Black's in this town should consider themselves fortunate. There's been no real problem with The Klan for a long time. But, from what I've heard, The Klan's activities are becoming more and more coordinated. It's said that members of The Klan may form an official organization. If that happens and if The Klan ever shows up in this town again the Negros will be in trouble," Sylvia opined.

"Brock told me about how he lost his father to The Klan," Lily said.

Suddenly, tears sprang into Sylvia's eyes. "Brock's father was murdered for helping those ignorant Negro slaves. He shouldn't have been killed. I miss him so much." Sylvia clutched her hand into a fist. Looking at Brock, she croaked, "I couldn't survive if anything ever happened to you, son. You're all I have left." She brushed away a tear that threatened to escape between her lashes and cleared her throat. "I'd...I'd better clean the dishes."

"I'll get the dishes for you," Lily stated when Sylvia started to rise to her feet.

Sylvia settled back in her chair with a nod.

Lily quickly collected the dirty plates and walked into Sylvia's cabin.

"You didn't say when the wedding was going to take place," Sylvia said to Brock once they were alone.

"We haven't discussed it yet. I just proposed last night."

"You should think about a long engagement. You don't want to rush things."

"I'll do whatever Lily wants."

Sylvia rolled her eyes.

"Mother, stop acting like that. Don't treat Lily like you've treated the others you didn't like."

"All I've ever done, I did for you."

"Just know I'm in love with Lily."

"In love with Lily or what's between her—"

"Hold your tongue!" Brock ordered.

"I thought you were interested in Angela Allen. I like her. She's a strong woman who knows her mind. She comes from a proper family. You'd do good to reconsider her," Sylvia remarked.

"Angela and I are two different people. We had our time. It didn't work. Marrying Lily is my decision."

"Your mistake you mean."

"Mother!" Brock snapped irritably. "I'm going to be with Lily. She is going to be your daughter-in-law. I suggest you accept that and work on getting to know her."

Sylvia gritted her teeth.

"Mother, please be civil. Once you make an effort to get to know Lily, you will like her. You'll see," Brock assured.

§

Setting down the plate she held in her hand, Lily looked at Sylvia as she walked into the room and came to stand beside her. "Dinner was delicious," she ventured.

Sylvia's reply was a grunt.

In the next moment, Brock's voice echoed through the cabin as he called Lily's name from where he sat on the porch.

"I have to go to him," Lily said to Sylvia and turned toward the door.

Suddenly, Sylvia reached out and clutched Lily's wrist halting her exit.

Lily raised surprised eyes to Sylvia.

Locking eyes with Lily, Sylvia hissed, "Stay away from my son. Brock's got his whole future in front of him. He needs to remain respected in this town."

"Mrs. Cunningham, I...I don't understand what you are talking about. I...I don't understand," Lily stammered, taken aback by the woman's words and petulant tone.

Sylvia's eyes narrowed into thin slits. "You stole my son from Angela. You did it to gain respect. You did it so you could pass for something you're not. But, I know what you are. I know who your mother is and I know what goes on in that house."

"My mother? What goes on in our house? What are you talking about?"

Sylvia dug her sharp nails into Lily's skin. "You will not marry my son. I won't let you. You're going to call off this wedding. Call it off! You hear me?"

"What?"

"If I could do it without hurting Brock, I would tell him what you are. Unfortunately, the more I try to tell him about you, the angrier he gets at me. I don't want to be the one who breaks his heart. But, I will tell Brock the truth if I'm forced to. So I suggest you do it. Call off the wedding because I know your secrets."

"What are you talking about?"

"Philip's wife and I were good friends when she lived in the States. We reconnected through letters not too long ago. In her letter, she wrote that she's never birthed a child for Philip. She said she never saw Marla in Europe. That's when I figured out the truth. So, if you know what's good for you, you'll call off this wedding."

41

"Mrs. Cunningham, I don't know what you're talking about. All I know is Brock and I are getting married," Lily stated firmly.

Sylvia grunted with irritation. "You're smug because you think my son loves you. Unlucky for you, I know what's going on between Marla and Philip. And, I know what's going on between you and Syrus. Once my son knows how you live...once he knows your secrets, he's not going to want you anymore."

"How I live? My secrets? I don't know what you're talking about."

"Save it Lily! My son is all I have left and I will do what I have to do to protect him! You're going to break it off with him if for no other reason than you can't be faithful to him! Your kind can never be! Your mother is a whore and you're going to turn out just like her! I will not have my son shamed by a half-breed Negro like you!"

Lily stared at Sylvia in stunned silence. "What did you say?" she asked when she managed to find her voice.

"You heard me, you mulatto mutt!" Sylvia spat.

"Lily? Did you hear me call you?" Brock appeared in the doorway.

Instantly, Sylvia released her hold on Lily and spun around to face her son.

"What the hell is going on here?" Brock questioned immediately aware of the tension that saturated the room. "Mother?" he looked at his mother. "Lily, what is it?" he demanded when he saw a tear roll from Lily's eye.

As her reply, Lily lowered her eyes then darted past him and ran from the cabin.

Brock shot his mother a menacing glare then turned his back to her and followed Lily.

"Take me home," Lily managed to say when she heard Brock's footsteps behind her.

"Lily, what happened in there? Talk to me," Brock prodded as she scrambled into his buggy. "Tell me what's wrong," he demanded after he jumped in the buggy and sat next to her.

"I don't want to talk about it!" Lily declared angrily.

"Sweetie, tell me. What did my mother say to upset you? What did she do?" Brock demanded.

"Your mother hates me! She said some horrible things to me! What she said is not true! It's impossible! She even said some horrible things about my mother!" Lily blurted out.

"Oh no," Brock groaned. "Don't worry. I'll take care of this." Brock started to rise from his seat.

Lily reached out and clutched his arm, stopping his exit. "No! Just take me home. Now!" she ordered fractiously.

Brock hesitated a moment, then, following her request, he sank back on the wooden seat and gathered the reins. Without a word, he guided his horse in the direction of Paradise Plantation.

§

Tears streamed down Lily's face as she raced up the steps of the mansion. Sylvia's words echoed in her mind as she searched the house for her father. *I will not have my son shamed by a half-breed Negro like you!* Half-breed? Negro? What was Sylvia talking about? Why would Brock's mother say such things?

You think my son loves you! Once he knows your secrets, he's not going to want you anymore! You can't be faithful to my son! Your kind could never be!

Lily shook her head to clear the thoughts from her mind. It was all so confusing. She loved Brock and would never be unfaithful to him. Why couldn't Sylvia see that?

Your mother is a whore and you're going to turn out just like her! What did Sylvia mean by that? Her mother had abandoned her father and moved to England. Sylvia said she was friends with her mother. So, why would she call her mother a whore?

"Father! Tell me the truth!" Lily demanded when she spotted him in the drawing room and hastened to him.

"What is it my dear?" Philip looked up from the newspaper he held in his hand. Concern wrinkled his brow when he saw tears run down Lily's face. Laying the

43

newspaper aside, Philip rose to his feet and reached for his daughter.

Lily stepped away from him.

"Who is my mother?" she questioned curtly.

"What?"

"You heard me!"

"Your mother? You know the answer to that question."

"What's her name?" Lily shouted cantankerously and stomped her foot.

"Your mother is my former wife. You know that," Philip replied nervously as he ran his hand through his graying hair.

"No Father! Tell me the truth!" Lily demanded impatiently.

"Why do you not think that is the truth?" Philip wanted to know.

"Sylvia Cunningham told me! She said some horrible things about my mother! She doesn't want me to marry Brock because of it!"

"Oh no," Philip groaned.

"She called me a half-breed Negro! She threatened to tell Brock if I don't break it off with him!" Lily explained.

"Daughter, let's discuss this later tonight. When Miss Marla comes back, I'll have her warm some tea for you and—"

"I don't want any tea! I want answers!" Lily yelled petulantly.

"Don't speak to me with that tone," Philip commanded stiffly.

Lily lowered her head and began to cry.

"Dear God. Daughter, please don't be upset," Philip pulled his daughter into his arms.

"Sylvia Cunningham thinks I'm a Negro...a mulatto. How can I not be upset?" Lily sobbed.

Philip patted Lily's back. "Precious child, don't cry. Dear God. I knew this day would come. Look sweetie. Go to Marla. She's down at the slave quarters tending the sick. Go to her. She will explain," he instructed wearily.

Turning swiftly, Lily retraced her previous route and ran down the steps of the mansion. She wiped the tears from her face as she took the sunlit path to the slave quarters. Eying the stone cabins, she scurried toward them. As she neared the slave cabins, she saw Syrus standing under a tree talking to a female slave.

"Syrus!" she called to him.

"Lily, what are you doing here?" he questioned when he saw her.

"Where is Miss Marla?" Lily asked anxiously.

"Why? What is it? You look upset," Syrus noted.

"Just tell me where she is!" Lily ordered.

Syrus nodded his head to a nearby cabin. "She's in there," he answered.

Brusquely, Lily turned from him and rushed to the cabin. Once there, she opened the cabin door and stepped inside. As her eyes adjusted to the light, she noticed a sleeping child lying on a bunk on one side of the room.

Marla was on the other side of the room standing next to a large stone fireplace. "Lily, what you doin' here?" she asked with a smile.

"I've just come from dinner with Brock and his mother," Lily answered stiffly.

Marla's smile faded to a frown. "Oh yes. How was dinner?" she inquired.

"Sylvia Cunningham hates me. She said some horrible things to me. She told me to end things with Brock."

"That meddlin' she-devil!" Marla hissed.

Locking eyes with Marla, Lily asked. "Who is my mother?"

"What?" Marla began to wring her hands nervously.

"You heard me!" Lily snapped.

Marla turned from Lily.

"Sylvia Cunningham called me a half-breed Negro!"

Marls spun around to face Lily. "That bitch!"

"Father told me you would explain."

Marla shook her head. "That's enough. I don't wanna talk about this."

"What's going on between you and Father? What are the two of you hiding from me? Tell me what Sylvia Cunningham is talking about!"

Marla rubbed her forehead apprehensively. "Things are gettin' too troubled..."

"Who is my mother? I want to know! I have a right to know!" Lily yelled.

"You don't need this stress. You're set to leave for Boston. Just go to Boston and forget this mess."

"I'm not going to Boston! I'm staying here and I'm going to find out what Sylvia meant when she implied things about my mother! Sylvia said Father's former wife never had a child! She said his wife never saw you in England!"

"Sylvia doesn't know what she's talking about. She's nothing but a judgmental—"

"Tell me the truth!"

"There's nothin' to tell."

"You don't want to tell me the truth! Fine! I'll find it out on my own!" Pivoting poignantly, Lily took a step toward the door.

"Lily wait!" Marla called out in alarm.

Coming to a halt, Lily turned to Marla.

Without a word, Marla walked to a nearby chair and sank into it. After many moments of silence, she finally spoke. "Everythin' I've ever done I done to protect you," she said.

"I don't need your protection! Just tell me what Sylvia is talking about! Tell me who my mother is!"

"I am your mother," Marla whispered ruefully.

"What?!" Lily exclaimed in astoundment.

Tears crowded in Marla's eyes. "I am your mother," she repeated somberly.

"No! That's impossible!"

"It's not only possible, it's true, Lily."

"That's a lie! It can't be! I'm white and you're a Negro!"

"You look white 'cause Philip is your father. But, Lily, you are my child."

"No! No! No!" Lily shook her head. "I'm white! I am white!" She rubbed her hands and arms. "I can't be black! I can't be!"

"Please understand. I didn't tell you 'cause I wanted to protect you. I just wanted you to be happy."

"Happy? You keep such a horrible secret from me and you want me to be happy!" Lily shouted belligerently.

"I hid the truth from you 'cause I thought you knowin' you were half black would be too much of a secret for you to bear. I didn't want to burden you with the truth. I thought if you thought you were white things would be much easier for you. And they have been." A tear rolled down Marla's face which she quickly wiped away. "I don't know how Sylvia found out I'm your mother. No one was ever supposed to find out. I didn't want anyone to find out 'cause I knew if anyone knew you had one drop of my African blood your life would be ruined."

"Stop saying such things! I was born in England! My mother lives there! You brought me here after Father convinced Mother to let him raise me!"

"No Lily. That's not what happened. That is the story I made up 'cause I didn't think anyone would find out the truth. You were born right here on this plantation."

Lily shook her head in opposition.

Marla continued to speak, "I've loved you from the moment I knew I was gonna have you. When the midwife laid you in my arms... I remember that day as if it were yesterday. You were the most beautiful thing I had ever seen. When I saw you looked white, I convinced your father to let you live as a white. If I hadn't, you would have lived a life as an outcast. Your life would have been tainted by the African blood that flows through your veins."

"No! No! No!" Lily shook her head and began to pace the floor.

"You know blacks are hated and seen as inferior. Just look around! You see it every day! Blacks are treated differently from whites! They are slaves! They cain't walk through front doors! They cain't go to school! I didn't want that for you! You would have experienced all of that if I didn't find a way to hide this secret!"

"Father told me I was born in England! Father told me you went there to pick me up! He lied to me!"

"After his marriage ended, your father needed a companion. Lily, we fell in love with each other. We didn't mean for it to happen. But, it did. I accompanied your father

47

on a trip to Europe when he traveled there to meet some European merchants. That's when you were conceived.

"When we came back home, I found out I was gonna have you. I never thought things would turn out like they did. But, once I realized you could pass for white, I knew I couldn't curse you with the truth.

"Since your father had been to Europe, I had him tell everyone his former wife had written him informin' him she birthed his child. I asked him to say she wanted him to raise the child in America and he was sendin' me to get you.

"Only one other person besides me and your father knew the truth and that was the old midwife. Your father told her he would free her and her family if she told everyone I lost my baby. She did. I left the plantation one night and stayed away for a few months. Philip told everyone I was in England gettin' you. People didn't question the story. When I returned, everyone believed both your parents were white, just as I wanted."

Sobs shook Lily's body.

"No…baby! Don't cry!" Marla rushed to her daughter and reached out to wrap her arms around Lily's shoulder.

Lily reared away from Marla as if she had been bitten. "Don't touch me you black witch!" she shrieked.

"Lily! Don't hate me!"

Lily shook her head. "You lied to me! You and Father lied to me!"

Tears began to roll down Marla's face. "We wanted to protect you! Please understand!"

"Protect me? No! I'll never understand!" Lily hollered.

Marla reached out to Lily again.

Lily reared away from her and ran toward the door of the cabin.

"Lily!" Marla's shriek was followed by the cry of the little boy who had awakened and now sat upright on the bunk.

Ignoring Marla's call, Lily buried her face in her hands and sprinted out of the cabin door.

§

As the door to the cabin swung open, Syrus ducked around the side of the cabin to remain out of sight. Leaning against the cabin, he watched Lily head for the copious fields of green tobacco plants. A frown crinkled his lips as the gravity of what he'd heard sank in. Marla was Lily's mother? Lily was not white but a Negro?

Suddenly, a smile curled Syrus' lips as he realized an additional truth. Due to his eavesdropping, he now had the ammunition he needed to get what he wanted. And what he wanted was Lily.

Overcome with elation, Syrus tilted his head back and let out a hearty laugh.

§

"What did you say to Lily?" Brock demanded after he returned to his mother's cabin and stomped inside.

"What makes you think I said anything to that girl?"

"Mother!" An indignant scowl coated Brock's face.

"You don't know that girl," Sylvia contended. "Why are you marrying her?"

"I know all I need to know about her! I told you to get along with her!" Brock growled.

"Is she with child? Is that why you feel obligated to marry her?"

"Damn it, Mother!"

"You don't have to marry her you know. She just did it to trap you."

"She's not going to have a baby!"

"Oh thank God! Now is the time to end things with her. You have to think about your future. You can't ruin everything you're working so hard to build."

"It never fails, does it? You always find something wrong with whoever I take an interest in."

"That's not true. I like Angela."

"Drop it, Mother! Lily and I are going to be together!"

"But you don't know her. Not really. I forbid you to marry her," Sylvia stated staunchly.

"You forbid me?" Brock scoffed. "I'm a grown man not a child! You don't get to run my life, Mother!"

Sylvia softened her voice. "Look, sweetie, you're all I have left. I love you and want the best for you. All I know is you can't have it with Lily."

"That's for me to decide!"

"Damn it!" Sylvia threw her hands up and shook her fist at the air. "She's got her claws so deep into you. Out of all the women who throw themselves at you... You can choose better than her. She's not right for you."

"Not right for me? You've seen Lily. She's so caring, sweet, innocent—"

"Innocent? Ha! Son, don't be so naïve. She just wants what you have."

"Which is?"

"Respectability for starters."

"That makes no sense. Lily is respectable. She's caring and loyal. I don't know why you have such a low opinion of her. There's nothing wrong with her."

"Nothin' wrong with her? Respectable? Honey, she and that mother of hers don't know the meaning of that word."

"She said you were implying things about her mother."

"She better be glad implying is all I did," Sylvia replied cryptically. "There's a lot more I could reveal about her. However, I see this is upsetting you. So I won't. I will just say it's time you faced reality. Trust me when I say, you don't know the truth about her."

"What truth?"

"For starters, why do you think Marla is staying in the main house and not a slave cabin?"

"Marla's the housekeeper."

"That's not all she is. Marla Jane is a lot more to Lily than that. And, to top it off, she's a no good whore whose bedding Philip."

Brock opened his mouth to utter a protest then closed it as he remembered what he had seen earlier that day. He had looked into two bedrooms. One had been Philip's room and the other...Marla's?

"Marla Jane seduced Philip when he was weak and vulnerable because she's a whore."

"How do you know it for sure?" Brock inquired skeptically.

"I make it my business to know," Sylvia replied firmly.

Brock turned his back on his mother and ran his fingers through his hair. He was quiet for a moment. Finally, he spoke, "That has nothing to do with Lily."

"You think not? Lily looks up to Marla. Is that not true? Do you not wonder just exactly what it is she's learning from that woman?"

"What are you saying?"

"Open your eyes son. Marla has never known her place. She's lived a lascivious life and she's exposed Lily to that kind of life as well."

"That's not true!"

"Really? Exactly what is Lily's relationship with that Syrus boy? She lives with him. But, they're not related. What do you think Marla taught Lily regarding him? How do we know Lily isn't involved with Syrus after what she's seen Marla do?"

Blood drained from Brock's face as the gravity of his mother's question sank in. Could it be? No... No... Brock's stomach began to turn.

His mother continued. "That kind of woman can never be faithful to you. She could never make a decent wife for you or mother for your children. You carry your father's name. He lived his life setting a good example for you. You've followed in his footsteps and built a good reputation for yourself. Having Lily in your life will bring you shame. Nothing but shame."

"No! I don't believe it!"

"Believe it!"

"How could you even think such a thing?" Brock challenged.

"Because I don't trust anything that goes on in the godless house at Paradise Plantation. I don't trust Marla. I don't trust Lily. And, I don't trust that Syrus boy. He's no good too."

There was silence.

"Damn it!" Brock seethed after a moment. "What you're thinking is impossible!"

"Is it? There's something perverse going on in that house. Think about it, son. Under all of the pretense, hasn't

51

Lily already given you some sign...some sign of how things really are?"

Brock sank into a nearby chair and began to let his mind wander. Lily was perfect in every way. But, his mother was insisting something was wrong. Was Marla Philip's lover? Could it be as his mother implied? Was Lily involved with Syrus? Was Lily's innocent yet flirtatious behavior nothing but an act? An act she had learned after years of observing Marla?

Brock recalled Lily leaping out of bed earlier that day and saying, *I don't want what we have to be cheap and sordid*. Cheap and sordid? Why had she used those words?

None of it made sense. Lily had presented herself as a good girl...an innocent...different than all of the rest. Her innocence had been what had intrigued him. It had been what lured him until his heart had succumbed to her snare. But, was it really innocence she possessed or skillful cunning?

What if things were as his mother suggested? She seemed so confident of it. Were Lily and Syrus lovers? If there was one thing he absolutely could not bear it was the thought of Lily being with another man. Especially Syrus. After all, even if they were not related by blood, for all intent and purposes, Syrus was her brother.

Quickly, Brock thought about his encounter with Syrus outside of Lily's room earlier that day. Syrus had not been happy to hear he had proposed to Lily.

"If she has been with that Syrus boy, can you live with that fact?" his mother's voice sounded in his ear.

Brock shook his head negatively. If Lily had been with Syrus, he couldn't live with it. He just couldn't. "Damn it!" Brock roared.

"For heaven's sake son think rationally. Bed Lily if you must. But don't marry her," Sylvia instructed.

Brock shot his mother a furious scowl. Without another word, he stood to his feet.

"I know I've given you a lot to think about. And, I don't want you to be angry with me. But, there is something else you need to know. It's about Lily and her real mother."

Brock shook his head and waved his hand dismissively. "I don't want to hear anymore of this!" he thundered and before Sylvia could continue to speak he stormed out of the cabin.

§

Sylvia hastened to her front door and watched her son stalk away. Her heart filled with pain at the sight. Closing her eyes for a moment, she thought of a time when there was no pain in her son's life or in her life. A time when her life had been filled with love. That time had been when Brock had a father and she had a husband. A husband who had been a hero to his son and the love of her life. There was nothing she would not give to have that time back...to have her husband back. To have one more day of seeing his smile...to have one more hour of hearing his voice...one more minute of touching him.

Instead of having any of those things, all she had now were memories. Beautiful memories. Bitter memories. No... She had more than memories. She had a physical manifestation of their timeless love. She had a reminder of the love she had once known. A connection to a love that would never die.

She had her son, Brock. He was the bond that now held her life together. The motivation that now gave her the strength to go on. Without her son, there was death and loneliness. Bitterness and resentment. There was immobilizing pain. Without her son, she knew she would sink into a place inside herself so dark she doubted she would ever see the light again.

Sylvia opened her eyes and looked at Brock. She had tried to protect him all of his life. But, despite her best efforts, he, like she, had felt more pain than any one person should feel. Sylvia told herself she had to do more to ensure that her son's heartache ended. If she was going to succeed in ridding Brock of any further anguish, she had to deal with the new menace developing in his life.

"I promise. I will do what I can to protect you," Sylvia whispered to her child. Then, shaking her head, she added, "I will stop that girl from hurting you."

Chapter Five

The loud knock that exploded on the front door was followed by a rapid session of even louder knocks.

Marla entered the foyer just as Brock burst through the door.

"Where is Lily?" he shouted.

"Brock!" Marla rushed to him. "Lower your voice. Your mother told you, didn't she? I can explain."

"You bet you will!"

"You can't believe everything you hear."

"So it isn't true?" Brock stared at her expectantly.

"It ain't exactly as you heard, I'm sure."

"What's the meaning of this?" Philip appeared in the foyer.

Marla spun around to face him. "Brock is here 'bout Lily."

"Let's go into the drawing room so we can talk in private," Philip instructed.

Brock followed Marla and Philip across the foyer to a room with a table and chairs that faced a large window which showcased a breathtaking view of the river.

"Anythin' I done was 'cause I had to," Marla said after she closed the door. "I never wanted things to happen like they did."

"So you go and shack up with Lily's father?"

"Watch it, Brock!" Philip growled.

"It ain't right I know," Marla acceded.

"You're damned right about that!" Brock affirmed.

"Don't judge me 'til you've walked in my shoes. I done what I had to do."

"So, is that what you're teaching Lily to do?" Brock questioned hotly.

"What? No? What are you talkin' about?"

"My mother told me the two of you are lovers! What message do you think that is sending Lily?"

"Lily has grown up her entire life not knowing," Philip stated.

"I just told her the truth today," Marla revealed.

"You expect me to believe that?" Brock grimaced.

"Believe it, Brock. I made sure Lily was sheltered from all of it. I seen to it she don't know 'bout the darker side of life," Marla explained.

"So Lily is truly innocent?"

"I swear to you, Lily has had nothin' to do with any of it. Don't punish her for my faults," Marla pleaded.

Brock turned from Philip and Marla, walked to a chair and sank down on it.

"Brock, you may not understand this but I've found happiness with Marla. I love her. We're happy together," Philip admitted, casting a loving glance at Marla.

Marla looked lovingly at Philip then turned to Brock. "What else did your mother tell you 'bout Lily?" she queried.

"Nothing. Why?"

"Lily told me your mother spoke of her mother."

"I left before Mother could tell me about Lily's mother."

Marla let out a long sigh. "Lily's done nothin' wrong."

"I know you love my daughter," Philip said to Brock.

"I do love Lily and I asked her to marry me last night," Brock revealed.

"You asked her to marry you!" Marla exclaimed.

"Yes. We were going to tell you two after we told my mother."

"So your mother knows you want to marry Lily?" Marla asked.

"Yes. She's not happy about it. But, Lily has my heart. I can never love anyone the way I love her," Brock assured.

"Then you two should get married. Tonight," Philip proclaimed.

"Tonight!" Marla exclaimed.

"Marla Jane, I know you haven't been fond of the idea of Brock and Lily getting close for several reasons. But, can't you see, this man really loves her. We both know she loves him. You've always done what you could to protect Lily so she could be happy. I know she will be happy with Brock"

"It won't—"

"No. It's time we step aside. You heard Brock. He loves Lily with all of his heart. We are both going to trust in that love."

"I don't think—"

"If Brock wants to marry Lily tonight, we're not going to stand in his way," Philip stated interrupting Marla's objection.

"I do want to marry Lily," Brock declared.

Marla shook her head. "But your mother—"

"I will deal with her. I want to marry Lily and we'll be married tonight." Brock stood up, a flicker of hope emerging in his eyes.

"Sylvia will be furious if Brock marries Lily," Marla insisted.

"What you're worried about won't be an issue after the two are married," Philip predicted.

Brock walked to Philip. "Thank you, Mister Frasier. You have always been very kind to me."

"That's because your father and I were close. I know he'd want me to watch out for you."

"Thank you," Brock said as he blinked back tears that smarted in his eyes.

Philip hugged him.

Brock cleared his throat and stepped away from Philip. "I'll go home and get things ready for Lily. Then, I'll return for the wedding," he said hopefully.

"Then, it's settled. I'll send for the minister. Marla Jane, wipe that worried look off of your face and go find Lily. Get her ready for Brock's return. We're having a wedding and it's taking place in a few hours!" Philip announced cheerfully.

§

Marla slackened her pace when she saw Lily sitting by the river. She had been searching for her daughter and now that she found her she breathed a sigh of relief. When she neared Lily, she cleared her throat.

"Stay away from me!" Lily ordered curtly.

"I've come to tell you some news," Marla said softly.

"I don't want to hear anything you have to say!" Lily bit out.

"You'll want to hear this," Marla insisted and lowered herself to the ground next to Lily.

Lily turned away from her.

"Brock was just here. He told us he asked you to marry him last night."

Lily did not respond.

Marla tried again. "I know you're angry 'cause of what I told you earlier. I want to make it up to you. So, I'm gonna put aside my objections and support your marriage to Brock."

"Really?" Lily turned to face Marla.

"Your father suggested the two of you get married tonight."

"Tonight!" Lily exclaimed then frowned. "Sylvia will be angry once she finds out I'm married to her son."

"Sylvia did not tell Brock I was your mother."

"She didn't want to tell him. She was afraid he'd be angry at her. That's why she wanted me to break things off with him so she wouldn't have to tell him. She's afraid if anyone finds out about me it will hurt Brock's reputation."

"Your father is right. You have to marry Brock tonight. Sylvia won't say anythin' to anyone after you're married to her son. She loves her son and won't do anythin' that will damage him. Once you two are married, our secret will be safe and Sylvia will have to keep her mouth shut."

"Once I tell Brock that you're my mother—"

"You can't tell Brock!"

"But why not? Brock needs to know."

"Brock don't need to know. Don't jeopardize your happiness. Please promise me you'll never tell him you're a mulatto. No good can come from it!"

"But I can't keep it from him," Lily protested.

"You know what happened to Brock's father. Because of what happened, he doesn't like blacks, you know that. There's no tellin' how he'll react if he finds out you're one of them."

"Brock loves me."

58

"Brock loves who he thinks you are. Once he knows you're half black..." A haunting look filled Marla's eyes and she lowered them. "What if Brock decides he can't handle the pressure your relationship is sure to cause him. Your father and I have managed to remain happy 'cause we been successful at keepin' our relationship a secret. But, if people find out... No one can find out. If they do I could lose your father and you could lose Brock. You don't want that.

"You don't know what it's like to live as a black. You don't know because I've always been there to make sure you ain't never had to find out. No, you don't know what it's like. But, I do. I know what it's like to never be given a chance. To have people look down their nose at you and treat you as if you're less than dirt." Marla clutched her fists together as tears slid down her face. "I've experience it all. I was never allowed to try and make somethin' of myself 'cause I'm a Negro. I can't go back to livin' like that." Marla shook her head and wiped back tears which were quickly replaced by more tears.

Lily opened her mouth to speak.

"Let me finish," Marla bade. "Your father is the only white who ever showed me any kindness. He's truly the best thing that ever happened to me. He gave me you and I want to protect you. That's why I'm askin' you to keep your race a secret. Once people find out, they will treat you different. They will! I don't want that for you. You have a chance to live a good life. Please tell me you won't tell Brock. No matter what."

Lily looked out over the crystal blue water. "You and Father have lied to me my whole life. Now you want me to lie to Brock?" she brushed back a wisp of hair that tickled her cheek.

"I know it may be hard to understand. You've found out a lifetime of information in one day. I don't expect you to understand it right now. I just hope after you've had time to think about everythin', you'll understand my actions and forgive me. I know you're upset with me now. But, let's forget about everythin' 'til after your weddin'. We'll talk more then. What do you say?"

59

Lily nodded her head.

"Just promise me you won't tell Brock anythin' until after we've talked again," Marla insisted gently.

Lily looked somberly at her mother, "I promise," she replied.

§

"Syrus, did you come to congratulate me on my wedding?" Lily asked when she saw him walking along the path toward her. Without waiting for an answer, she said, "I have a big night tonight. I'm headed inside. I'm going to get ready. Syrus what's wrong?" Lily asked noting his placid expression.

"I know," he said stiffly.

"Know what?" Lily inquired and took a step toward the house.

"I know you're a Negro," he said lightly.

Lily halted her steps.

"I listened at the door of the cabin. I heard Marla tell you she's your mother. I never would have guessed though I probably should have by the way she's always fussing over you."

"Syrus, no one can know. After I marry Brock, none of it will matter."

"You think you're going to marry Brock? You can't marry Brock. Not after what you found out today."

"Of course I can!" Lily affirmed.

"Brock won't marry you once he knows you're a Negro."

"That's not true! Brock loves me!"

"You can't believe Brock will still love you after he finds out the truth."

"Brock will still love me!"

"So you're going to tell him?"

Lily shook her head. "I'm not going to tell him."

"If you really believed he loved you, you'd tell him you're black," Syrus hedged.

"I do believe it! There are just certain reasons why I can't tell him," Lily muttered and stepped away from him.

60

"You really don't get it. Do you? You being a Negro changes everything. Brock doesn't like Negros because of what happened to his father. I guarantee you, he does not want to be married to one."

"I am white. I'm not—"

"You have bad blood flowing through your veins. African blood. It's contaminated blood and no self-respecting white man is going to want you now let alone marry you. That includes your precious Brock."

"Brock isn't like that!" Lily argued taking another step from Syrus.

"You're living in denial," Syrus insisted as he followed her to the house.

"I don't want to discuss this with you!" Lily revealed.

"Now, that you know your parentage, you should give some thought to my proposition. I'm willing to over look that cursed blood that runs through your veins," Syrus disclosed.

Lily turned to him. "As my brother—"

"I'm not your brother!" Syrus bellowed. "I am a man! A man who's willing to offer you more than you should expect now that you know you're black!"

"How can you say such things?" Lily challenged.

"There's no reason you and I can't try to find pleasure with one another. I've had plenty darkies from the fields. It would be nice to have a white woman to warm my bed. Or shall I say, half white."

"That's disgusting!"

Syrus grabbed her arm. "Disgusting! You dare say you find love in my arms disgusting?"

"Get your hands off of me!" Lily jerked her arm away from him. "Stop this nonsense! You're upsetting me!"

"Don't resist my offer. It's the only rational solution to the turn of events," Syrus contended harshly.

"Syrus, I don't know what's come over you. There's no way in hell anything is ever going to happen between us! Not now not ever! Now, I'm going to marry Brock and if you breathe a word of my secret to anyone, Father will make you pay!"

Upon hearing her words, Syrus took a step backward.

Emboldened, Lily continued to speak. "Now for the last time, leave me alone!"

Suddenly, Syrus reached out, jerked Lily's arm and pulled her close. His hot breath brushed her cheeks as he hissed, "You can't dismiss me as if I were one of the darkies! You can't turn your nose up at me and think that will be the end of it! You best think again, sister dear! I won't let you turn me down and run to Brock's bed! You do and you will rue the day you slighted me!"

"Father!" Lily screamed loudly.

Instantly, Syrus pushed her away from him. "You're going to pay for rejecting me!" he spat then turning on his heels he stomped down the path away from the house.

§

Brock's eyes focused on Lily and the stunning vision she created as she stood at the top of the grand staircase. Dressed in an elegant white gown made of shimmering silk he watched as she began a slow descent down the stairs.

"God help me you're beautiful," Brock whispered to Lily when she came to a stop beside him. "How could I have ever doubted you?" he asked as he took her hand and led her the short distance to the drawing room where the minister, Marla and Philip waited.

The minister nodded approvingly when the couple entered the room and came to a stop in front of him. After a nod, the minister began the marriage ceremony. He spoke about love and said love was faithful and loyal. He reminded those present that love was patient and endured. That love never failed.

"Lily Frasier, do you take Brock Cunningham as your wedded husband?" the minister asked.

"I do," Lily replied happily.

"Do you promise to love, obey and be faithful to him as long as you both shall live...until death do you part?"

"I do," she affirmed.

The minister looked at Brock. "Brock Cunningham, do you take Miss Lily Frasier as your wedded wife?"

"I do," Brock answered in a strong steady voice.

"Do you promise to love, protect and be faithful to her until death do you part?"

"I do," Brock promised.

"Because both of you have come of your own free will before God and man to be married. And, since you both are willing to commit to the sanctity of marriage. By the authority vested in me, I now pronounce you man and wife. Brock Cunningham, you may kiss your bride," the minister smiled.

Tears crowded in Lily's eyes as Brock turned to face her. She tilted her face to him and he placed a tender kiss on her lips.

Marla and Philip began to clap in approval.

Tears of joy moistened Lily's cheeks.

The minister proclaimed, "I present to you Mister and Missus Brock Cunningham."

Brock and Lily turned to face Marla and Philip.

"What God has joined together, let no man put asunder," the minister proclaimed.

Smiling happily, Marla scurried from the room.

Philip stepped forward and hugged Lily. "I love you, daughter," he said tenderly.

"I love you too," Lily replied and kissed her father's cheek.

Marla appeared carrying a double layered cake covered in creamy white icing which she sat on top of the table.

After the delicious cake was consumed and congratulations given, the newlyweds said their goodbyes. Marla threw rice at the couple when they ran down the steps of the mansion. Lily squealed and Brock laughed as they settled in Brock's wagon, already packed with Lily's belongings. Lily turned and waved to her parents who stood on the veranda in an embrace.

"We love you, Lily!" they shouted in unison.

"I love you too!" she called back to them as Brock jostled the reins and started the horse forward.

§

Stars twinkled radiantly in the night sky as The Cunningham Ranch came into view. As the buggy rolled forward, Lily looked at Brock's cabin in the middle of a large field. To the right of the cabin, several yards away, was a large barn. Behind the barn there were wooden fences where quarter horses and mustangs were corralled. Some distance away, cattle huddled together after a day of grazing in acres of brown grass. Farther out, past the cattle, Lily saw Sylvia's cabin which had smoke curling from the chimney.

Two large brown dogs appeared and began to bark happily and wag their tails as they ran along side the wagon. Brock brought the wagon to a stop in front of his cabin then ordered the dogs to be silent. The dogs fell silent and sat on their tails. Brock jumped out of the wagon. Lily followed his lead and the dogs sidled up to her sniffing her feet. She patted their heads.

"They're glad to see you again," Brock said. Then, without warning, he scooped Lily into his arms.

"Put me down," she giggled even as she wrapped her arms around his neck.

"My love, don't you know it's only proper that I carry you over the threshold," Brock chided before making his way toward the cabin. "This is your new home," he announced after he opened the cabin door and stepped through the threshold. "I know it's not like what you're used to at Paradise Plantation. But it's mine and I like it."

"It's wonderful," Lily sighed and placed a loving kiss on his cheek.

"As you know, the kitchen area is over there." He nodded toward the area that served as the kitchen. "There's a bedroom there and here's my room." Brock walked to his bedroom which contained a large dresser and a large bed. He dumped her on his bed. "This is where you belong," he proclaimed. "Now, I have to go unhitch the horses and unload your trunks. Make yourself comfortable," he said then headed from the room.

As Lily watched Brock exit the room, she smiled and stretched out over the bed. She was now Mrs. Brock Cunningham and it felt so good. Sighing with satisfaction,

Lily said a quick prayer of thanks that she was now married to the man she loved. After the prayer, she climbed out of the bed and lit the lantern so she could dress in her nightgown before Brock returned.

It was a while before Brock returned.

When he did, Lily knew why. He smelled of vanilla soap and a white towel hung loosely around his waist. Lily thought he looked a lot like a Greek god as he stood before her, his upper torso tanned and rippled with endless muscles.

Her heartbeat quickened.

Brock cast a disapproving look at her nightgown. After he sat on the side of the bed, he pointed to the offensive material. "Take that off," he ordered.

Without a word, Lily stood from the bed and obeyed her husband. Surrounded by the soft light of the lantern's flame, she slowly lifted her nightgown to reveal her feet, followed by her shapely legs then the smooth curve of her hips. She finished by pulling the nightgown over her head exposing her breasts to his view.

Brock moaned then his deep voice rumbled, "Toss it on the ground."

Lily dropped her nightgown to the floor.

"Come here," he commanded.

Lily took the few steps to where Brock sat then came to stop in front of him. In the next moment, he clasped his massive hands on her hips, pulled her to him then slid his tongue over her stomach and across her belly button. Gently, he nudged her down onto his lap and popped one of her breasts in his mouth. He suckled on the soft mound and flicked her nipple with his tongue while his finger slid between her thighs to the warm wetness along her folds.

Lily moaned and ran her fingers through his hair.

"You are my wife. Everything is acceptable now," Brock stated in a low timbre. Then, gently lifting her, he laid her on the bed, placed his hands on her hips and slid her to the edge of the bed so that her legs dangled over the side.

His towel slipped away as he knelt to his knees.

A moment later, to Lily's amorous delight, he placed his tongue where his finger had been. The feeling, so thrilling, made Lily moan. She closed her eyes, clutched the bedding and arched her pelvis to him. Her sensitive bud responded to his prodding and before long, molten tremors rippled from her maidenhead forcefully engulfing her body.

Satisfaction glimmered in Brock's eyes when he stood to his feet. The bed sagged as he climbed into it. Lily felt an accelerating sensation when his massive hands possessively circled her waist and pulled her underneath him. She sighed when his rigid shaft began to prod the entrance of her treasure. A cry left her lips when his manhood drove into her.

Adeptly, Brock moved his hips in a measured motion so that she took in the full length of him. He repeated the thrust, pressing her to find a rhythm of her own. Slowly, Lily began to move her hips to meet his strokes. Seeing the thirst in her husband's eyes, she quickened her pace until a carnal groan rumbled from his throat and her name escaped his lips. She moved underneath him until he collapsed on top of her with a salient sigh.

When Brock raised himself to kiss her lips, Lily whispered, "Who's the only woman who can make you feel so good?"

"You are, my love," came his lusty reply.

§

The next morning, the sun's shining rays found their way through the windows much too early for the newlyweds. The couple stayed in bed intertwined with each other's arms until noon. When they finally emerged from their room, they ate the food Marla had packed for them. As they finished the meal, Brock announced he had to take a horse to the blacksmith's in town. He asked Lily if she would like to go with him. She declined saying she needed to stay behind and unpack.

After Brock left, Lily prepared a bath and washed the remnants of the previous night of lovemaking from her body. She smiled as she remembered her night in Brock's arms and relished the thought of the many nights she would spend there in the years to come. Once her bath was concluded, Lily dressed and began to unpack her belongings. As she rummaged through her things, she thought about how perfect everything had turned out. She and Brock were now married. They were going to be together forever. Nothing was going to tear them apart.

Annoyed squawks from the chickens outside alerted Lily to a visitor's presence. A knock sounded a moment later and Lily traipsed to the cabin's door and swung it open.

Abruptly, the smile disintegrated from her face when she saw Angela standing before her.

"Well... well. What do we have here?" Angela asked. Then, without waiting for an answer, she pushed past Lily and stomped into the house.

Chapter Six

"Where is Brock?" Angela asked exasperatedly.

Lily took a deep breath, "He isn't here," she replied and shut the door.

Raising her chin, Angela sneered, "You're waiting for him, aren't you?"

"I have every right to be here," Lily asserted.

"You pretend to be so innocent. But the truth is you're a spoiled, manipulative creature, Lily Frasier. The spell you have Brock under won't last. One day, he'll see you for what you are and break it off with you. When he does, I'll be there to pick up the pieces."

"Brock is with me because he wants to be with me. He'll never leave me," Lily responded.

Angela shook her finger. "I'm warning you Lily. Back off or—"

"Or what?" Lily cut in.

"Or so help me, you'll be sorry. I'm the one who is going to end up with Brock. I don't care how long I have to wait. I'll do whatever it takes to make him mine again."

Flicking her hair from her shoulders, Lily remarked saucily, "I guess you haven't heard."

"Haven't heard what?"

"Brock and I were married last night."

Angela's expression transformed to one of astonishment. "Liar!" she shrieked.

"Am I?" Lily asked. Placing her hand on her hip she strutted to the trunk that contained her belongings. Reaching in, she pulled out a dress and leisurely ran her hand over the material. Slowly, she pulled out another dress, then another. "You see these? These are my things. You want to know why they're here? They're here because last night Brock and I were married. So, Angela, you are the one who needs to get it through your head. Brock is not in love with you. He's in love with me and he always will be," she proclaimed haughtily.

"Damn you Lily! Damn you, you manipulative bitch! You're going to regret this!" Angela hissed.

Locking eyes with her foe, Lily stated, "You will be the one to regret it if you don't stay away from my husband!"

"You're going to pay for this!" Angela spat then spinning on her heels she stormed from the house.

§

Brock was standing outside the blacksmith's when he saw Angela heading toward him. As she advanced, he could see the doleful expression on her face. So, he walked out to meet her.

"Tell me it isn't true," she pleaded.

Brock instinctively knew what she meant. "I wanted to speak to you before you heard it from someone else," he said.

"So it is true?"

"Yes. It's true."

Angela lowered her head. "Why Brock why?"

"I'm sorry about the way things ended between us."

"I thought that in time…" Tears began to flow freely down her cheeks.

Brock wrapped her in his protective embrace. "God Angela. I didn't know you still felt so strongly. The last thing I want to do is hurt you."

"Then why? Why did you do it?"

"I wanted to tell you about the wedding before you heard it from someone else. Angela you are an incredible woman but I love—"

"No! What about us? If you'd only give us another chance." Angela wrapped her long arms around Brock's neck. She pressed her succulent body against his and began to kiss his face and neck.

"I love her," Brock stated softly.

"No! Don't say that." Angela stopped kissing him and looked longingly into his eyes.

"Please don't make this difficult," Brock requested gently.

"Damn you Brock! Damn you! You've made a fool of me!" Angela lamented angrily.

"I didn't mean to hurt you. The timing just wasn't right for us."

"But, I love you," she confessed.

"And I love Lily. Please understand," Brock's words were a plea.

"I will never understand! Lily is not right for you! Your marriage won't last. I'll wait for you." Angela buried her head in his chest and hugged him tightly.

"Don't say things you don't mean," Brock chided.

"Oh I mean it. I really do mean it," she assured staunchly.

§

"You conniving scheming floozy! You married my son!" Sylvia spat after she burst through the front door of the cabin.

Lily stiffened as her mother-in-law stomped toward her.

"Angela stopped by and told me you married my son! I told you to break the engagement! Instead, you married Brock last night!"

"Missus Cunningham, I love your son."

"Love? Love! You know nothing of love! All you care about is yourself! You don't give a damn about how your lies will affect Brock! You think by marrying him you can silence me and force me to keep your secret! I should have never trusted you to do the right thing! I should have told him the truth about you as soon as I found out!"

"Please, Missus Cunningham. I had no idea Marla was my mother. But, now that I know, it doesn't affect the way I feel about Brock or how he feels about me."

"After his father died, I saw to it that Brock turned against blacks! When he finds out you are one, he's not going to want you! When I tell him you manipulated him into marriage in order to hide the fact you're black and to keep me from telling what I know, he's going to hate you!

"You think you're going to be able to keep your secret buried? Well, you're not! I'm not going to let you white wash

70

your lies and manipulate my son! I will see to it that he sees you for the lying whore you are! I'm going to find my son and I'm going to tell him about your lies and see to it that he has your marriage annulled!" Sylvia announced.

Horror clouded in Lily's eyes. "No!" she screamed and rushed to her mother-in-law who was headed out of the front door. "Please don't tell him!" she begged and grabbed the woman's arm.

Sylvia looked at Lily with a hate-filled glare. "Get your hands off of me you insufferable creature! I'm going to see to it that you never lay those hands on my son again!" she swore then lifting her chin high, stalked from the cabin.

§

Lily folded the letter she held in her hand as a tear ran down her cheek. She lay the piece of paper on the table and ran her hand over it. It was a note containing her explanation as to why she had not revealed her secret. Brock would find it when he came home. Hopefully, after reading it, he would not want to end their marriage.

At that very moment, Sylvia was no doubt telling Brock she was half black. Lily wondered how he would react after he heard the truth. Would he react as Syrus, Sylvia and her mother predicted? Would he say he hated her? Would he say she had inferior blood running through her veins? Would he tell her that he didn't want to be married to her any longer? Or would he tell her he still loved her and did not want to live without her? Was the pain of his past too deep to be healed by their love?

Lily didn't know.

What she knew was she loved Brock and did not want to live without him.

But, did he want her?

She'd find out after he read her note.

In the note, she explained she was going to check into the hotel in town and stay there that night. She asked Brock to think things over. If he found he could forgive her and wanted to continue their marriage, she asked that he come to the hotel to see her. If he did not come, she wrote, she

71

would know he could not forgive her for hiding the secret of her race and no longer wanted her as his wife. She explained in the letter that if he did not come, the next morning as planned, she would head to Boston and spend the summer with her aunt while she tried to sort things out.

Lily stood to her feet and looked around the room. Would Brock come for her at the hotel that night? Or would now be the last time she stood in his cabin as his wife?

A knock sounded at the door.

Brock?

Lily flew to the door and swung it opened.

"What do you want?" Lily questioned with a frown when she saw Syrus standing on the porch.

"I came to see you." Syrus stepped into the cabin. "You going some place?" he asked pointing to the packed luggage by the door.

"I'm going to town. I'm spending the night at the hotel."

"Why?"

"As we speak, Sylvia Cunningham is telling Brock everything and I'm afraid—"

"Brock won't want you anymore," Syrus finished for her.

"I've asked him to come to the hotel tonight if he wants to stay married to me. I put it all in a letter." Lily nodded to the letter lying on the table. "I hope he'll come." She lowered her head.

"You should have listened to me. I told you a marriage between Brock and you wouldn't work. Not since you're a Negro."

"I have to believe Brock won't let me down. In my heart, I know he won't. I know he'll come to the hotel tonight."

A wrinkled creased Syrus' brow. "We're a lot alike, you know? I'm an illegitimate whelp abandoned by his whore of a mother. And, you're an illegitimate whelp deceived by your whore of a mother. Hopefully, now you see, you belong with me. After all, never again will you enjoy Brock's hands on you. Never again will you feel Brock's kiss. But, if you let me, I can take his place."

Lily shook her head. "Don't start, Syrus!"

"Brock's always been the golden boy who gets everything he wants. I won't let him have you too."

72

Reaching out, Syrus drew her to him.

"Syrus, let me go!" Lily shrieked and pulled against him.

"Oh Lily! You feel so right in my arms," he said and ignoring her resistance he leaned down to kiss her.

Lily turned her face from him. His lips pressed into her cheek.

"How dare you do this!" she spat angrily.

"Just give me a chance."

"No! Now, let me go you beast!"

Syrus bristled. "You have contaminated blood flowing through your veins and you dare continue to reject me?" he bit out.

"Get your filthy hands off of me and get out of my house!" Lily yelled extracting herself from Syrus' grasp.

"I offer you something Brock will no longer give and you insist on repaying me by throwing me aside as if I were the trash!"

"There can never be anything between you and me! Since you can't remember that, I am going to tell Father what you've said and done and he'll make sure you keep your hands off of me!" Lily shouted angrily.

"You can't tell Father! I won't let you turn him against me!"

"I warned you to leave me alone! You refused! Father has to know!"

"I can't let you do that." Syrus moved to block her path when she took a step forward.

"You can't stop me!" Lily yelled and pushed past him.

Hastily, she stomped to the door and picked up the bags she had packed earlier.

"You walk out that door and there's no going back. I will stop you from telling Father. You will pay a price for rejecting me. A dear price. I promise you that," Syrus warned.

"We'll just see about that!" Lily remarked then stomped out of the house without looking back.

§

"Syrus, what are you doing here?"

Syrus looked up at the sound of his name and saw Angela standing in the cabin door.

"I could ask you the same thing," he said dryly.

"I went to see Sylvia. But, she is not home. So, I thought I'd stop back by here to talk to Lily. That bitch has to pay for stealing Brock from me."

Ignoring Angela's words, Syrus looked down at the note he held in his hands.

"What's that?" Angela walked to him and snatched the note from his hand.

"Give that back to me!" Syrus snorted and attempted to grab the letter from Angela.

Waving her hand swiftly, Angela managed to keep the note from his reach. "This is a note from Lily," she said as she quickly read the writing.

"Give it back!" Syrus reached for the letter once again.

Angela turned her back to him and continued to read the note. "Lily is black!" she exclaimed with a gasp.

"Angela! She left that letter for Brock!"

"That bitch is black! This is unbelievable! I would have never known!"

"No one knows."

"So Marla Jane is Lily's mother? I guess I should have figured that one out. Sylvia told me Lily was no good for her son. But, she wouldn't tell me exactly why. Now, it all makes sense."

"Brock is not going to want her once he knows she's black," Syrus predicted.

"Why did she write this letter?"

"Sylvia confronted Lily. She told her she was going to tell Brock the truth. That's what she is doing now. Lily wrote the note for Brock so he could get her side of the story."

"And if he still wants to continue their marriage, he is to meet her at the hotel in town tonight," Angela said after she finished reading the note.

Syrus took the note from her.

"I can't believe this!" Angela screeched.

"Brock won't show at the hotel," Syrus guessed.

"But if he does?" Angela shook her head. "There's no way I'm going to lose Brock to a black bitch."

74

"Do you really think Brock will go to her after he reads this?" Syrus asked.

Angela shook her head. "I don't know."

"I've got to figure out how to stop her."

"What?"

"Seeing as how Brock will probably reject her once he finds out, I offered her my companionship. She rejected me and threatened to tell my father that I told her I wanted her. Philip is my life. I don't know what I'd do if Philip rejected me. I can't let that happen. I told her I would stop her."

"How far would you be willing to go to stop her?" Angela wanted to know.

"What do you mean?" Syrus questioned.

"Lily took the man I love away from me. I say it's only fair that something is taken from her. She should be punished for crossing me and silenced before she ruins your relationship with Philip. Do you agree?"

Syrus nodded his head.

"So I ask you once more, how far are you willing to go to stop her?"

"I'm willing to go as far as I'd have to go."

"I was hoping you would say that. You want Lily silenced and I want Brock. I think we could be very useful to each other," Angela submitted.

Syrus arched his eyebrow and looked at Angela as if he was seeing her for the first time. "You've intrigued me. What do you have in mind?"

"Something that would ensure Lily can't interfere between you and Philip and also ensure she can never come between me and Brock."

"Deciding how to handle Lily will be a big problem."

"A problem I can handle," Angela assured.

After a moment, she held out her hand. "Give me that note," she instructed.

Syrus handed it to her.

"If we put our heads together, who knows what we can come up with. Are you with me, partner?" she asked and held out her hand to Syrus.

"I'm with you," Syrus said. Then, reaching out, he took her hand in his and shook it.

Chapter Seven

Three years later...

The arms of darkness slithered around Lily's legs and snaked their way upward. It weaved a murky patchwork across her waist and stomach and overlay her arms with a malignant weight. Climbing like a vine, darkness reached its tentacles around her throat and squeezed until she bowed her head in submission.

Lily let out a plaintive wail and yanked on the chains that bound her. Despondently, she closed her eyes in hopes she could prevent the blackness from suffocating her. It has been three years since the nightmare began and there seemed no end in sight. But in spite of it all, the spark of hope that remained inside her refused to be extinguished. Lily knew she couldn't forget...didn't want to forget.

Brock's face appeared in her mind's eye. His brooding blue eyes...his swarthy skin...she'd never forget. She'd find her way back to her husband no matter what hell sent.

Images of the dark alley, her kidnapper's face and the glistening knife made her tremble. She had thought she was going to die when she saw the knife lunged at her chest. The assailant had used the knife to cut the excess rope that dangled from her arms. But she had fainted before she knew that. When she woke up, she remembered the panic that seized her after she realized she was shackled and in the back of a moving wagon.

Tears slipped from Lily's lashes and she fruitlessly tried to gulp back the desolation that rose in her throat. She was living a horrible nightmare. She wished she was home in Brock's loving arms that very instant. Lily shook her head in opposition to the oppressive heat in the small shed that drenched her and made it unbearable to breathe. She wished she could wipe the perspiration from her forehead. She yanked desperately on the chains. But to no avail. Her defiance had gotten her imprisoned. Alone and confined in endless blackness for refusing to accept her new reality.

For three years, the sun had risen over the horizon. For three years the moon had winked at her from its place in the sky. All the while, she had lived life working as a handmaid to a wealthy widow on a cotton plantation. Her life had been tolerable until a year ago when the woman remarried. Since then, Lily had spent much of her time spurning the groom's advances and for her refusal, locked in the shed as if she were an animal.

Oh what she would give to be in Brock's arms... To tell him she loved him... To hear him tell her he loved her... To live one more day as his wife... To make love to him again...

A loud scrape caused Lily to raise her head and open her eyes. A moment later, resplendent sunlight filtered into the darkness arraying its light against the aphotic shadows. Lily blinked to ward off the lucent rays that stung her eyes. A second later, the form of a man stepped into the entryway of the shed, walked to her and unlocked her chains.

"Time to go girl!" the man bellowed.

Lily recognized the voice as that of the overseer. A second later, she felt his hand on her arm then she was pulled onto her wobbly feet.

"Get going!" he ordered harshly and followed her out of the shed.

When Lily exited the noxious confines, she saw the mistress of the plantation standing with folded arms glaring at her. The woman's husband stood behind her with a doleful expression on his face.

In a voice filled with indignation, the woman looked at the overseer and said, "See that this minx is made ready for the auction! She needs to be sold so she can no longer be a distraction to my husband!"

"Yes ma'am," the overseer replied dutifully. Then, turning to Lily, he barked, "You heard your mistress! Get going!" and pushed her toward the slave quarters.

§

Lily watched as the overseer stopped the wagon at the rear of the auction house and dismounted from his seat. Indignantly, he strode to the rear of the wagon and unhooked the latch on the door.

"Come on girl! Get out of there!" he bellowed.

Lily shook her head and scooted away from the door. "I can't be auctioned! I'm free! Please let me go!" she pleaded desperately.

The overseer let out an irritated growl, reached inside the wagon and pulled her out of the wagon and onto her feet.

Lily screamed in panicked distress and twisted against his iron grip. "Please, let me go! I'm not a slave! I'm free—"

The palm of the overseer's hand smashed across her face cutting off her words.

Lily's hand flew to her burning cheek and her eyes smarted with tears.

"Shut up you stinkin' half-breed!" the man fumed. "If you say another word, you'll feel a sting on more than just your pretty little face!"

Hearing the anger in his voice, Lily knew it would do no good to continue to speak. So, she lowered her head and remained silent when she was pushed toward the entrance of the auction house.

The moment Lily stepped inside the building, the smell of animals and filth stung her nose and the sound of sorrowful wails met her ears. A quick scan of the room revealed horses and cows on one side of the room and humans chained together on the other.

A tall man who wore a black shirt tucked under a thin belt approached. "You're late," he grunted to the overseer.

The overseer cocked his head in Lily's direction and replied, "This is the girl I told you about."

The tall man eyed Lily from head to toe. "You're right, she don't look like no Negro," he confirmed. Then, to Lily he said, "We're almost ready. Follow me," and begin walking away.

Realizing she may not have another chance to plead her case, Lily found her voice, "I can't be sold! I'm not a slave!"

Abruptly, the man turned to face her, his eyes tightened into seamless slits.

"Please sir! No one has listened to me! But, I asked that you do," she said hopefully then announced, "I am not a slave. I can't be sold because I'm free! Please, I just want to go back to my husband."

His eyes never leaving hers, the auction worker reached for the belt around his waist and in one quick motion yanked it from around his waist. When he did, Lily realized it was not a belt, but a whip. With a twist of his wrist, the leather whip unraveled and sliced through the air. A second later, its talons crackled against the ground.

"What did you say?" the man blustered.

Fear churned painfully in Lily's stomach. But, she willed herself to ignore it. Inhaling sharply, she managed to muster her retreating courage and said, "I...I said I...I want to go back to my husband."

The auction worker twisted his wrist.

A painful scream ripped from Lily's lips when the talons of the whip sank through her thin blouse and bit into her back. Unprepared for the sting, Lily fell to the ground and landed on her hands and knees.

Ignoring her scream, the worker pulled her to her feet and jostled the whip. "You'll never see your husband again! Now, I said get moving!" he thundered belligerently before pushing her to a door at the back of the room.

When the worker opened the door, a large outdoor area that contained a wooden platform became visible. Atop the wooden platform, a bearded man was speaking to a crowd assembled below him. Upon closer inspection, Lily realized the crowd was made up of men whose dissatisfied grumbling for the gray haired woman in the middle the stage permeated the air. As the bearded man continued to speak, Lily realized he was the auctioneer.

The auctioneer said a few more words. Then, he motioned for the old woman to leave the stage. The woman, quick for a woman her age, scurried from the platform.

"Why don't you ever have any beauties?" a loud voice shouted toward the stage.

"What does it matter to you? You never buy!" the auctioneer shot back.

"Hey, you show us some beauties! Then we'll buy!" came the response which was followed by declarations of agreement.

"I don't think your wife would let you buy a beauty, Bob!" a voice called out.

There was a splatter of chuckles.

"What would you know about beauties when you're into boys?" was the reply.

Laughter exploded from the crowd.

"Gentlemen! Gentlemen!" the auctioneer chided in opposition to the sounds of amusement. "Let's get back to business. It just so happens that today, and only today, I've been told we *do* have a beauty. Soon, she will walk atop this block and you will be awed by her beauty. She's not like anything you expect to see on this stage. For you see, she is a rare find. A mulatto. Incredibly, as you will soon see, she looks completely white. Only one lucky soul will be fortunate enough to take her as a mistress."

"I'm feeling lucky!" one of the men yelled.

Snickers of merriment followed the revelation.

"Bring her out!" came the holler.

Grunts sounded followed by a chant of, "Bring her out! Bring her out!"

Upon hearing the chant, the auction worker nudged Lily forward. However, Lily found she could not move her feet. She swallowed back the fear turned panic that now rose in her throat. A scowl enveloped the worker's face. In the next instant, the worker flicked the whip against her legs causing her to stumble out of the auction house and into the sunlight.

Not wanting to face the mass of men, Lily looked back the way she'd come. The worker, the scowl still on his face, marched to her and pointed to the steps of the auction block. Her heart pounded rapidly in her chest when he grabbed her arms and pushed her toward the steps. Uncontrollable shivers began to course down her spine as he shoved her up the steps and hauled her to the center of the stage.

A buzz of excitement erupted when he swirled her around to face the crowd.

"Well fellas, is what I said not true? Have you ever seen a wench with such beauty as this?" the auctioneer wanted to know.

"You weren't lyin' this time!" someone proclaimed.

"God knows we're going to have fun tonight!" another person shouted.

"I can see the beauty meets with ya'lls approval!" the auctioneer exclaimed. Turning to look at Lily, he said, "You won't find a healthier broad this side of the Mississippi. Her teeth are healthy and strong..."

Upon hearing the words, the auction worker who stood beside her slid his dirty finger between Lily's lips and rubbed his finger along her gums and teeth.

She jerked away from his touch.

The auctioneer continued, "Never have you seen beauty such as this grace our humble stage before. Take a look at her."

Placing his fingers on Lily's chin, the worker lifted it upward. Suddenly, the man brought his hands to the front of Lily's blouse and tore her blouse apart exposing her breasts to the men's view.

Instantly, whistles and catcalls erupted from the crowd.

Encouraged by the response, the worker yanked on Lily's skirt causing it to slither down her legs and bunch around her feet.

As cheers erupted from the onlookers, Lily whimpered and attempted to cover her most intimate parts with her hands. Finding the effort futile, she hung her head in shame.

§

Brock Cunningham took a gulp of beer from the cup he held in his hand then sat it on the counter in front of him. Gingerly, he placed his hand over his pocket in an effort to feel the money he had put there. It was his life's savings and he felt uneasy carrying such a large sum. However, the bills he carried were needed to pay for the horses he had come to the town to bid on. It had taken three years. Finally, he had managed to save the money he needed to buy a pair of thoroughbreds. Once he had the thoroughbreds to add to his stock, he would began breeding thoroughbred horses as he'd always dreamed.

After arriving in town that morning, he had planned on stopping by the auction house to inspect the horses before the auction which was to take place late that afternoon. However, his plans had been interrupted when the wheel on his wagon cracked. Instead of going to the auction house, he had been forced to go to the town's wheelwright to get the wheel fixed.

Brock took another gulp of beer as his attention turned to the conversation of the men who sat at the table behind him. The men were raucously conversing about the auction of a beautiful mulatto female that was taking place a few blocks away. While they drank their whiskey, the men revealed their fantasies for the slave. Brock pitied the woman unlucky enough to fall prey to the lascivious men of the town.

Lily's face flashed in his mind and for a moment he could hear her voice call his name. He wondered where she was and what she was doing at that moment. He hoped she was somewhere safe. But, after three years and no word, he couldn't be sure.

Laughter erupted at a table behind him wrenching his thoughts to the present. Unable to listen to any more of the men's talk, Brock laid coins on the counter for his drink then made his way out of the saloon.

Wooden boards creaked under his feet as he walked down the boarded walkway. When he came to the end of the walkway, he turned the corner and saw a crowd of men gathered in front of an auction block some distance away. He let his eyes scan over the assembled to the female atop the platform. But, due to the distance, he could not see her clearly.

Brock took a moment to adjust his hat.

Shifting his gaze, he looked down the dirt street that led to his hotel and contemplated returning there instead of becoming a part of the commotion ahead.

A loud cheer erupted from the crowd.

Brock looked back toward the auction block.

This time, as his eyes settled on the female atop the platform, a prick of familiarity needled him. A frown encased his lips at the feeling that prodded him to take a closer look.

As if drawn by an unseen fetter, he began to erode the distance between he and the female. As he neared, it became clear the female was nude. Remembrance flickered in him when the girl's shapely legs came into focus. Pensively, Brock let his gaze travel up the female's legs and over her curvy hips to her flat stomach. As he drew closer, his eyes rested briefly on the mounds of her small breasts, partially covered by her hands. Though she had her head bowed, he strained to catch a glimpse of her face which was partially obscured by long chestnut colored hair.

Suddenly, the man in black who stood on the stage next to the female pulled her hair back.

Instantly, Brock came to an abrupt halt as recognition doused his memory.

"Holy mother of God!" he exclaimed.

Chapter Eight

Lily kept her eyes lowered to the ground as the auctioneer continued to speak.

"It's my duty to inform you gentlemen, whoever is lucky enough to purchase this minx will be in for a special treat. I assure you she won't disappoint."

Howls of excitement pricked Lily's ears.

"Gentle sirs, just think of all of the ways this wench can amuse you. Just look at her breasts. They are as ripe as fresh peaches," the auctioneer contended.

The auction worker reached out and unclasped Lily's arms from around her chest then tapped her breasts until they bounced.

"Her breasts are firm when you need them to be and jiggly when you want," the auctioneer proclaimed with a smile.

Snickers of merriment rippled through the mass of men.

"Her skin is as soft...as soft as a baby's bottom," the auctioneer assured as the worker ran his hands gingerly over the curves of her breasts before playfully swatting her bottom.

"To top it off, she's clean. You won't find a finer specimen of femininity anywhere," the auctioneer promised. Then, looking at Lily, he muttered, "Turn around and bend over, girl. Show 'em you're clean."

Lily looked at the auctioneer with a repugnant glare.

"You heard the man! Turn around and bend over!" the worker barked.

Lily shook her head and attempted to step backward. However, the worker reached out, pushed her hair from her face and grabbed the back of her neck. The worker tightened his grip when she started to pull away from him. A second later, he pushed on her neck until she bent her head. He added more pressure until she bent forward at the waist. A moment later, the worker wedged his calloused hand between her legs and jammed his finger between her folds. Lily winced as he quickly circled his finger within her then extracted the digit out of her and held it out to the crowd.

Lily straightened her stance and tears smarted in her eyes as whistles and gleeful calls rang out.

"Let the biddin' begin!" the auctioneer proclaimed.

"I bid five hundred dollars!" an enthusiastic voice called out.

"Five hundred? That is a fine bid. But, I see you gentlemen need to get a better look at this specimen," the auctioneer concluded and pointed to Lily.

"One thousand dollars!" an eager voice shouted above the noise of individual conversations.

"One thousand dollars?" the auctioneer questioned. "For this beauty, the price is nice but not good enough."

"Twelve hundred!" came another bid.

"Fifteen hundred!" someone else yelled out.

"One thousand five hundred. I have a bid of one thousand five hundred dollars. Can I get five hundred more?" the auctioneer goaded.

Loud whispers echoed through the air.

"Can I get two thousand?" the auctioneer prodded again. "I have two thousand from the gentleman to my right... No bids for five hundred more?"

"Five thousand dollars!" a commanding male voice pierced the rancorous bidding.

Instantly, a hush fell over the crowd and Lily's heart skipped a beat.

Could it be? The voice. Was the voice that called out the familiar voice that lived in her dreams...the voice she so desperately wanted to hear again...longed to hear again...needed to hear again? What were the chances that after all of the years that separated them he'd be in the crowd?

Slowly, Lily lifted her eyes and scanned the crowd for the provocative bidder.

As her eyes roamed the mesh of faces which had gleefully leered up at her, the sea of bidders slowly parted and turned in unison to look at the man who had bid the large sum. Lily strained to view the bidder at the end of the newly created pathway. The man stepped forward and Lily

85

took in the sight of the tall muscular male with blonde hair and blue eyes. Her breath caught in her throat.

Lily blinked and stared in speechless amazement. Could it be? Was it really Brock? After three long years, had he come to rescue her? Or was her mind playing tricks on her?

"I bid five thousand dollars!" Brock's voice rumbled again.

Elation erupted inside Lily. It was Brock! He was standing there! He had come to rescue her! It was a miracle! Now, she could be free of the bondage of slavery! Now, she could finally be with the man she loved! Now, she could return home! Just as she dreamed, she could be in Brock's arms again! She let out a sigh. Finally, her prayers were being answered. Finally, things could go back to being as they had been. As they should be.

"Did I hear you right? Did you say five thousand dollars?" the auctioneer questioned after Brock came to a stop at the foot of the auction block.

"I did," Brock replied.

"Haven't seen you 'round these parts. Who are you mister?" the auctioneer inquired.

"Don't worry about who I am. Just know, I have the money and I don't hear anyone matching my bid." Brock reached into his pocket, pulled out a wad of bills and held it up to the auctioneer.

The auctioneer snatched the money from Brock's hand. "Sold to the stranger!" the man exclaimed and hurriedly began to count the cash.

"Brock!" Lily called out to him.

Brock shot her a silencing glance then motioned for her to come to him.

Instantly, Lily dashed across the platform. As she scurried down the steps, she opened her arms to hug her husband. Abruptly, he turned his back to her, grabbed her skirt and blouse from the floor of the platform and threw them at her.

"Put your clothes back on!" he ordered curtly. "Put them on! Now!" he thundered when she did not move to cover herself.

Daunted by the unexpected abrasiveness in Brock's tone, Lily frowned and hastily stepped into her skirt. Hurriedly, she slid on her blouse careful to tuck it in her skirt to keep it from falling open.

Brock clasped his hand over hers. "Let's go!" he instructed tightly and stepped to lead the way.

Daunted by the impertinent gazes of the men, Lily squeezed Brock's hand as they made their way through the taciturn crowd.

"Damn outsider don't have no right comin' in here and buyin' up our women," one of the men blurted out breaking the deafening silence.

Brock led Lily out of the crowd and down the street behind the auction house.

"That was horrible!" Lily exclaimed after she and Brock were a short distance from the auction house.

When Brock didn't respond, she looked at him and saw he was looking back the way they'd come. She glanced over her shoulder and saw the crowd of men from the auction spill into the street after them.

"What are we going to do?" Lily asked as their disgruntled grumbles wafted to her ears.

"Follow me!" Brock instructed before heading into a nearby stable.

Lily scrambled to keep up with Brock's quickened pace.

When she entered the stable, she saw Brock speaking to the man inside.

"Some of those men are drunk and they're carrying guns. It's best if we leave now," Brock said in answer to the question she was about to ask.

At that moment, the man who worked in the stable led a saddled horse to the entrance. Brock walked to the horse and tugged the straps of the saddle in place. Hastily, he climbed upon the animal.

"Don't just stand there! Climb up!" he called to Lily.

Lily walked to him. He reached down and lifted her upward.

After he positioned her in front of him, Brock prodded the steed forward. As they exited the stable, Lily saw the mass of men rushing their way.

Brock jostled the reins and nudged the horse into a trot up the street away from the men. Tugging the reins, he urged the horse into a gallop causing Lily to slump against his chest. She smiled. She was in Brock's arms and she was headed home. Grateful for the blessing, she said a quick prayer of thanks as Brock guided the horse safely out of the town.

§

Streaks of purple and orange light from the waning sun faded into grey as the sun slipped behind the horizon. Lily leaned against Brock's chest to garner his warmth and stave the feel of the cool breeze that had begun to blow. She closed her eyes and savored the feel of his arms around her. She wanted to laugh, cry and scream for joy all at once. After years of being apart from her one true love, she was back in his arms and they were heading home.

"What a wonderful night," she said happily as they continued on their journey.

After what seemed like an eternity, Brock turned the horse off of the dusty road and guided the steed to a small clearing. He brought the animal to a halt, dismounted then reached up and helped Lily to the ground.

In the next instant, their arms slid around each other in a cherished embrace and their bodies melded together.

"Oh Brock!" Tears began to stream down Lily's face.

"Lily, sweetheart! I can't believe it's you! I can't believe you were on that goddamned block!" Brock's voice faltered as a tear slipped from his eye.

"I knew this day would come," Lily croaked. "I knew I'd see you again. Oh! I've missed you so much."

"Why did you leave?"

"I tried to get back to you. I—"

Brock's lips covered her cutting off her words.

"I love you so much," Lily whispered and pressed her cheek against his after their lips parted. "I've done nothing but dream of the day I would see you again. I've prayed for this day."

Their lips met once more.

"I can't believe this! Are you all right?" Brock questioned.

Lily nodded her head. "I'm happy beyond belief."

Brock brushed the tears from her cheek. "You must have been through hell."

"I was abducted by some slavers. I couldn't get to you."

"Abducted? What do you mean?" Brock questioned blinking back his tears.

"After I received your note, I went to meet you. That's when a slaver grabbed me."

"My note? What are you talking about?"

"The note you sent to the hotel."

"I didn't send a note. What hotel?"

"Didn't you read my letter?"

"What letter?"

"I wasn't sure how you would react once your mother told you about me. I explained it all in a letter I wrote for you."

"I didn't see any letter."

"Oh no! You didn't get my letter!" Lily lamented in astonishment.

"After my mother told me your secret and I returned home, I realized you had packed your bags and left. I didn't know where you'd gone. I kept thinking you'd come back. But, no one knew where you'd gone. Not even your mother."

"I wanted to come back," Lily assured as her stomach growled loudly.

"You're hungry!" Brock exclaimed.

Lily nodded her head. "I haven't eaten properly in a few days," she said.

Hastily, Brock dug into his saddle and pulled out dried jerky and a canteen. "See if you like this," he said and handed her a handful of meat and the canteen.

"I'm not sure I can eat much due to all of this excitement. But, I'll try," Lily replied and took a bite of the beef.

"Tell me what happened. Where have you been all this time?"

"Somehow, the slaver who kidnapped me knew I was half black. I was sold to be a handmaid for a widow who lived on a cotton plantation. It was horrible. I felt so powerless. I had no money or rights. The woman who bought me was tolerable. However, she remarried a man who thought I had no right to my own body. But, I never let him take me. I was faithful to you."

Brock kissed her forehead. "Sweet innocent Lily. You've been through hell. You must be exhausted. I will get the tent set up so you can rest," he said tenderly.

"How are my mother and father?" Lily asked as Brock took two small bundles off of his horse.

"Your parents are doing fine. They will be very glad to see you," he surmised and unrolled the two bundles which unveiled a small tent and a bedroll.

"I guess everyone now knows that Miss Marla is my mother?" Lily remarked as Brock began to erect the tent.

"No. Your secret is still safe," Brock revealed.

"But your mother—"

"After my mother told me Marla was your mother, I went to see Marla and she confirmed it. She made me promise to keep the secret for fear you could be hurt if anyone found out. I agreed and swore to my mother if she ever told anyone your secret I would never speak to her again. I guess it was enough to scare her because she promised not to tell a soul.

"I searched for you for weeks. But there was no trace of where you'd gone or what happened to you," Brock said as he placed the bedroll inside the tent.

"And now, you've found me. I can't believe this is not a dream."

"It's not a dream," Brock affirmed.

Lily walked to Brock, wrapped her arms around him and lay her head against his chest. "There hasn't been a day that's gone by that I haven't thought about being where I am now. In your arms."

Brock buried his face in her hair.

"How did you find me?" she wanted to know.

"Actually, I was in that town to buy a pair of thoroughbreds."

"But fate brought us together instead. I knew it would happen. You said our love could withstand anything. Oh Brock," Lily sighed. "Now things can go back to the way they were before I left. We can start over as man and wife."

Suddenly, Lily felt Brock's body stiffened against hers. She raised her eyes to his in time to see a tormented shadow cloud his face. "What is it?" she questioned.

Brock extracted himself from her embrace. "It's getting late. I've got to secure the horse for the night."

"But—"

"You should get some sleep," he said then walked away before she could continue to speak.

Lily frowned as she watched Brock's retreating form. Why had he pulled away from her? Had she upset him? She opened her mouth to speak then decided against saying a word. Instead, she knelt in front of the tent and crawled inside the small structure.

It took a second for her eyes to adjust to the darkness within the tent. When they did, she turned and peered through the opening. She saw Brock tying the horse's reins to a tree. After a moment, she moved back into the darkness and shed herself of her skirt and blouse then slid into the bedroll.

She told herself to relax because in a few minutes time she would be snuggled in Brock's arms. When Brock crawled in the bedroll with her, she would make him forget any reservations he had about their reunion. She'd show him that things could return to the way they had once been.

Lily's eyes fluttered in deference to the sleep that beckoned her. She pressed her eyes closed then opened them wide. She did not want to fall asleep before her husband lay beside her. After all, once he was next to her, she'd be able to run her hands over the rippled muscles of his chest, just like she had done before. She'd be able to trail her fingers up his arms…just like she had done before. She'd beckon him to return her touch…just like she used to. And oh how she wanted him to touch her. For only his touch could erase the feel of the auction workers hands on her body.

91

Tonight would be the night things returned to the way they were three long years ago. Yes. Tonight would be the night things returned to the way she needed them to be…the way she wanted them to be. No. She did not want to fall asleep before that could happen.

§

When Brock crawled into the tent, the soft sound of Lily's breathing informed him she was asleep. After his eyes adjusted to the darkness, he saw her sleeping form underneath the bedroll. Unwilling to climb into the bedroll with her, he stretched out beside her. He lay still as Lily stirred a little and rolled against him. With a sedated moan, she draped her arm across his chest and snuggled her head against his shoulder.

After a moment of hesitation, Brock wrapped his arm around her.

Suddenly, an image of Lily standing on the auction block flashed in his mind. A feral shadow blanketed his face as he thought about how he felt when he realized it was Lily who stood on the block. There were no words to describe the way he felt seeing her stripped in front of those men. He had felt such anguish and helplessness the depths of which he never wanted to feel again.

After three years and no word, he'd never expected to see her again. Nor had he expected to find such a ferocious wave of love still idling inside of him for her. Over the years, he had worked to bury memories of her at the bottom of his heart. But now that she was back and in his arms, memories inundated his mind.

Brock closed his eyes in an effort to suppress his thoughts only to open them a short time later. It seemed having Lily nestled against him was bringing to life more than just memories.

Brock groaned and rolled away from her in an effort to gather his composure. He would not be able to sleep in the tent next to Lily. After all, things had changed in his life over the past three years and he couldn't be so quick to forget that. There were reasons why he couldn't allow himself to think of the past. There were reasons why he could not succumb to Lily's allure.

Not now.

Not ever again.

§

The sun's warm rays slowly heated the tent compelling Lily to open her eyes. When she did, it took a moment for her to remember where she was and how she had gotten there. She reached her hand to the empty place beside her. Too tired to raise her head, she closed her eyes and let sleep claim her once again.

§

"Lily, it's time to wake up."

Brock's words sounded a moment before Lily felt him gently nudge her.

Fighting grogginess, Lily's eyes fluttered opened and she saw Brock hovering above her.

"What time is it?" she mumbled and yawned.

"Almost time for dinner."

"Dinner?"

"You've been asleep all day. We need to get moving," Brock said.

Lily sat up in the bedroll yawning as she did so. "I woke up earlier and you weren't here. Where'd you go?" she wanted to know.

"I went to look for food. You ate all there was last night."

"You didn't go back to that town, did you?"

Brock shook his head. "No, though I was tempted since my wagon's there and my clothes are still at the hotel."

"We left in such a rush you didn't have a chance to get them."

"No. But while I was gone I managed to get some food and look what I got for you." Brock tossed an article of clothing at her.

Lily caught the garment then held it out for inspection. When she did, she saw it was a white dress that buttoned down the front. She lifted her eyes to Brock. Noticing the glint in his eye, she followed his gaze to her bare chest. Blood rushed to Lily's face reddening her cheeks. She picked up the blouse she had thrown aside the previous night and held it against her chest.

Brock smiled slightly. "I suggest you put that blouse back on for now. We should come to a stream in a day or so. We'll stop by it and then you can bathe. Once you refresh yourself you can put the dress on."

"So where'd you get the dress?" Lily questioned.

"I went to a farm house a few miles from here and asked the farmer who lived there if he could spare a couple of items. And guess what? I even got a bar of soap." He held up a bar of soap.

"You got a farmer to give me this dress?"

"Actually his wife did that. She was a very sweet woman. She even talked her husband into giving us a horse."

"So, we now have everything we need to make it home?" Lily asked inquisitively.

"Yes. At least, I hope so since I'm out of money."

"Out of money?"

"Yep. I gave the auctioneer my life's savings. You were not cheap, if you'll remember," he replied.

Lily lowered her eyes.

"Well, we best get going. Hurry up and dress," Brock instructed then started to rise to his feet.

Lily put a staying hand on his arm. "There is one thing you forgot," she proclaimed.

"What's that?" he asked as he turned to look at her.

"You forgot to kiss me good morning," she whispered. Flirtatiously, tossing her blouse aside, she began to unbutton his shirt.

"Lily…" Brock's words fell away as she slid her hands under his shirt and ran them over the taut ripples of his chest.

"I've missed you. Tell me you missed me," she implored gently and slid her arms around his neck.

94

Once her hands locked behind his neck, Lily fell back onto the bedroll pulling Brock down with her. When his body flattened against hers, she pressed her lips to his and moaned when he returned her kiss.

"Oh Brock," she breathed when she felt his arm slide around her waist. "I've missed you... I've missed this..." She inhaled sharply when she felt his member swell against her leg. "I don't want to wait any longer. Make love to me," she pleaded softly.

"We...We can't," Brock rasped after a moment. Pulling away from her, he raised himself up on his knees.

"What do you mean we can't?" Lily questioned bewilderedly.

"This just can't happen," Brock said flatly. Then, clenching his shirt together, he crawled out of the tent.

Hurriedly struggling into her skirt and blouse, Lily crawled out of the tent and rose to her feet. "Brock, what is it?" she questioned as she tucked the end of her blouse in her skirt.

"I don't want to talk about it," Brock answered sternly.

Lily bristled at his tone. "But why?"

Brock's cutting gaze killed the words on her lips.

"If you want to eat, there are boiled eggs and biscuits in my saddle," he said briskly then turning his back to her began to disassemble the tent.

Lily bristled at Brock's abrupt behavior. Squaring her shoulders, she turned from him and walked to his saddle. She reached inside and pulled out a small bag. She opened the bag and saw half a dozen boiled eggs and half a dozen biscuits. Lily picked up a biscuit and took a bite out of the soft bread as she thought about Brock's behavior. What was keeping Brock from being with her? Why had he refused to make love to her?

Lily looked at Brock as he disassembled the tent. His long legs, glistening blonde hair and broad shoulders were just as she remembered. She thought about the last time they had made love. It had been on their wedding night. Yearning consumed her as she thought about the feel of Brock's bare skin on hers. Over the past three years, she'd dreamt of making love to him. She'd ached to feel his unyielding muscles under the palms of her hands. She wanted to make love to him...needed to make love to him more than words could say. Nothing could be allowed to get in the way.

Crossing her arms, Lily decided she would persuade Brock to realize he wanted to make love to her just as much as she wanted to make love to him... and she'd do it before the day was through.

§

Neither said a word as they began their journey that evening. The silence between them remained as the sun began its slow descent and the moon rose to take its place. Several hours passed before they stopped for the night. After they dismounted, Brock began to gather sticks for a fire. Once the sticks were gathered, he placed them in a pile and started a fire with a match he had gotten from the farmer. Next, he put a small pot on the flames and poured stew from the farmer's wife into it.

While Brock erected the tent, Lily sat by the roaring fire and braided her ruffled hair. When the homemade stew began to bubble, she stirred the delicious smelling fare then poured a small portion in a bowl and handed it to Brock. He took the bowl she held out to him and began to eat.

When she could no longer take the silence, Lily lifted her eyes to glance at Brock and saw him looking at her with an expression she couldn't read. When her eyes met his, he quickly looked away and sat down his bowl. Encouraged by the realization Brock had been watching her, Lily sat down her bowl and leisurely stretched her arms.

"I'm getting tired. I'm going into the tent. You going to join me?" she asked.

"You go ahead. I'm going to sleep out here," Brock said.

Lily frowned. "You're not going to join me in the tent?" she questioned.

Brock shook his head negatively.

"Why not?"

"Do I really need to answer that?"

96

"What do you mean?" she queried.

Brock let out an agitated huff then responded. "You walked out on our marriage, remember? You hid your secret from me and then you walked out on me."

"I...I wanted to tell you. But...But I was afraid," Lily stammered.

"You were afraid? Afraid of what?"

"My mother asked me not to tell and your mother said you'd hate me. I didn't want to see the hate in your eyes after you found out," Lily explained.

"You were my wife! How could you think for one minute I would turn my back on you?"

"How was I supposed to know you still wanted me or loved me? I had just found out I had black blood in me. The same black blood that you despise because of what happened to your father. I didn't know what to do. I left you that note explaining I still wanted to be with you."

"I didn't get any note, Lily. *I'm half black.* If you had only stayed and said those words... Now, we'll never know what could have been."

"What do you mean *what could have been*? We're back together again. We can start where we left off."

Brock shook his head. "If you had stayed at home, like a loving wife and explained yourself, maybe things could have been different. But, you didn't tell me because you wanted to keep your secret. I think you married me because you thought by doing so, you could keep your secret safe. You thought you could manipulate the love I had for you. But, it all fell apart after my mother found out. I went against my mother and married you because I thought you were different. I thought I could trust you."

"You can trust me!" Lily proclaimed.

"Look Lily, we've been apart for three years. We can't get that time back. Even if we could, I've learned I can't trust you to be completely honest with me and there's no fixing that."

With that said, Brock rose to his feet then curtly turned his back to her before walking away.

97

As Lily watched Brock walk away, tears crowded in her eyes. One slipped down her cheek. Lowering her head, she made her way to the tent and crawled inside.

§

The next morning, as they had the day before, Brock and Lily rode in silence. As before, the sun slowly climbed in the sky. When the sun was high above them, they stopped for lunch. After a brief rest, they continued on their way. Eventually, the sun gave way to dusk. Hours after the silver moon was high in the sky, they came upon a stream. Brock directed the horses along the babbling brook for an additional hour before he finally stopped.

"We'll rest here for the night," he announced then dismounted.

Following his lead, Lily dismounted to find her legs sore and stiff.

Brock removed the saddles and the horses ambled to the stream and began to drink.

As before, Brock gathered sticks for a fire. Lily poured the last of the stew in the pot and put it over the fire Brock started.

"You going to eat dinner?" she asked him when he moved from the fire.

Brock shook his head negatively then knelt by his saddle and rummaged through it. A second later, he pulled out the bar of soap and headed to the stream.

Lily served herself some stew then turned to look at Brock. She saw him take off his shirt and begin to wash it. She watched him as she continued to eat. Her eyes widened when she saw him shed his pants and begin to bathe in the stream. Gulping down the remainder of her stew in no time flat, she sat down her bowl and collected the dress Brock had given her the day before. By the time she made it to the stream, he had rinsed his body of trail dust and exited the water.

"Leaving so soon?" she questioned as he fastened the buttons on the pants he had slipped back into.

Brock nodded his head.

"You won't be needing this." Lily brushed her fingers over his and took the bar of soap he held in his hand.

Brock dropped his hands to his side and stepping past Lily walked the short distance to the camp fire.

Lily laid the cotton dress on a nearby rock and quickly glanced at Brock, she saw he was serving himself some stew. Fed up with the silent treatment and remembering her earlier vow to get him to succumb to her, she began to slowly peel off her blouse. Next, she leisurely stepped out of her skirt. Tossing the tattered garments to the ground, she dipped her foot in the cool water and let out a brazen squeal. A satisfied smile curved her lips when out of the corner of her eye she saw Brock raise his eyes to look at her.

A frown encased her lips when he hastily shifted his gaze to the bowl he held in his hands. Her frown melted away when a second later he raised his eyes to look at her again.

Lily took a few steps into the water then turning so that she was facing Brock, lowered herself to her knees. Zealously, she began to splash water on her body causing it to cascade over her shoulders, down her arms and over the curve of her hips. With slow deliberation, she began to rub the bar of soap over her arms and shoulders until she worked up a small lather. Seductively, she rubbed the soapy suds across the mounds of her small breasts then over her flat stomach. Slowly, she lathered her legs. Lily locked her amber eyes with Brock's blue ones then rubbed the inside of her thighs.

After a moment, she rinsed the suds from her gleaming skin then quickly lathered soap in her hair. Once her hair was rinsed clean, Lily stood to her feet and exited the water. She picked up the dress from the rock and slithered into it. With hips swaying, she walked to where Brock sat and stood above him. "Are you going to join me in the tent tonight?" she asked.

Brock looked at Lily unable to ignore the way the thin material, soaked with water droplets, clung to her rounded curves and rigid nipples. He clenched his teeth. Suddenly, he reached out and tugged Lily's arm causing her to fall on her hands and knees in front of him. "I'm not in the mood to play your silly game," he hissed testily.

"I...I have no idea what you're talking about," Lily replied saucily.

"Stop it. I'm not going in that tent with you. So, you just stop it."

"Stop what?"

"Stop being a tease," Brock barked.

"And if I don't, what are you going to do about it?" she asked then quickly pushed Brock's shoulders causing him to lean back. Hastily, she fell against him then stretched on top of him after he fell to the ground and landed on his back.

Letting out a grunt, Brock wrapped his arms around Lily and flipped his body so that he was on top and she was buried beneath him.

Lily laughed lightly and brushed her fingers through his moon stained hair.

Brock swatted her hand away. "Stop it!" he growled.

"No!" Lily replied and defiantly wrapped her arms around him. "Does having me in your arms bring back memories?" she asked, ignoring his scowl.

Brock did not answer.

"Why won't you make love to me?" The words tumbled out of her mouth.

Brock started to pull himself off of her.

"Tell me!" she ordered holding him tight.

Brock opened his mouth to speak. Suddenly, not trusting his voice to speak, closed it. How could he explain that all he could feel was the pain he felt when she left? How could he explain he hadn't intended to be angry with her? He hadn't intended to be so irrational. So hurt.

"Why didn't you trust me with your secret?" The words were out before he could stop them.

"I wanted to tell you. I just didn't think I could."

"You were my wife! You should have stayed! You should have trusted me! Isn't it ironic? You left me because you didn't think you could trust me. Yet, when you were on that auction block and needed me the most, I was the only one you could trust."

100

"Can you look me in the eye and tell me the moment you found out I was black you still wanted me?"

Brock was silent for a moment. Finally, he spoke, "I thought I hated blacks. But, I realized my love for you was more than the hate I held in my heart."

"You're saying that after three years. You've had three years to get used to the idea," Lily retorted.

"When I told you I loved you I meant it."

"Good. Then, you won't mind if I do this..." Lily reached up and pressed her lips to his. Eagerly, she kissed him beckoning him to respond to her touch.

"No. Lily. No. I told you, this can't happen." Brock pushed away from her.

"But why?"

"Just leave me alone, Lily," he ordered staunchly.

"I—"

"Leave me alone!" he bellowed and rose to his feet, refusing to look at her.

Lily rose to a sitting position. "But why?"

"Just go to the tent, Lily. You've done enough for tonight," he instructed sharply.

Chapter Nine

Lily lay awake in the lonely tent as the moon crawled across the night sky. Thoughts of Brock and his rejection crowded her mind banishing any thoughts of sleep. This was not the reunion she had envisioned. She had envisioned being reunited with Brock and drowning in his arms. But, he did not want to kiss her let alone make love to her. He was angry at her because he thought she abandoned him. But she hadn't abandoned him.

Tormented by her thoughts, Lily pushed aside the bedroll and sat up. She had to make him see that she loved him and wanted to be with him more than anything. She had to get Brock to make love to her. Squaring her shoulders, she crawled out of the bedroll and poked her head out of the tent. Aided by the moon's bright light, she saw Brock sleeping near the waning flames of the campfire. Silently, she crept to where he lay. She paused a moment. Then, with nimble fingers, she quickly loosened his pants. Eagerly, taking his flaccid member in her hand, she popped it in her mouth.

A moment later, Brock let out a drowsy moan.

Encouraged by the sound, Lily let her tongue slide down his shaft.

She slid her tongue upward then down again until his member grew rigid against her finger tips.

She smiled when Brock moved his hand to rest in her hair.

Edaciously, she let her tongue skim his flesh until she heard him suck in a ragged breath.

Lily raised her eyes and saw he had opened his eyes and was staring down at her.

"Go back into the tent," he ordered in a low voice.

Lily shook her head and ran her mouth over his flesh once again.

Suddenly, Brock reached down and pulled her upward so that her eyes were even with his. Acting swiftly, he flipped her so she was embedded beneath him.

There was a moment of silence between them.

Finally, he whispered, "I can't resist you."

"I'm glad," Lily replied a moment before their lips met in a searing kiss.

"Oh Lily," Brock breathed after he stripped her of her clothing.

"Brock, I've missed you," Lily inhaled and worked to pull off his shirt and pants so he was nude as she.

Hot liquid warmth rolled over Lily's body when Brock's lips moved to cover every inch of her. She let out a happy sigh when his hardened tower began to prod the entrance of her intimate place. Lily felt herself expanding. Willingly she accepted her husband. He thrust himself fully within her and she thought the feel was just as she remembered...had dreamed of...had wanted. She breathed Brock's name as a second later, he placed his hands on her waist and began to move her hips.

Lily arched her hips to her husband and braced herself for his response. An instant later, he drove his member into her slick passage tethering them together. He plunge deeper within her and she thought she would die from the pleasurable feel of it. Unrestrained passion she had not felt since the last time they made love cascaded over her smothering her self-restraint as he thrust his member into her over and over again. Rampantly she moved her hips to match his pace. She heard her name escape his lips a moment before she was sent spiraling toward ecstasy.

It was over too quickly.

Intertwined, they both lay panting as the beads of perspiration that lined their bodies quickly cooled in the night breeze.

Lily looked up at Brock and smiled at him.

A turbulent look flashed across his face. Without a word, he rose on his knees and picked up his pants and shirt.

"Go back to bed," he said in a ragged voice. Then, climbing to his feet, he walked away without speaking another word.

Astounded, Lily watched Brock walk away and thought about the expression that had flickered on his face. It had

103

not been one of happiness. But, one of guilt. Why would he feel guilty about making love to her? Why did he not want to be with her?

Lily rose to her feet.

As she redressed, she thought about the years of anguish she had spent away from her husband. She couldn't believe that in three years he had completely stopped loving her. But, it seemed he had. After the years that passed, did she still have the power to make him remember he loved her? Reflecting on the look that showed on his face, Lily realized she didn't know. However, one thing she did know was that she still loved him. No matter what it took, Lily promised herself, she would find a way to make Brock remember the love they shared. She'd be damned if she couldn't find a way back into her husband's heart...and into his bed.

§

The couple started traveling at daybreak the next morning. Just as the previous days, neither person spoke.

No one spoke all day.

Finally, after sunset, they came to a river and stopped for the night.

For dinner, Brock opened a can of beans and they ate the beans along with beef jerky and the last of the biscuits.

When Brock headed to the river, Lily waited until he had undressed and entered the water before she walked to the river's edge. She stood at the bank and silently watched him bathe.

After a moment, he looked up and saw her watching him.

"What do you think you're doing?" he called from his place in the water when she began to unbutton her dress.

"What does it look like I'm doing?" Lily asked slipping out of her dress.

"Lily!"

"What?" she asked as she tossed her dress to the ground.

"Don't get into the water," he commanded.

104

"What? I can't hear you," Lily called out and waded into the water.

"Don't come any closer," Brock ordered.

Lily responded by disappearing under the water. She broke the surface of the water a few feet from him.

"What...what are you doing?" Brock sputtered when she circled her arms around his shoulders.

"Brock, my darling, make love to me again," she coaxed.

Brock shook his head negatively.

Lily wrapped her legs around his waist and pressed her body against his causing a wave of attraction to ease between them. Seconds later, Brock's manhood harden against her cool skin.

"Lily, no," he protested and attempted to extract her legs from around his waist.

"Kiss me and I'll leave you alone."

Brock remained still.

"Kiss me one time and I'll leave you alone," she said again then added, "I promise."

Brock let out an exasperated sigh and leaned in to kiss her.

Lily pushed away from him before his lips touched hers.

"Oh so you want me now?" she scoffed and swam a few feet away from him.

"Damn it!" Brock growled, waded toward her and reached out to grab her.

"Tell me you want to make love to me!" she called and moved out of his reach.

"Damn it Lily! You're being a tease!" Brock declared before submerging himself under the water.

Lily began to swim toward the bank.

A splash sounded.

Lily glanced behind her and saw Brock quickly gaining on her as he swam toward her. With rapid strokes, she neared the water's edge. When she made it to land, she began to scramble out of the water.

Reaching out, Brock grabbed her ankle and tugged it.

Lily fell onto the soft grass.

"Temptress," Brock growled and lowered his nude body atop hers.

Lily struggled slightly. "What do you think you're doing?" she asked mockingly.

Brock ground his mouth into hers.

"I thought you didn't want to kiss me," she rasped when their lips parted.

"I don't."

"I thought you didn't want to make love to me."

"I don't," Brock said then rolled onto his back and dragged her to a sitting position on top of him. "I've moved on with my life. Your seduction doesn't affect me anymore," he breathed.

"I see," she said and curled her fingers over his hardened manhood.

Brock inhaled sharply. "Lily...we shouldn't..." he murmured when she moved her fingers along his shaft.

Lily leaned down and covered his mouth with hers cutting off his words. "We should," she whispered mulishly as she raised herself slightly then lowered herself onto his pulsating tower.

Brock moaned and cupped her bottom.

"Promise me, there will be no more secrets between us," he coaxed.

"There will be no more secrets between us," Lily stated and began to move her hips. She ran her fingers over his wet chest and through his hair. "Oh Brock. I've missed you so much. Tell me you missed me," she begged.

"I've missed you," he revealed.

"Tell me you've missed making love to me," she pleaded softly.

"I've missed making love to you," Brock replied.

Lily smiled and quickened her pace.

Faster and faster she flexed her hips increasing the tension that mounted between them. Effortlessly, she rode him until he called out her name and released himself inside her. Lily tossed her head back and let out a lustful cry.

"Who's the only woman who can make you feel this good?" she asked as she collapsed on top of him.

"You are, my love," he answered with a smile.

§

Later that night, Lily was awakened by the feel of Brock's manhood prodding the entrance of her intimate place. She pressed her back into his chest and moaned drowsily when he kissed her neck. He entered her womanhood from behind and Lily breathed his name as he placed his hands on her waist and began to move her hips.

When it was over, the couple drifted off to sleep.

Later as the sun came up the next morning, the couple made love yet again.

After they were spent, Brock looked down at Lily whose head rested on his chest. "We've got to get going. We can't spend the whole day making love," he said.

"Can't we?" she questioned then followed her query with a kiss.

§

The sun shown brightly when Brock and Lily climbed onto their horses. A couple of hours after lunch, they came upon a small wagon train. Three wagons were a part of the small entourage. The man in the head wagon was a black man named James Porter. James explained he was a free man traveling with his new wife and some of their extended family. He invited Brock and Lily to travel with them as far as they could.

Brock accepted.

The man's wife was young and pretty and the other adult relatives were friendly as were several children who laughed and played contently. After Brock and Lily joined the group, James rode ahead to hunt for food. He returned hours later with game strapped to his horse. The group stopped for the night and a fire was started. As the venison roasted over the fire, light from the flames glowed against the canvases that covered the wagons. When the meat was served Lily relished every delicious bite. After dinner, the hum of relaxed conversation ceased when James took

107

out his guitar and began to play a harmonious tune which the children danced to.

One of the children grabbed Lily's hand indicating he wanted to dance with her. She danced with the little boy until the group began to urge Brock to dance with her. In response to the prodding, Brock took Lily's hand and twirled her around several times. Happiness swelled in her when she heard Brock laugh. She said a quick prayer of thanks that she was back in her husband's arms and in his bed and they were on their way home.

The next day seemed to go by quickly since traveling with the wagon train seemed to make the trip much less tedious. At dinner, the left over venison was served in chili. Once the meal was consumed, songs were sung around the campfire then the group bedded down for the night.

That night Lily and Brock rested quietly in their tent.

The next morning, James rode out ahead of the group while Brock stayed behind to lead the wagon train.

Near noon James galloped back to them.

"Get off the trail!" he yelled. "Get the wagons off the trail! Now!"

Lily was sitting next to James' wife Lorraine when he galloped to the wagon.

"What is it, honey?" Lorraine asked her husband.

"It's The Klan! 'Bout a mile up the road!"

At the mention of The Klan, a shudder went through the group. Immediately, the wagons were turned off the road and driven into a thicket of trees and over-grown grass. Everyone piled out of the wagons to search for a place to hide.

"Over here!" Brock called to Lily.

Taking her hand, he led her in the opposite direction from the others. They crossed the road, walked into the brush and came upon a huge log that had fallen to the ground. Stepping behind the rotting log, Brock helped her onto her stomach and he lay on his.

As they waited, the only sound to break the silence was that of leaves rustling in the warm breeze that swept the dusty road.

Eventually, the sound of horse hooves snaked its way through the air. Deep voices wafted through the breeze long before the invaders could be seen.

"Carl Junior, take a look at this," one of the men said when they appeared on the trail.

Lily raised her head and peered over the log. When she did, she spied three men dismounting from their horses. The insignia on their saddles denoted they were members of The Klan. Lily realized James must have seen it and been alarmed.

One of the men pointed to the tracks in the dirt that showed where one of the wagons had made a sharp turn off the road. The men headed into the thick grass then disappeared behind the thicket of trees near the place where the wagons were hidden.

Brock reached out his hand and pulled Lily back down to the earth. He motioned for her to remain silent.

Lily lay back down on the dry grass and waited.

After what seemed like an eternity, the voices sounded again. Brock and Lily listened as the men returned to their horses then rode away.

Minutes passed.

Finally James' voice beckoned everyone out of their hiding places. "It's okay. They've gone," he announced.

Everyone emerged a bit unnerved.

"I reckon, you two probably don't know much 'bout The Klan. But, we black folks have to watch out. The Klan hates us and would kill all of us if they could. I'm not sure if they would've done anything to ya'll 'cause ya'll are white. But, when it comes to hatred, you can never tell," James explained.

"I know all too well what they will do to whites who side with blacks. My father tried to help blacks and was killed because of it," Brock revealed.

Lorraine gasped in horror.

James placed his hand on Brock's shoulder. "I'm sorry to hear that," he said. Then, turning to the group said, "We've all had quite a scare. Since it's close to midday, I say we stay here and eat lunch. Brock if you don't mind, can you go huntin' for tonight's dinner. I'd like to stay here with my wife."

James placed his arm around Lorraine's waist.

"Do you want to go hunting with me?" Brock asked Lily.

"Mercy me. Of course, she wants to go with you Brock," Lorraine answered sweetly before Lily could speak.

Lily blushed.

"Tonight is going to be our last night with you," Brock informed the pair. "Tomorrow we have to head our separate ways. We're almost home."

"I can't wait to get home," Lily revealed taking a step to stand by her husband.

"It's been a pleasure travelin' with ya'll," James commented and handed Brock a rifle.

Brock nodded his head then he and Lily began to walk away.

James called out to them.

Brock and Lily stopped and turned back to look at him.

"There's only two bullets left. Make sure you use them sparingly." James waved and called out a goodbye.

Brock and Lily waved at him then turned and headed through the trees.

"Do you think we're going to catch anything?" Lily asked Brock after they walked awhile.

"We're going to try," he answered.

"Remember, there're only two bullets left."

"You best be glad I'm a good shot," Brock drawled.

Lily chuckled.

"I've got to rest," she said after they came upon a large rock.

"We might as well. I haven't seen anything I can shoot," Brock commented and sat beside her.

"That was scary today when The Klan showed up," Lily mused.

"Those men will put the fear of God into anyone. They detest blacks and are very inhumane."

"I'm glad I've never had to deal with them before today," Lily sighed.

110

"Men with that much hate in their hearts are very dangerous. If they knew you were half black who knows what they would do."

A chill went up Lily's spine. "Let's change the subject," she suggested. "There's something I would like to do." She scooted next to Brock and nibbled on his ear.

"Lily...Lily..." he protested and pulled away. Becoming very serious, he said, "There's something we need to talk about. You need to know what's happened in my life before we get home."

"This sounds ominous."

"I've asked you not to keep secrets from me. So, I won't keep any secrets from you. I want you to know, I didn't think I would ever see you again. I held out hope that you'd return home. But the years went by... I made some decisions. I should have just told you from the beginning. It has been unfair of me not to."

"I don't care about any of that," Lily cut in.

"It's important I tell you," Brock insisted.

Standing up, Lily wrapped her arms around his neck and put one of her legs on each side of him. Her eyes fixed with his as she lowered herself on his lap and brought her lips close to his. "Kiss me," she commanded softly.

"Lily, I'm trying to have a serious conversation with you," Brock scolded.

"Don't make me beg," she whispered.

"We have to talk about how things will be when we get home. Things have changed in my life..."

Ignoring his words, Lily pressed her lips against his.

"God Lily. It's impossible for me to resist you," Brock admitted in response to his body's instant reaction to her.

"We'll talk...after dinner. Right now, I want you to make love to me. After all, we couldn't make love to each other for three years," Lily said before she pulled his shirt off and pushed his pants down. She caressed his hardened member then guided it into her slickened treasure and settled on him. "Is this like you remember?" she questioned.

Brock nodded his head.

"I'm glad you remember," she murmured.

With her still connected to him, Brock rose from the rock and walked to the shade of a towering magnolia tree.

Lily's warm skin tingled against the cool blades when he lowered her on a thick patch of grass. Her insides tingled as he began to make love to her.

When it was over, Brock lay his head on her stomach and she ran her fingers through his hair. Leaf covered branches swayed in the wind fanning them as somewhere in the distance a bird chirped.

They both breathed deeply savoring the moment and wishing it would never end.

Suddenly, Brock put his fingers over his lips and slowly raised himself to a sitting position.

Lily watched confused as he noiselessly reached for the rifle. "There's a rabbit right over there," he uttered under his breath.

Lily followed Brock's gaze to a rabbit that had hopped nearby.

The rabbit was looking about, its ears in the air, while it nibbled on several blades of grass.

Slowly, ever so slowly, Brock brought the rifle to his shoulder and pointed it at the rabbit. The rabbit started to hop away. He fired once then twice. He stood up. There was the clicking sound of the release vibrating against an empty chamber when he tried to fire the gun a third time.

"Damn it! It got away!" He lowered the gun.

Lily sat up and ran a short distance the way the rabbit had gone. "Come back rabbit!" she called out.

Brock laughed at her antics. "Looks like we won't be having meat for dinner tonight," he commented.

Lily turned and started to walk back to him.

A gleam appeared in his eye and in the next moment, he swooped up her dress.

"Brock." Lily lunged at him. "What are you doing?"

"If you want your dress back you have to get it back!" he proclaimed and took off in a run.

"Brock! Come back here!" Lily howled.

"You have to catch me!" he hollered right before he disappeared into a thicket of trees.

Lily ran to the place where he disappeared and stopped. She stood naked in the sun and called, "Brock, give me back my dress!"

The reply was the rustle of the wind.

"You're in trouble!" she exclaimed.

There was silence.

"AARRR!" Brock wrapped his arms around her waist and pulled her so that her back was against the wall of his chest. "I've captured you. Now you can never leave me," he whispered against her hair. "You look so cute nude," he admitted when she grabbed her dress out of his hand.

"You're going to pay for your tricks!" Lily turned to face him and playfully swatted his bottom.

Brock kissed her nose. "Let's head back," he instructed after she put her dress back on.

Brock took her hand in his and the pair began the trek back the way they'd come.

As they neared the encampment, the sound of turbulent commotion met their ears. A tumultuous cry rang out amongst a fury of havoc. Lily and Brock looked at each other then picked up their pace. Their strut transformed into a sprint as they maneuvered through the trees. The sound of churlish screams and frenzied gunfire assaulted their senses.

Brock released Lily's hand. "What the...!" His voice trailed off as he bolted ahead.

He entered the clearing then came to an abrupt stop.

When Lily entered the clearing, she ran to where Brock stood then stopped dead in her tracks as well. Her mouth fell open in disbelief.

"Oh my God!" they rasped in unison.

Chapter Ten

The Klansmen Brock and Lily had seen on the trail earlier that day pushed over barrels and pounded on the bed of an over turned wagon as they ransacked the camp. Several men they had not seen before sat atop horses and the horses were circled around James. James, his hands tied behind his back, sat atop a horse as well. A rope, one end tied to a tree branch and the other formed into a loose noose, hung around his neck.

Brock started to charge forward, rifle in hand. But, Lily wrapped her arms around his waist.

"No!" she shrieked.

The Klansmen who weren't involved with James' hanging, tired from their destruction, climbed on their horses and trotted to where James sat. One of the men grabbed the reins of the horse that held James. A moment later, with a click of his tongue, the man led the horse forward.

Horror showed in James' eyes as the horse walked forward. Desperately, he shook his head and tightened his legs around the animal. But to no avail. The horse disappeared beneath him and his body fell like a heavy sack toward the ground. His feet dangled above the ground and he thrashed frantically about as the noose tightened around his neck.

"Die Nigga!" one of the Klansmen bellowed.

"The only good nigger is a dead nigger!" another of the Klansmen hollered.

After firing their guns in the air, the Klansmen galloped off.

Brock broke away from Lily's grasp and hurried to the foot of the tree. He grabbed James' flailing body and hoisted it up so that all of his weight would not be on his neck.

Lily scurried to Brock and pushed a broken barrel near his feet. Brock stepped onto the battered wood. With a grunt he reached up, loosened the noose then pulled the man's body down.

Falling to his knees Brock groaned, "God save him! Save him please!"

Lily's stomach turned violently and she felt as if she were going to be sick. Her feet gave way underneath her and she fell to her knees. "Oh my God!" she groaned.

Brock unbutton James' shirt and placed his hands on the wounded man's chest in search of a heartbeat. Finding none, he dropped his hands to his side.

"There was nothing we could do. We were out numbered and out of bullets," Lily found her voice.

"Where are the women and children?" Brock asked matter-of-factly.

Lily stood and looked around. None of James' family was in sight.

Brock rose to his feet and scanned the items that had been thrown to the ground. Shifting his gaze to look off in the distance, he lamented, "I should have done something."

"There was nothing you could've done."

"Yes. I could've been here."

"Brock if you had tried to do anything I'm sure you would be dead too. They would have done to you what they did to your father. They would have killed you for trying to save a black man."

Brock lowered his head.

"We just saw him alive. We talked to him a couple of hours ago. Why did he ask me to go hunting today? He always went hunting. I should've been the one to stay behind. This shouldn't have happened."

"You're right, Brock. This shouldn't have happened to him. But, he sent you hunting and you're alive because of it."

"It's my fate to go at the hands of The Klan. My father died that way and I have a feeling the same will happen to me."

"Ssshh! Don't say that," Lily instructed.

"Damn The Klan! Damn them and all they stand for!" Brock cursed before kneeling down to touch James' neck. "Oh my God!" he exclaimed.

"What is it?" Lily asked kneeling beside him.

"Oh my God!" he exclaimed again. This time he lowered his head so that his ear was close to James' nose. "He's breathing! He's still alive!"

Lily gasped in shock. "Alive?"

"Yes! He still has a heartbeat!"

"I can't believe it!"

"He's alive but barely. Unless a doctor sees him, I doubt he will last the night."

"What do we do now?" Lily asked.

"We pray," Brock said. After a moment, he said, "We need to find a safe place for James to rest."

Lily quickly walked around and looked for items to salvage. She picked up a blanket and managed to salvage a bag of food and other items needed to continue their journey. Brock picked up James and as the last of the sun's light disappeared from the sky, they began to walk away from the campsite.

As they trudged forward, a coyote's howl echoed on the wind. Lily shivered with fright and scurried to keep up with Brock's long strides.

Finally, Brock turned toward a dense growth of trees. He lay his burden down on the ground. "Wait right here," he commanded before disappearing into the overgrowth.

Lily looked into the darkness. Suddenly, the night became much deeper and foreboding. Rustling leaves scratched in the wind.

"Lily!"

Lily jumped with fright as Brock appeared out of the dark.

"I found a small clearing. Follow me," he said and collected James' body.

Lily picked up the bag of food and the few items she had collected from the overturned wagons and followed Brock to the clearing.

"We can rest here for the night," he explained.

Brock laid James on the ground and covered him with the blanket. Wearily, he lowered himself onto the ground a short distance away. Lily sat down next to Brock and laid her head against his chest. He wrapped his arms around her and buried his head in her hair.

In the next instant, he began to cry.

§

The next morning it was obvious James' condition had worsen during the night. His face was ashen and his breathing shallow.

"He has to get to a doctor," Brock asserted then disappeared through the knot of trees.

He returned a few hours later with news that there was no sign of Lorraine or her relatives. But he said he had spotted some travelers on the road who just happened to be a minister and his wife. He explained that after he told them about James they agreed to take James with them and seek medical attention for him.

Brock loaded James in the minister's wagon. As the couple departed, they waved and promised they would do all they could for James.

After they rode away, Brock left the clearing and returned an hour later with news his horse and James' horse had come back to the encampment sometime that day.

Without delay, Brock and Lily climbed on the steeds and once again headed for home.

§

Brock and Lily arrived in their hometown around lunch time several days later. Lily's heart raced happily in her chest as they rode through the bustling town. It had been three long years since she'd left and she was so glad to be home. Tears crowded in her eyes at the thought of seeing her mother and father again.

Brock stopped the horses in front of the water trough at the livery stable. As the horses began to drink, he dismounted then helped her to the ground. Several passersby said hello to him and looked inquiringly at Lily.

"Lily! Is that you?"

Lily looked up at the sound of her father's voice and saw him rushing across the street toward her.

"Father!" Lily squealed and ran into his warm embrace.

"Oh my God! Lily! Where have you been? Where did you go? You shouldn't have left!" Philip blinked back tears.

"I didn't leave! I was as abducted by slavers!"

"What? My dear child!" Philip held his daughter close. "I'm so glad I came to town today. I was just at the planter's wharf. Had to check on a shipment of hogsheads that were brought in for inspection." Philip looked at Brock. "What are you doing with Lily?"

"I saw her when I left town to purchase thoroughbreds."

Philip laughed. "So Brock, dear boy, you didn't bring back a thoroughbred. But, you sure bought back a filly." Philip kissed Lily's forehead.

"Brock rescued me off of an auction block," Lily revealed happily.

"Dear God! You will have to tell me all about it. But, right now, I've got to get you back to Paradise. Your mother will want to see you."

"Where are you going?" Lily asked Brock when he started to turn from them.

"There are some things I have to attend to. I'll be by to see you later tonight. We can talk then," he said coolly.

"I'll wait for you to finish up here in town. Then, we can go see my mother. After that, I'd like to go home so I can relax."

"No, Lily. You can't stay with me," Brock stated.

"What do you mean?" Lily questioned.

"We'll talk when I get to Paradise. Go with your father," Brock instructed firmly.

"Let's go daughter," Philip muttered gently.

Lily lowered her head and held on to her father as he led her to his awaiting carriage. She climbed in the carriage unsure of her emotions. She wanted to see her mother of course, but why did Brock not want her to wait and go with him?

Lily heard her father direct the coachman to a nearby store before he climbed into the carriage. "I need to make one quick stop before we head home," he revealed after he settled in the seat beside her. "Your mother will be very happy to see you," her father wrapped his arm around her then frowned. "Why do you look so sad?" he inquired.

"It's a long story," Lily replied dryly.

"I always have time to listen to you, my dear," Philip admitted gently.

Lily was quiet for a moment. Finally, she said, "Brock's been distant from me since the day he rescued me off of that auction block. He said there was something he wanted to tell me. We were going to talk about it at dinner one night. But we ran into some trouble on the trail and we never got around to talking about it."

"Do you have an idea what he wanted to tell you?"

"He told me things had changed in his life. He said things happened that I don't know about."

"Oh, so that's it," Philip said solemnly.

Lily extracted herself from her father's embrace and turning her back to him looked out the carriage window into the street. She was jerked forward as the carriage started to move. But she hardly noticed. All she could think of was the fact that with each turn of the wheel she was going farther from Brock.

Brock had tried to warn her that there was something different in his life. What was it and why would he not take her to their cabin? Whatever the reason, she was back in town and they would have to deal with it. They would deal with it together because she was determined to get things back the way they had been before she was abducted and ripped from his life.

When the carriage came to a stop, her father exited the carriage and disappeared inside the general store. As Lily waited, she looked out of the window toward the river and saw the wharf alive with activity. She watched men scurry up and down planks loading and unloading cargo from shipping vessels. In the distance, row barges and shallops dotted the water. She thought about how different the river looked illuminated by the midday sun compared to the ominous way it looked the night she was kidnapped. An image of the darkened alley flashed in her mind which was followed by an image of a shroud appearing out of the dark.

She remembered the knife glistening in the moonlight then a crimson haired man stepping out of the shadows.

The door to the carriage opened cutting off her thoughts. Her father climbed in and rapped on the ceiling of the carriage.

Upon hearing the sharp taps, the coachman started the carriage forward once again.

As the carriage rolled through the town, Lily look out the window amazed at all of the new construction that had taken place. Some of the new construction included a second general store, a cobbler shop and even a newspaper office. Lily turned her attention to the people who scurried about intent on conducting their business for that day. She noticed a woman walking down the boardwalk with three children in tow. In front of them, two men stood talking to each other.

Lily sat up in her seat.

Coming into view, on the boarded walkway, was Brock. She followed the direction of his gaze and saw he was looking at a female who was scurrying toward him. The female was blonde, dressed in a white dress trimmed in lace and she held a white lace parasol that hid her identity. As the carriage rolled by, Lily watched the woman stretch out her arms then wrapped them around Brock's neck. She stared in disbelief as the woman stepped on the tip of her toes and leaned inward.

For a moment, the parasol blocked the pair from view. Then, the female loosened her grip on the parasol causing it to dangle precariously from her hands. It was then Lily saw that the woman was kissing Brock. In the next moment, the kiss ended. At the same instant the wind blew between the strands of the female's hair causing the locks to flutter upward allowing Lily to see the woman's face clearly. Lily gasped with shock when she realized the female was Angela Allen.

Immediately, all of the blood drained from Lily's face.

"He didn't tell that little detail."

For a moment, Lily thought she had said the words out loud until she realized it was her father who had spoken them.

120

The buggy rolled past the scene of Brock with Angela and when the couple could no longer be seen, Lily yelled, "Stop! Stop this carriage now!"

She banged her hand on the roof of the carriage.

The carriage came to a screeching halt.

"Wait a minute my dear child." Philip put a staying hand on his daughter's arm then tapped the roof of the carriage. "Keep going!" he shouted to the coachman.

The carriage jerked sharply as it began to roll again.

"Listen to me for one second and try to understand. A lot has happened since you left. I know you loved Brock and Brock loved you. But he's with Angela now. They are engaged."

"Engaged?" Lily gasped, suddenly feeling as if she had been punched in the stomach.

"She's been after him since you left. He resisted for years. Finally, he gave in to her."

"But they can't be engaged! Brock's married to me!"

"We didn't know what happened to you. Some people began to think you were dead. Brock didn't want to believe it. But after so much time and no word, I guess Angela and his mother convinced him he would never see you again."

"Oh my God!"

"You're my daughter so I'm going to tell you what I know. I know for a fact that Angela will do whatever she has to do to get her claws into Brock. I think Brock cares for her. He made a commitment to her. He told her when he returned from this trip with new horses he would end his marriage and they would set a wedding date."

"But he didn't come back with horses! He came back with me! I'm still his wife!" Lily protested.

"Lily, I know you two loved each other before you disappeared. I remember that well. You must remember, you two were only married for one night before you disappeared. A lot has gone on since that time," Philip stated.

Lily groaned and shook her head upon hearing her father's words. Suddenly, Lily recalled the look of guilt that clouded Brock's face the first time they made love on the trail. With new clarity on the reason behind the look, her heart broke into a thousand pieces. Did Brock really care for Angela as her father suggested?

Maybe everyone thought she had abandoned Brock or was dead. Maybe Brock had finally accepted those theories. However, the facts were she had not abandoned him and she wasn't dead. She was alive! She was back in town and he was her husband! After all she'd done to get back to him, they were going to be together. After all the years of hoping and praying to be back in his arms, she would not give him up. Not without a fight.

"Listen to me daughter. Brock was devastated when you left," Philip said after seeing the glib expression on her face. "He felt you had abandoned him. It really hurt him."

"But I didn't leave! I was kidnapped!"

"None of us knew that. None of us knew a thing. All we knew was we never heard anything from you. Brock told us you had packed your bags. So he thought where ever you went, you went willingly. He thought you wanted to use him to hide the secret of your birth. Now, three years later, you're back and you're telling us you didn't leave on your own. This means Brock's got a lot of decisions to make. And, so do you. I suggest you both rest before you do any deciding."

Lily sank back in the seat suddenly drained of all will. Maybe her father was right. Maybe she did need to rest before she made any decisions. Truth be told, she was too tired and upset to think clearly. After she rested, she'd figure out a way to get things back the way they were before she left. The way she dreamed things would be. The way they should be.

Lily's thoughts were interrupted when her father wrapped his arm around her.

"You still love Brock, don't you?" he asked.

Lily nodded her head.

"You are going to try to win him back?"

Lily shook her head.

Philip kissed her forehead then said, "You are a beautiful person inside and out. Brock will remember that and you will get your husband back."

Lily rested her head against his shoulder. "You think so?" she asked.

"I'm sure of it," Philip answered.

§

Brock raised his head and looked down at Angela's pretty face. Her green eyes sparkled intently as she smiled lovingly at him.

"Hi suga," she cooed. "It's so wonderful to see you. I heard you just got back into town." She reached up and kissed him again. Pressing herself against him, she asked, "How was your trip? You alone? You all right?"

"I'm fine," Brock answered dryly as he recalled the look on Lily's face when he told her she had to go to Paradise alone instead of waiting for him. He thought about the shabby way he treated her on the trail. Angela, the woman who stood in front of him with her arms around his neck, was the reason why. Their plans were for her to be his wife.

Brock thought back to the way it had happened.

For him, Lily's disappearance had been devastating. When days had gone by without her contacting him or her parents, he knew something was wrong. He had saddled up a horse and even though he had no idea where she was, he set out to look for her.

Thoughts of her invaded his mind night and day as he contemplated where she was and the fate she had endured. But, after almost four weeks on the trail and no leads, he had been forced to take the long disheartening trip back home.

When he returned to town, Angela had been waiting for him. She told him she wanted to be there for him. At first, he refused her invitations to dinner. However, she was persistent. After months of encouragement from his mother, he finally consented to have a dinner. As she had on previous occasions, Angela proved to be pleasant company and one dinner turned into two. Then two turned into three. Soon, the pair shared many dinners together.

Angela became his constant companion. She hung curtains in his cabin and planted flowers around the

123

outside. Night after night, she pressed her supple body against his and pleaded with him to forget Lily and move on. His body reacted to her soft yielding flesh. Her provocative kisses seemed to suppress the ache that permeated his heart. When she touched him, he found that at least for a little while he could ignore the emptiness he felt. His mother, overjoyed to see him with Angela, insisted that Lily was gone for good and was never coming back. Finally, his hopes of seeing Lily began to fade even as memories of her plagued his thoughts and dreams.

One year turned into two and Angela began to urge him to settle down with her. After much persistence, and another year, he finally consented to her appeal and told her they would marry. He explained that after he returned to town, he would end his marriage and they would set a wedding date...

Angela wrapped her hand around his upper arm bringing him back to the present. As they walked down the boarded walkway, Brock's thoughts returned to Lily. He hadn't told her he was engaged to Angela. In a short while, he'd have to tell her.

He remembered the nights of passion they shared on the trail and he gritted his teeth. Those nights should not have happened for they only served to complicate things.

§

As the carriage neared Paradise Plantation, Lily's heart began to pound in her chest. When the carriage rolled through the plantation's iron gates, Lily looked toward the two story mansion. It seemed larger than she remembered. Its white brick and black shuttered windows sparkled amidst rolling acres of green crop and the back drop of the brilliant blue green river. Lily looked toward her old room on the second floor. A rocking chair was on the upper veranda just as she remembered.

"We're home!" Philip announced happily.

"I can't believe it," Lily breathed.

"Miss Lily's back in town!" The coachman's voice called to a female slave walking along the pathway leading to the house.

"Miss Lily back?" the slave repeated in disbelief.

Lily waved out of the window, "It's me!"

The slave whispered something to the little boy by her side and the little boy sprinted toward the group of slaves working a short distance away. After the boy spoke to the group, the group sprinted toward the wagon. Lily recognized many of the faces and accepted the smiles and good wishes they called out to her.

Just as the wagon was about to come to a stop in front of the mansion, Marla emerged from the front door, tears streaming down her face. "Lily? Lily! My baby! You're back! Welcome home!" she cried.

The carriage came to an abrupt stop and Lily jumped out. Tears streamed uncontrolled down her face as she ran to her mother's open arms.

"My baby! My baby, finally you home!" Tears splashed down Marla's face as she captured her daughter in an embrace.

"My God!" a familiar voice rumbled a few moments later.

Lily looked up and saw Syrus strutting toward her. Like always, he had a whip hanging from his belt. She wiped tears from her eyes and stepped from her mother's embrace.

"How did you get back here?" Syrus questioned when he came to a stop beside her.

"Brock rescued me," Lily explained.

"Really?" Syrus arched his eyebrows. "Are you angry about the things I said and the way I acted before you left?" he asked.

"That was a long time ago, Syrus. All is forgotten," she assured and embraced him.

"Syrus, you and Lily can talk later. Right now, she needs to tell me everythin'!" Marla proclaimed. Tenderly encircling her arm back around Lily's shoulders, Marla led her away from the group that had gathered and to the mansion.

When Lily entered her old home, her eyes devoured everything within her view and she noted that from the table in the foyer that held a bouquet of wild flowers to the lingering smell of tobacco everything was just as she remembered.

Her mother ordered a tub of hot water drawn for her and she took a long relaxing bath. As she washed the remnants of the trail from her body, she smiled and said a quick prayer of thanks that she had made it home.

After her bath, she found a huge dinner waiting for her. However, Lily could not eat much of it.

"I'm too excited. My stomach's a little uneasy," she told her mother.

"I understand," Marla replied contently from her seat next to Lily before she listened intently as Lily recounted the story of what had happened to her over the past three years.

"I don't understand how that slaver knew you were black," Marla fretted.

"I don't understand it either," Lily replied.

"None of it makes sense. You shouldn't have had to go through such a horrible experience," Marla insisted.

"It's a miracle Brock found me. I'm so glad that I made it home. I must say, I'm really sorry about the way I acted when you told me you are my mother."

"Oh, honey child, you don't have to apologize. I'm just happy you ain't still angry with me."

"I could never stay angry with you. I guess in my heart I've always known you were my mother. I felt the love you had for me even when the words could not be spoken."

"Brock and Sylvia know the truth. But, Brock has forbidden Sylvia to say a word. No one else knows I'm your mother. So, things will go back the way they were before you were taken."

"Oh Mama, I'm just happy to be able to see you again," Lily explained.

"What did you just call me?" Marla questioned shyly.

"Mama," Lily repeated.

Marla smiled. "I'm so glad to hear you call me that."

Lily buried her face in her mother's neck and hugged her tight. "I love you so much," she whispered.

"Only half as much as I love you," came Marla's reply.

§

A short time later, Lily headed up the stairs to her room.

Back in her old room, she smiled as she lay across her old bed. After all she had been through; the kidnapping, living as a slave and the auction block, it felt good to be back at Paradise. She would have much rather gone back to her own home. But for now, she wouldn't dwell on that. She was free and she was still married to the man she loved. That was all that mattered.

Despite everything that had happened in their lives, Brock still loved her. She was sure of it. She had felt it when he kissed her and when he made love to her. Part of him resented her for leaving that was very obvious. But, she told herself, with time she could make him understand she had not wanted to leave him. Then maybe he'd forgive her. And so what his life had moved on. What had she expected? Was life supposed to stop for him just because it had for her?

Brock had once said their love could survive the odds. Fate agreed. For despite the odds, it had brought them back together. They had their future in front of them. She had cried herself to sleep for years. Now, she told herself, there would be no more tears. Lily vowed she would not feel sorry for herself. Instead, she would do whatever it took to make her husband see the love they once shared was still between them.

Lily told herself to relax and not worry about the future. She told herself to focus on the present.

At the present moment, there was no heartache, no engagement and no rejection. It was just her in her old room and in her old bed. And for that, she was truly grateful.

Chapter Eleven

Brock raised his hand and knocked on the door in front of him.

Marla opened it moments later and smiled when she saw him standing before her.

"Lily's asleep upstairs in her room," she said and nodded toward the stairs when he stepped into the house.

Taking the stairs two at a time, Brock strode down the long hallway to Lily's old room. Noiselessly, he opened her bedroom door and stepped inside.

Soft light from the lantern by her bed flickered against the wall casting a burnished glow over the room staying the murky shadows invited by the fading sun.

Noiselessly, Brock walked to Lily's bed. As if suspended in time, he stood watching her as she slept. A cool breeze wafted through the door that led to the balcony and teased the strands of hair that lay against her cheek. In the deep recesses of Brock's heart, something stirred. As if he could hear her beckoning him, he sat on the edge of the bed and with the back of his hand brushed the hair from her cheek.

Lily stirred. Her eyes fluttered several times before she managed to keep them open. Drowsily, she sat up and smoothed back the wisp of hair that fell against her face. Without a word, she leaned toward him and softly melded her lips to his.

After several moments, she peeled her lips from his and silently stared at him. She leaned toward him again.

Brock began to lean inward then paused. After a moment of hesitation, he lowered his eyes and refused to look at her.

Lily raised her hand and slapped his cheek. "I am your wife! I am your wife! How could you do this to me?" she fumed and slapped him again.

Brock reached for her wrists.

She managed to evade his clutches and her fists landed against his chest. A wail escaped her throat and she began to cry. Brock grabbed for her wrists capturing them in his grip. He pulled her to him. Lily wrestled against him causing them both to fall onto the bed. Brock flipped her so that her back was pressed against his chest. He pinned her arms to her side and rested his chin in the nest of her hair.

Lily squirmed in protest. But he held her close.

"No Lily! No! Don't do this! Please, don't do this!" he pleaded in a voice laden with anguish.

"How could you? How could you do this to us? I saw you with Angela! I saw you kissing her!" she sobbed.

"I didn't think I would ever see you again," Brock confessed.

"She's the reason you didn't want to make love to me!" Lily extracted herself from his arms and sitting up turned to face him. "You are with her! That's what you wanted to tell me the day James got hurt, didn't you? You wanted to tell me you were engaged to her!" Lily accused.

Brock sat up and nodded his head

A sob caught in Lily's throat.

"I should have told you earlier, I know. It's just things got complicated real quick. They're still complicated."

"No! No! Things are not complicated! I am still your wife! We promised each other we'd be together until the day we died!"

"That's just it, Lily. I waited for you to return. I hoped you would return. But eventually, I thought you were dead. It was a very hard time. Angela was there for me during each painful minute. She has been by my side during my lowest moments."

"Angela is not a part of this!" Lily argued wiping her tears.

"Angela and I have been together all these years. I've made her a promise I can't ignore."

"You made *her* a promise? What about the promise you made me!"

"Angela and my mother—"

"Your mother? Your mother hates me! She would do anything to keep us apart!"

"She thinks too much time has past and we both should move on."

129

"I accept I should have known life would go on for you. But, for the record, I never stopped loving you. I tried to get back to you. I went through three years of hell to get back to you and our marriage. For three years, I've done nothing but dream of the day we'd be together again. I dreamed about being home and you loving me. It's what kept me alive."

"Oh Lily…"

"We belong together," she insisted. "It's as simple as you want to be with me and I want to be with you. No one else matters."

"It's not that black and white. You have to understand—"

"Understand what?"

"Angela has given up a lot to be with me. She put her future on hold for me."

"Angela's important to you? That's funny. If Angela is so important to you, how is it you're willing to forget about her when it suits you? When we were on the trail, you were more than happy to perform your husbandly duties with me! You could've told me about her anytime! But you didn't!" Lily stood. "You conveniently forgot to tell me you had another woman waiting for you!"

"Lily that's not how it was and you know it! You were the one coming on to me! Look Lily, I don't want you to be hurt. I never wanted things to turn out this way. I—"

"You never stopped loving me," Lily cut in.

Brock rose to his feet. "Lily don't make this any harder than it already is."

"I know you never stopped loving me because I felt your love every day even though I was a million miles away," Lily insisted.

"Look, we need to talk about the way things are going to be."

"Fine. We can talk about everything when we get home," Lily stated and took a step toward the door.

"Lily, I can't take you home."

"You can't take me home? Why?"

Brock shifted on his feet.

130

"It's because of Angela? Isn't it? For the record, in the eyes of God, we are still man and wife! I don't care if you thought I was dead! I'm not dead! I'm alive! I'm back in town and there's no way I am going to let another woman end our marriage! I know you, Brock. I know what we shared and I want it back. The love we have, it's still there. I could feel it when we made love on the trail. When we made love, it was as wonderful as it's always been."

"Don't say that."

"Can you deny it?" Lily asked.

Brock did not answer.

"Take me home, please. Just tell Angela I am back. Tell her to leave you alone."

"I can't."

"You can!" Lily wrapped her arms around her husband and buried her face in his neck. "Please," she begged.

Brock brought his arms around Lily noting how snuggly she fit in his arms. The scent of her powdery perfume fluttered about him bringing back heartwarming memories of the past. Like quicksand, the memories unexpectedly threatened to gobble him up. In that moment, he wanted to surrender to her. He wanted to give his heart to her just as he had many years ago. He wanted to succumb to her silky arms which beckoned him. But could he risk loving Lily again? If he did, would he end up with his heart on the floor once more? Could he really forget the past? Could he focus on moving toward the future?

Brock looked down at Lily and frowned. Slowly, he pried her arms from around his neck then kissed her forehead. In a sad voice, he said, "Sweetie, now it's my time to walk away."

Lily gasped in protest as he stepped from her embrace.

In the next moment, he turned his back to her and headed for the door.

"Then go! I don't ever want to see you again!" Lily yelled hysterically as he stepped out of her room and closed the door behind him.

§

Brock shook his head to clear it but to no avail. Thoughts of Lily continued to plague his mind. He thought about the hurt that had shown in her amber eyes when he walked away from her and his heart sank. He had practiced walking away from her a million times in his mind. Then, it was payback since she'd walked away from him. Was that the reason now? If he was over her, why was it he could still feel warmth where her body touched his? And, why could he still feel the soft touch of her hair where the wind had blown it against his cheek?

"Where'd you go?" Angela's demanded as she walked toward him when he arrived at his mother's cabin.

"I went to see Lily," he replied after he dismounted from his horse.

"Of course. You're wearing her perfume," Angela sneered and reared back from him then placed her hands on her hips.

"She's still my wife, Angela."

"So where does that leave us? We've been sharing a life together for almost three years. Are you going to give that up for a woman who packed her bags and walked out on you after one day of marriage? Lily didn't care enough about you to stay and be your wife. But, I care. You asked me to be your wife and I can stand right here right now and promise you, I will never leave you. I will never walk out on you."

"Lily didn't mean to leave me. She left me a note telling me where she'd gone. But, for some reason, I never got the note. She was abducted. She's been through a lot. This is very upsetting for her."

"There's no need for you to rush to comfort her. If she hadn't walked out, she would not have been abducted. Look, Brock, you two are not married in any way that counts. I love you, Brock. We belong together and I will do whatever I have to, to protect our relationship."

"There's a lot to sort out. I have some tough decisions to make."

"It's over between you and Lily. Listen to me when I say, I've loved you too long and I won't let you go. I won't let you or Lily make a fool of me," Angela warned then swiveling on her heels she stomped inside his mother's house to eat the awaiting dinner.

§

The next day, Lily stayed in her room most of the morning sleeping. After Brock left the previous evening, she had fallen on the bed and forgetting about her previous vow to be strong, she had cried herself to sleep.

Around noon, her mother called for her to come downstairs for lunch. Dejectedly, Lily made her way down the grand staircase. Her mother's voice called from the drawing room. When she walked into the drawing room, she saw the table set with sandwiches. She sat down and looked out the window at the cerulean river arrayed along the horizon.

"Why do you look so sad this mornin'?" Marla asked as she poured a cup of lemonade.

Lily looked at her mother through tear filled eyes. "Brock won't leave Angela."

"You're still crazy 'bout him even after all these years," Marla observed.

"I should have told him that you were my mother before we got married. He deserved to know the truth. Because I didn't tell him the truth, he thinks he can't trust me. He thinks I was manipulating him. If I had told him the truth none of this would have happened."

"You wanted to tell him. I'm the one who told you not to. I should have let you do it."

"Brock doesn't care that I'm half black. I told you he wouldn't care."

"Brock's a good man. A very good man. I know that now. But, at the time, I didn't know how he would react, especially 'cause of what happened to his father."

"Yesterday, when I woke and saw Brock looking at me…the way he looked at me… For a moment, I thought he was going to tell me things could be the way they used to be. Instead, he made it plain where his loyalties lie. It was a delusion for me to think that after three years apart Brock would still care about me."

"Mercy me. Don't be so dramatic. Don't you reckon if Brock didn't want to be married to you, he would've annulled your marriage a long time ago? But, he didn't. If he didn't end the marriage when you weren't here, I don't think there's a chance in hell he's gonna do it now that you're back. He'll come back to you once he's had time to sort things out."

"You think so?"

"I know so," Marla smiled and patted Lily's hand.

A knock sounded at the front door.

Seconds later, a slave scurried past the drawing room on her way to answer it. A moment later, the young female appeared in the doorway and smiling at Lily said, "Mista Brock's here ta see ya."

Lily's mouth dropped opened. Brock was here! He had returned for her! Now she could go home and they could restart their lives together as man and wife. Why had she doubted him? She squealed and hugged her mother. "Oh Mama! He's back!"

"Calm down. Relax. Act natural," Marla advised after Lily sprang to her feet.

Lily took two measured steps. Abruptly losing her cool, she flew toward the front door.

Brock looked larger than life to Lily as he stood on the veranda.

"You're back!" she breathed happily and stepped onto the porch next to him.

"I need to apologize for the way things were left yesterday. I don't want there to be any more hurt between us," Brock stated.

"Me either. We do need to talk. Just let me say goodbye to my mother then we can talk about everything on our way home."

"No, Lily. You don't understand. I'm not here to take you home," he said.

"What? Then why are you here?"

"I'm here to see if we can find a way to be civil to one another."

"Civil? You refuse to take me home. You refuse to let me be your wife and you want me to be civil?"

134

"It's best if we both keep a level head about this."

"You think so, huh?" Lily twisted her lips. "Well, I'll start being civil the moment I get home. I fought the gates of hell to get back to you and our home and that's what I want. I want to be with you. I want to go home. Take me home. Now!"

"Lily, please…"

"I'm not going to take no for an answer!" she insisted.

"There's no need to get upset about—"

"Don't lecture me! The only words I want to hear from you are those telling me you're going to take me home and you're going to let me live as your wife!" Lily screamed, losing her cool.

"I can't do that."

"Why not?"

"Things need to be figured out first."

"Take me home and then we'll figure things out!"

Brock shook his head negatively.

Lily arched her eyebrow and stepped back inside the mansion.

"Let's discuss this."

"There's nothing to discuss!" Lily shouted.

"Let's discuss this rationally."

"Rational? You want rational? I'll show you rational!" she shouted then slammed the door shut.

Once the door was closed, Lily leaned against it and burying her face in her hands, she began to cry.

§

The next day, feeling bad about the way she acted, Lily decided to go to the ranch and apologize to Brock. She told herself she would remain calm and try once again to get him to consent to her moving into their home.

When she arrived at the ranch, she looked around for Brock but did not see him. She took a minute to watch two ponies, one palomino and the other sorrel in color, romping playfully in one of the corrals. As she walked up the steps of her old home, one of Brock's dogs ran to her barking and wagging its tail. She reached down and affably petted the dog.

"Well, well…look what we have here."

Lily looked up at the sound of the voice and saw Angela peering out one of the windows of the cabin.

"Lily, I heard you were back in town. Come in," she smiled and motioned for Lily to come into the house.

Lily straightened herself then opened the door to the cabin and stepped inside. Once inside, she couldn't help but notice how beautifully decorated the cabin was and knew Angela was responsible for it.

"Do you like what I've done to the place?" Angela asked when she saw Lily's gaze scan the room.

Lily did not answer.

Angela smiled. "I'm glad you showed up because I've been doing some thinking. I've come to the conclusion we should put our differences aside."

Angela glided to the large table in the corner of the room.

"Come here. There's something I want to show you," she said sweetly.

Lily followed Angela to the table.

"It took me a long time to find this. However, when I saw it, I knew I had to have it." Angela picked up a brown paper package that was lying on the table. "After all, special events like this one only come along once in a girl's lifetime," she announced happily then ripped the paper uncovering a bolt of shimmering white silk.

"It's for my wedding dress," she said sweetly as she shook the creamy white silk causing it to spread like an undulating wave over the table.

At the sight of the glimmering material billowing over the table, Lily's breath caught in her throat and she found she couldn't say a word.

A smirk creased Angela's lips and in a voice filled with pleasure, she said, "I just know Brock will love it. Being engaged to him is wonderful. Knowing he loves me and wants to marry me is an indescribable feeling. That's why I'm obsessing over every little detail. I want our wedding to be perfect. Just like it is between Brock and me."

Lily lowered her eyes, desperately hoping the anguish she felt did not show on her face.

Knowing she was having the desired affect on her competition, Angela continued, "There was a time when you had Brock wrapped around your finger. You manipulated him with your feminine wiles and mind games. I assure you that will not happen again. You will never be with Brock again. Not ever."

Angela lifted her chin and stared down her nose at Lily. "I told you once I would get Brock back. You made it easy for me by abandoning him. Now, I have him and he is going to leave you and marry me. He is going to spend the rest of his life with a woman who is his equal. And, on our wedding day, I'm going to be dressed in a perfect wedding dress made from this silk. After the ceremony, I'm going to come back here to your old home and make love to your husband in your old bed. By the time the sun comes up the next morning, I'm going to be carrying Brock's seed in my belly."

Infuriated by Angela's vicious jab, Lily yelled, "You have some nerve saying these things to me! You can't marry Brock because he's still married to me! I'm still his wife and I won't let him end our marriage! I won't let you come between us!"

"For all intent and purposes, you two aren't married! You abandoned Brock after one day of marriage and now he wants nothing to do with you! He loves me! That's why he won't live in the same house with you!" Angela shot back.

"He loves you? That's news to me. I guess Brock was too busy kissing me to tell me that when we were on the trail together!"

Lily watched the confident expression on Angela's face evaporate. Seeing her words hit their mark, she spat, "I see he didn't tell you that juicy detail."

"Because it isn't true!"

"Oh it's true all right! Now, tell me, if Brock loves you so much, why do you think he made love to me over and over again? Night after night."

"You hussy!" Angela hissed.

"Brock is my husband and I won't let you come between us! I'm taking back my rightful place in Brock's heart and in his home!"

Suddenly, Lily reached out and yanked the silk off the table then threw it on the ground and stomped on it.

Angela's eyes became dark with ire. "Why you—!" She raised her hand to strike Lily.

Reacting quick, Lily caught Angela's arm in a vice like grip and dug her nails into the woman's skin. Locking eyes with her foe, she proclaimed, "I'm back in town and I'm here to stay! So back off! Stay away from my husband! If you don't, your face is going to end up like your silk!"

Lily kicked the silk with her feet.

"Crazy bitch! You dare threaten me?" Angela seethed. "You had your chance with Brock and you blew it! I was with him a long time before you came between us and I won him back! I will not let you steal him from me again! I am going to do whatever I have to do to keep you away from him!" Angela jerked her arm from Lily's grasp.

"Brock is my husband and he will never leave me! Think about it Angela! He didn't leave our marriage when I was away! There's no way he's going to leave me now! So give it up! There's nothing you can do to keep me from Brock! There's nothing you can do to come between us!"

Spearing Lily with a loathing glare, Angela retorted, "Don't be so sure I can't keep you from Brock! You aren't good enough to kiss Brock's feet! All I have to do is make Brock see that and your life will be a living hell!"

"I'm not afraid of you!"

"You should be, pretty one!" Angela hissed. "You should be!"

Chapter Twelve

"I hate her!" Lily fumed after she returned home and stepped onto the veranda outside her bedroom.

"Hate who?" Syrus asked as he patted the hip of the slave girl who sat in his lap.

The girl jumped from his lap and smiling shyly scurried away.

Casting an exasperated glance at the girl's retreating figure, Lily muttered, "I'm talking about Angela Allen!"

"What's wrong with Angela?"

"She's evil!" Lily walked to the railing, leaned on it and looked out at the sea of slaves scattering toward their shanties now that their day's work had ended.

Laying down his cigar, Syrus rose from the rocking chair. "What did Angela do?" he asked inquisitively.

"It's what she won't do that's the problem."

"And what's that?"

"Leave Brock alone," Lily replied.

"I'd rather not hear about Brock. I'm interested in you and what happened to you. I can't believe you were abducted and forced to live as a slave. Tell me what happened and how you happened to make your way back home."

"Remember that night we ran into each other in town? I was staying at the hotel and I told you I'd received a note from Brock and was going to meet him?"

Syrus nodded his head.

"It turns out Brock never sent me that note."

"What? So who sent the note?"

Lily shook her head. "I don't know. I went to the warehouse because of the note. Some slavers were waiting for me. My hands were tied and I was taken. For the last three years, I've lived as a slave." Lily trembled.

"Have a seat." Syrus nodded to the rocking chair.

Lily sat in it.

"Tell me how Brock found you," Syrus prodded.

"I was on an auction block about to be sold when he saw me. He had come to the town to buy some thoroughbreds."

"How much did he spend?"

"Five thousand dollars."

"That's a lot of money."

"It was his life's savings. He has nothing left."

"It was a stroke of luck that Brock found you."

"It's a miracle. I was happy until we witnessed a man being hung."

"What?"

"When we were on the trail, some Klansmen tried to kill a man. We saw them hang him... To see his body hanging like that..." Lily's voice faded as she recalled the sight.

"I can tell by the look on your face it was a horrendous ordeal," Syrus said gently.

Lily rubbed her forehead. "It was very hard on Brock. His father was killed by members of The Klan if you'll remember."

"Oh yes. He was killed for hiding some slaves."

"Brock's afraid that he will die at the hands of The Klan too. If Brock and I had to face The Klan again, I don't know what we'd do."

"The Klan can be a bit cruel."

"It's a good thing they didn't know I have black in me. Oh, I wish we could forget about all of it. I wish Brock and I could go back to the way things were between us before I was taken."

"Why do you worry yourself with Brock?"

"When did you stop liking Brock?" Lily asked.

Syrus rubbed his forehead. "You've still got it bad for that lout."

"He's my husband."

"But, he's with Angela. He's taking her to The River Room tonight."

"How do you know?"

"I know," Syrus replied cryptically. After a moment of silence, he said, "You don't have to be stuck at home tonight. I'll take you to The River Room."

"You would?"

"Sure. I haven't been in a while."

"I...I don't know," Lily replied skeptically.

"What could it possibly hurt? Brock will be with Angela. Maybe after you see those two together, you will realize you shouldn't have rejected me."

"Syrus! Don't start that again!"

"All right! All right! They'll get to see you enjoying yourself."

"I'm not sure..."

"It'll be all right. Trust me," Syrus prompted.

§

Spirited music streamed from the piano on stage at The River Room. However, it barely drowned out the sounds of the individual conversations and sporadic laughter that erupted throughout the large room.

From where he sat near the piano, Brock cast a glance across the table and looked at Angela. She looked pretty as she sat quietly listening to the music. He thought about the many times she had sat across a table from him. Whether it had been here at The River Room or at his cabin, she had always been there for him. She had always stuck by his side.

Always.

So, why at this very moment was he thinking about Lily? Why was he thinking about how good it felt to have her in his arms? Why could he not forget the feel of her smooth skin, the tenderness that showed in her amber colored eyes or the heat of her kiss?

"You're thinking about Lily, aren't you?" Angela's question pierced his thoughts.

Brock lowered his eyes to his mug.

"You've been holding out for her for too long. It's bad enough you haven't made love to me since you got married. But, since you came back to town, you have not so much as kissed me. I'm not so naive that I don't think it has something to do with your wife." Pausing briefly, Angela eyed him suspiciously then queried, "You slept with her, didn't you?"

141

Brock rose to his feet.

Pushing back her chair, Angela followed his lead and rose to her feet. "We need to talk about it! You have to choose! You need to make it clear who you want! Where are you going?" she called to Brock when he started to walk away.

"Lower your voice!" Brock ordered then clutching her hand he led her to a corner.

When Brock turned to face her, Angela said, "Look, I know the excitement of seeing Lily again may have made you do some things you regret. I don't want to focus on that. What I do want to focus on is our relationship now that you're back. I feel you withdrawing from me. Why can't you see that I've never stopped loving you? I've always been there for you. Always." Angela shook her head as tears crowded in her eyes. "I just wish I knew you loved me as much as I love you."

Seeing Angela's tears, Brock brought her gently into his arms. "I realize I'm sending you mixed messages. But how can I not when I'm all mixed up myself?" he asked.

"Oh, Brock," Angela buried her head in his chest. "I don't want to lose you."

Brock rested his head on top of her golden curls. "I proposed to you because I wanted to put the past to rest and focus on the future."

"It feels so good to hear you say that," Angela whispered.

Brock opened his mouth to speak then closed it when he spotted Lily standing across the room talking to Syrus. His eyes narrowed as he watched the pair. Immediately, he noticed the lecherous glint in Syrus' eye as Syrus looked at Lily.

"Do you love me?" Angela's voice interrupted his observation.

"Of course, I care for you."

"But do you love me? Tell me you love me," her words were a plea.

When he did not answer, Angela lifted her lashes to look at him. She turned her head to follow his gaze. "You're still in love with her!" she accused.

142

"She's still my wife."

"What is it going to take to make you see, she's no good for you? What is it going to take for you to realize you can't relive the past? Don't let her back into our lives. Don't let her steal your heart again," Angela pleaded.

"Angela, I can't make any promises to you until things are settled between me and Lily."

"No! Don't say it! You can't cast me aside again! I won't allow it!"

"I don't know what will happen."

"Just tell me you love me and we can get through this together," Angela implored.

Brock lowered his eyes.

"Damn you!" Angela seethed. With a brutal shove, she extracted herself from Brock's embrace. "You go back to her and you both will pay!" she spat before spinning on her heels and stomping away.

§

"Syrus, I'm not so sure this was a good idea," Lily said as she scanned the crowded tavern in search of Brock.

"Nonsense. Just forget about your problems and have fun," Syrus coaxed.

At that moment, musicians began to play their instruments from the stage.

"Come on!" Syrus grabbed Lily's hand and led her through the smoke filled room to the dance floor.

Once there, he turned to face her and began to shake his body erratically to the unrestrained beat.

Lily couldn't help but laugh.

"Come on move it! Move it!" Syrus exclaimed merrily and bobbed his head with a rhythmic tempo.

Lily smiled at him as one of the musicians began to pound a drum.

"All right," she sighed and started to move her hips to the beat.

When the musical piece ended a few minutes later, Lily inhaled deeply to catch her breath.

"That was fun. But I've had enough," she panted.

143

"Don't stop now. We just got started!" Syrus declared.

"All right," Lily relented as another uninhibited tune began to permeate the room.

"Relax and have fun!" Syrus exclaimed then he contorted his shoulders with an exuberant bounce.

An uncontrolled giggle escaped Lily's lips. "You win. I'll forget about my problems for one night," she conceded and began to dance.

"You're having a good time. I can tell," Syrus remarked after they danced several sets together.

"Oh, Syrus, I'm having a wonderful time. But, there's something I want to do." Lily stopped dancing.

Syrus placed his hands on Lily's shoulders when she took a step backward. Leaning inward to be heard over the music, he questioned, "You're going to try to find Brock, aren't you?"

"I want to talk to him."

"Don't go chasing after that boar."

Lily opened her mouth to speak. However, Syrus placed a finger under her chin and lifted it so her eyes met his. In a low tone, he asked, "Do you remember what I told you before you left?"

Lily jerked her chin dismissively away from his touch. "I don't want to talk about that. It makes me uncomfortable."

"I may have come on a little strong then. But, now that you're back and Brock is with Angela, I was thinking, maybe you'd reconsider my proposition."

"I'm a married woman, Syrus. I will never consider any such thing," Lily responded.

"Brock's with another woman! You're his wife but he's with another woman!"

"I've been gone for three—"

"If you were mine, it wouldn't matter to me how long you'd been gone."

"He's my husband Syrus! I still love him! Nothing's going to change that! I'm not going to give up on my marriage!"

"You can't continue to live in the past! You've got to move on! I'm willing to take you even though you're black. That's got to mean something!" Syrus insisted.

"Syrus!"

"Don't reject me again. Bad things happen when you reject me," Syrus reproved in a harsh voice.

Shoving brusquely against Syrus' chest, Lily broke from his grasp. Hastily, she spun on her heels then came to a curt halt when she saw Brock standing on the edge of the dance floor. Her gaze locked with his. A wave of hope rose in her when she realized he had been watching her.

In the next instant, Brock shifted his gaze from her.

As the plaintive wail of a violin faded, Lily thought about Brock's refusal to let her return to their home and live as his wife. She grimaced and thought of Angela and Angela's assertion that she would never be with Brock again.

A drumbeat began to echo through the room.

Lily began to move her hips to the beat. Slowly at first, she swung her hips from one side to the other. Surrendering to the rousing rhythm, she moved faster gyrating her body to the beat.

Brock looked at her.

With a smoldering stare, Lily searched the depths of Brock's eyes and parted her lips. A smile curled her lips when he took a step toward her. Then another. She lowered her lashes.

When she looked up a moment later, she saw Brock had halted his advance. The crowd of dancers closed around her and for a moment she lost sight of him. A second later, when the dancers parted, she saw him turning away from her.

Squaring her shoulders against her bruised pride, Lily twirled around and glided back to Syrus. In an audacious move, she took Syrus' hands in her own and placed them on her hips. Indignantly, she shook her hips to the seductive drumbeat and let her hands curl around Syrus' neck.

Brock clenched his teeth. He knew Lily was deliberately trying to get under his skin and told himself to look away and not play her game. But, he found he could not look away. No matter how he tried, he found he could not take his eyes off of her as she moved lithely in Syrus' arms. God help him! What was wrong with him? After all of the years

145

that had gone by, hadn't he inoculated himself from her affect? Hadn't he learned not to keep from falling into her trap?

The answer came when, in the next moment, Syrus grabbed Lily's bottom and swept her against his middle. In the next instant, Lily tossed her head back and let out a boisterous laugh.

Unable to restrain himself any longer, Brock stomped to the pair and angrily tapped her shoulder.

Lily wiggled her bottom refusing to turn to him.

Syrus stepped back slightly and Lily saw a hint of trepidation in his eyes.

The tap came again on Lily's shoulder.

This time, Lily gracefully swirled around to face her husband. Continuing to gyrate her body, she batted her lashes. "Oh, hello Brock," she purred demurely.

"Stop it, Lily!" Brock snarled.

"Stop what? Dancing?" she questioned coyly.

Spearing her with a cold glare, Brock growled. "Stop playing your silly little games."

"Silly little games? I'm afraid I have no idea what you're talking about?"

"You're embarrassing yourself!" he hissed.

"What do you care? You care about Angela. Not me. Remember?" she retorted.

Brock's eyes narrowed. In the next instant, he grabbed her arm. With an irritated growl, he dragged her from the dance floor and steered her out the back door of the building. When they stepped into the star splattered night, Brock whirled her around to face him.

"What the hell do you think you're doing?" he growled.

"I have no idea what you're talking about."

"What are you doing here with Syrus?"

"What does it matter to you?" Lily questioned hotly.

"Don't be so naive Lily. Syrus is not your biological brother. I see the way he looks at you. Teasing him is not a good idea!"

"Are you jealous?"

"You're playing a dangerous game, girl. Don't you know that?"

"You're with another woman and you dare question me about who I'm with and what I do!" Lily yelled, suddenly angry. "We're still married! Have you forgotten that? You have no right to be with another woman! You have no right to disrespect me in such a way! I'm your wife! Not Angela! As long as you are with her, I will do what I want when I want and I'll do it with whoever I want!"

The back door of The River Room swung opened and the man and woman who exited glanced inquisitively at Brock and Lily.

Impatiently, Brock grabbed Lily's arm and hauled her around the side of the building.

Once they were alone, he clenched his teeth and snarled, "I don't trust Syrus!"

"Syrus brought me here because he likes having me around which is something you've obliviously not wanted!"

"Stay away from him!"

"I'll do as I please!" Lily fumed mulishly.

"You're still my wife and you aren't going back in there to dance with him. So you might as well go home," Brock surmised.

Lily folded her arms. "Which home are you referring to? Are you talking about Paradise Plantation? Paradise is not my home! My home is with you! At our cabin! If I can't go back to our house…my home…I'm not leaving!"

"Lily, do as I say!"

Lily dug her heels into the ground. "I leave by myself and you go home with Angela, is that it? You said yourself Syrus can't be trusted. So, why do you want me to go back to Paradise Plantation? Syrus lives there too, remember? Seems to me, if you really want me away from Syrus, you'd let me return home. So tell me, do I go home with you. Or do I go back inside and leave with Syrus?"

Brock studied her through hooded eyes. Finally, he muttered. "Damn it, Lily! I'll take you home…to the cabin!"

At his words, happiness swelled in Lily and a delighted smile curled her lips.

Brock looked at her with a scowl.

"Lily, are you all right?" Syrus called out as he rounded the corner of the building.

147

"I'm just fine Syrus. My husband is going to take me home. To our cabin," she stated gleefully and smiling placed her hand on Brock's arm.

Without speaking, Brock stomped forward nearly dragging Lily behind him.

As the couple rounded the front of The River Room, music and laughter exploded into the night as a man exited the building.

Lily hummed happily to the music and scurried to keep up with Brock's long strides.

§

"Are you going to let Brock do that?"

Syrus turned at the sound of the female voice and saw Angela standing next him.

"Are you going to let him drag Lily out of your arms?" she asked.

"Somehow Lily found her way back to him. She's in love with him," Syrus answered.

Angela was quiet a moment. Finally, she spoke. "I see the way you look at Lily. You still want her for yourself."

"Nothing will come of it. She won't let it," Syrus stated.

"You've gone a long time without getting what you want. Don't you think it's time you finally get what you want?"

Syrus was silent.

"You should know by now, I can make things happen. I can see to it that you get what you want," Angela stated.

"I know where you're going with this and I'm not sure I want to be a part of it this time," Syrus hedged.

"Brock should be mine. I will do anything to get him back. You can join with me and get what you want. Or, you can stand on the side and be left out. But, if you join me, I'll see that you get what you really want."

"What will you do this time?"

"I wish I could tell the whole world Lily's a nigger. But, Sylvia asked me not to because having people know might hurt Brock. So, I will have to come up with something. We will come up with something."

148

"What do you want me to do?"

"Tell me everything you know about Lily. Then we can formulate a plan."

Syrus lifted his arm slightly. "All right partner," he acquiesced.

Placing her hand on Syrus' arm, Angela looked up at him and batted her eyes invitingly. "It's time we discuss a new strategy. With your help, we will have Brock and Lily right where we want them."

Syrus clasped his large hand over Angela's slender one. "I have a feeling I'm going to like working with you…again," he said and then began to laugh.

§

During the ride home, all Lily could think about was in an hour or so her dream would come true. She would be back home in her bed with Brock lying beside her. When the cabin came into view, she had to stop herself from squealing. She managed to keep a straight face as she followed him inside the cabin. A few seconds later, the sound of a match being struck was followed by a sizzle. A small burst of light softened the shadows within the room and Lily watched Brock light a lantern.

The room filled with light.

"You should be comfortable now that you're home like you wanted," Brock said.

Lily looked around the room noting the things that hinted at Angela's touch. She promised herself she would discard the items the very next day. At the moment, however, she told herself to enjoy the fact she was home.

With this in mind, she walked to the large table in the corner of the room and ran her hand along the top of it. "I feel very comfortable," she muttered wistfully.

"Good. Then I'll be going," Brock said.

"You're not staying?" Lily questioned.

"No. I'm not staying," he replied solemnly.

"But—"

"Look Lily, I promised to bring you here. I didn't promise to stay with you."

Lily let out a rueful sigh. "Why are you doing this to me? I didn't know I'd be kidnapped. I left you a note in hopes you'd come after me. It's not my fault I was taken. All I want to do is be with you…to be your wife again."

"All the time you were gone, when I was hurting, Angela was good to me. She was there for me. She never left me. Now that you're back, you want me to forget all that. You want me to forget everything. You want me to pretend the last three years didn't happen. Well, they did happen Lily and I can't pretend I didn't bond with another woman because I did."

Lily gasped suddenly fearful.

"You and me, we said our vows and we planned for it to last forever. Unfortunately, fate had different ideas. You want me to let Angela go and continue our marriage? There's only one problem with me doing that. I can't live my life wondering if you're going to betray my trust and try to manipulate me again. I can't spend my life wondering if you are going to hide anymore secrets from me."

Lily started to speak. However, the look of anguish in Brock's eyes rendered her speechless.

"There was a time when I thought you living here in this house with me was all I wanted. Now, I'm not so sure due to the fact I know I can't take being hurt by you again," Brock said sadly then he turned and walked out the front door and closed it without looking back.

Chapter Thirteen

Lily's eyes were wide open when the sun came up the next morning. She had not been able to sleep a wink after Brock walked out of the cabin the night before. Her pride bade her not to run after him. But, the grueling night she'd spent alone spurred her out the door the next morning after she looked out the window and saw him feeding the horses.

"Why won't you come home?" she asked after she came to stand beside him.

Brock didn't speak.

"Please, Brock. At least come by for dinner," Lily pleaded.

"When I finish here, I have to go by the Morgan farm. Their mare is foaling. Won't be back in time," he stated and walked away.

§

"How is your meal?" Syrus asked Angela as he sipped brandy from the glass he held in his hand.

"The food here is delicious. Thank you for ordering it for me," Angela responded.

"It's the least I can do considering we're partners," Syrus grinned.

Angela smiled in return then wiped the edges of her mouth with her napkin. Casting a quick glance out the restaurant's window, her smile faded. "Look who's there." She tilted her head to one side.

Shifting his gaze in the direction Angela indicated, Syrus looked out of the window and saw Lily walking into the grocers across the street.

"Wonder why she is in town?" Syrus mused.

"Go find out," Angela ordered.

"Are you sure?"

"Yes. Find out what happened after she and Brock left The River Room last night. And, find out where they plan

151

on being tonight. Tonight may be the night we put our plan into action."

"Tonight? Isn't tonight kinda soon?"

"The sooner the better."

"You think we can get everything ready on such short notice?"

"I can. Now, if you play your cards right, you will have what you want tonight. And I will have what I want real soon."

"Fine. I'll see what I can find out," Syrus said and placed his napkin on the table.

"Find out what you can then come back here," Angela instructed.

Syrus pushed back from the table and stood up.

"I'll be waiting," Angela called as he made his exit.

Syrus strutted out of the restaurant and across the street to the grocers. He stepped inside the store and looked around.

"Syrus, what are you doing here?" Lily asked when he came to stand beside her.

"I was about to ask you that question," Syrus smiled.

"I'm here because I'm going to fix a nice meal for Brock tonight."

"So, you and Brock worked everything out?" Syrus inquired.

Lily shook her head negatively. "Not exactly."

"I could stop by the cabin this evening and tell Brock what a cad he is if you'd like."

"Syrus, don't be silly. Besides, Brock will not be home."

"What do you mean?"

"He's going to the Morgan farm to help deliver a foal."

"Are you going to the Morgan place to see him?" Syrus asked.

Lily nodded her head. "I'm going to fix a meal and take it out to him so we can talk."

Syrus rubbed his chin. "So what time are you going to see Brock at the Morgan farm?"

"I have some things to do around the house then I am going to take him the food for dinner."

"Very interesting. Well, I won't keep you from your task," Syrus said. Then, bowing poignantly, he backed away from her and made his way out of the store.

Once he exited the grocers, Syrus retraced his earlier steps and headed back across the street to inform Angela of Lily's plans.

§

A contented smile graced Brock's lips as he looked down at the tiny colt nuzzled against its mother. Turning, Brock ambled to the bucket of fresh water and began to rinse his hands. The baby colt had been born, the farmer overjoyed and now his assistance was no longer needed.

As Brock dried his hands on a clean towel, his thoughts drifted to Lily. He thought about her request that he have dinner with her. He knew her request for dinner was an effort to get him to move home and be with her. There were several reasons he hadn't stayed with her. The least of which was he couldn't be sure how he would respond once the lights were out. But, now that he'd had a whole day to ponder it and now that it was night, he did not feel good about leaving her alone. He was beginning to wonder if he should go back to the cabin to see her.

"Brock?" A sultry voice sounded.

Brock turned toward the sound of the voice and saw Angela standing in the entrance of the small barn. Her bright yellow dress seemed to glow against the darkness just beyond the door.

"What are you doing here?" he asked her.

"We need to talk," Angela answered and took a step toward him.

Brock laid down the towel and wiped his brow with the back of his hand. "What are you doing here so late? How did you know I was here?" he asked.

"A woman always finds a way to know what she wants to know. For instance, I know you let Lily stay in the cabin last night," Angela revealed as she came to a stop in front of him.

"That is her home. I couldn't keep her from it," Brock stated informatively.

"Damn it Brock!" Angela screeched and folded her arms across her chest. After a moment, she waved her hand in a dismissive jester and said, "Fine. Try to work it out with Lily all you want. You just mark my words. It'll end up the same way it did before. Lily will hurt you again. She betrayed your trust and walked out on you. She will betray you again and when she does maybe then you'll finally see her for what she really is."

Angela reached out and took Brock's hands in hers. "I know you're struggling with the feelings you have for her. You should remember, those feelings are for ghosts of the past. Life has moved on and so should you."

Angela gently kneaded his hands then pressed them to her breasts. "Feel me Brock. Feel me. I'm flesh and blood. I'm not a ghost and what we have is not a memory. I've loved you since the first day I laid eyes on you. I will always love you. So, don't let a dream from the past tear us apart."

Her lips found his.

"Angela..." Brock leaned away from her. "Listen to me, Angela. I'm still a married man. I can't forget that. Until I figure things out, I think it's best if we don't see each—"

Angela rolled her lips hungrily across his cutting off his words. "She's not good enough for you and I won't lose you to her. Not again," she muttered.

The sound of a wagon rolling to a stop outside the barn echoed through the thin walls. In response to the sound, Brock moved to step away from Angela. Acting quick, Angela took hold of his shoulders at the same moment she locked her foot around his ankle. Hastily, she pressed her body against his frame and shoved him causing him to lose his footing and fall backwards.

Keeping her grip on his shoulders, Angela landed with a squeal on top of Brock as he fell to the ground. "I remember this position very well," she giggled playfully and slid her arms across his chest. Then, she leaned down and pressed her mouth on his stifling the protest that formed on his lips.

"Brock!" Lily's voice called from the entrance of the barn.

Brock and Angela turned in unison to see Lily standing in the doorway of the barn with an astonished look on her face.

"Oh, hello Lily," Angela purred with a look of satisfaction.

"Lily!" Brock frowned and tried to sit up.

Angela splayed her alabaster hands on his shoulders and pushed him back down with a playful laugh.

Lily gasped and turning abruptly ran from the barn.

"Angela!" Brock snapped angrily.

"All right! All right!" Relenting, Angela rolled over and sat up with a sigh.

Quickly, Brock rose to his feet and raced out of the barn. He exited the barn in time to see Lily direct their wagon onto the dirt road in front of the farm house.

"Brock!" he heard Angela call to him.

Ignoring Angela's call, Brock leapt on the stallion which he had tethered nearby and urged the animal into a gallop.

Dust from the wagon greeted him as he steered the stallion in the direction Lily had taken. He leaned forward and entwined his fingers in the horse's mane as the night air whipped about his face. Fervently, he prodded the stallion into pursuit until it felt as if he was flying like the wind. When the horse galloped to the wagon, Brock steadied the animal's pace to run alongside it. Glancing at Lily, he motioned for her to slow the wagon.

She responded by slapping the rein's urging her horse into an even faster pace.

Brock prodded his horse until it was neck and neck with Lily's horse.

When both animals ran in unison, he leapt from his steed.

Lily's gasp met his ears as he sailed in the air then landed an instant later on the horse she directed.

"Whoa! Now!" Brock commanded as he reached out and gathered the horse's bridle. "Easy boy, easy!" He pulled on the bridle and the horse slowed a bit. He reached for the reins and yanked them from Lily. Then, he brought the horse easily under control. Once the horse came to a stop, he turned and looked at her.

Without saying a word, Lily jumped from the wagon and began to run down the middle of the road.

"Lily! Come back here!" Brock called after her.

Lily shook her head and continued to run away from him.

Brock jumped from the horse and sprinted after her. He could hear her crying before he caught up to her. When he did, he reached out and clutching her arm spun her around to face him.

"How could you? How could you?" Lily sobbed as he pulled her into an embrace. "I can't do this anymore! If you want to be with Angela, you can be with her! I can't fight you anymore! It hurts too much!"

Brock shook his head. "Lily, listen to me. I..." His words fell away when a horse neighed near his ear. He lifted his gaze and his heart began to pound in his chest at the sight before him.

Lily felt Brock stiffen and lifted her gaze as well. She let out a terrified shriek when she saw three men with hoods covering their faces sitting atop horses. The emblem stitched on two of the men's attire denoted them as members of The Klan.

Fire from the torches they held licked hungrily toward the darkened sky. Two of the Klansmen dismounted and planting their torches in the ground took a menacing stance in front of Brock.

Lily began to tremble at the sight of the perilous horde surrounded by the ghostly glow of firelight.

Brock moved his impressive frame protectively in front of her.

"We don't want any trouble!" he called to the masked men.

"You don't always have to want trouble. Sometimes trouble wants you," one of the masked riders responded.

Brock clenched his teeth. "If you all have something to say, say it and leave. We've got nothing you want."

Lily clutched Brock's arm.

He motioned for her to stay behind him.

Looking at Lily, one of the men sneered, "You girl, you the black bitch? We don't need your kind around here."

"Leave her alone!" Brock's voice rumbled.

Turning his gaze back to Brock, the man snorted, "What did you say you nigga lover? Huh?"

Brock gritted his teeth.

"You're a traitor to your own kind, boy. We're here to rid this town of vermin like you and we're going to start the clean up tonight."

Suddenly, the man who remained on his horse pulled a whip from a hook on his belt. Lily let out a terrified scream when she saw the thread of the whip hurl toward Brock. In a flash, Brock pushed her away from him. An instant later, the long cord slithered around his waist.

Brock groaned as the cobra-like fangs of the whip bit into his skin.

The cord unraveled and a second later the man on the horse flicked the whip again. This time, Brock sidestepped to the left but not before the thick cord snaked around his right wrist, searing his skin. He let out a bitter groan and grabbed the cord. With a growl, he jerked the lash causing the rider who held it to nosedive off of his steed.

A snarl of protest erupted from the masked men who stood in front of Brock. They grabbed Brock's arms and twisted his limbs behind his back. The man who fell from the horse stood to his feet. With a boorish curse, he kicked his torch aside then clutching his hand into a fist the man strutted to Brock and rammed his fist into Brock's stomach.

"You nigga lover! You're gonna die boy!" one of the men who held Brock blustered as blow after blow was hammered into Brock's stomach.

Lily ran to the man who punched Brock and grabbed his arm. Effortlessly, the man pushed her from him. Unprepared for the brutal shove, she fell to the ground.

Brock let out a growl and tried to break from his captors' grip.

The man who punched Brock straightened and reached into his back pocket. Remaining silent, he pulled out a thin rope, tossed it at Brock's feet then motioned to the men who held Brock.

157

"We got to tie his hands!" one of the men who held Brock hollered.

While the two men who held Brock tied his hands, the man who had beaten Brock walked to his horse and unhooked a long thick rope from his saddle.

"No! No!" Lily screamed as she scrambled to her feet.

One of the men who had been holding Brock rushed to her and grabbed her arm.

Lily jerked against the man's grasp.

The man responded by sliding his hand around her waist.

Lily screamed and flailed about as the man who had unhooked the rope walked to Brock and tied it around his neck. "God! No! Please don't!" Lily pleaded and let out a shrill wail. "Please don't do this!"

"Lily!" Brock called to her.

"She'll be in good hands with us, boy," the man who held Brock remarked as he dragged Brock toward one of the horses.

Lily began to wail in anguish as the two men struggled to lift Brock onto the mount. When Brock was on the horse, the horse was led to a tree and the long end of the rope was thrown over a low hanging tree branch. Lily let out an anguished scream as an image of James Porter hanging from a tree flashed in her mind. She knew any moment the Klansmen would pull the horse out from under Brock. A second later, Brock's body would fall, the noose would tighten around his neck and his feet would dangle inches above the ground.

Lily closed her eyes against the image. "Please! Please! Let him go!" she begged desperately.

"Settle down bitch or you gonna take his place," the man who held her drawled in her ear and twisted her arm behind her back. Then lifting her off her feet, the man carried her close to Brock. "Don't worry yo self with this here mulatto wench. She's in good hands with me."

Brock growled.

The man laughed.

His two friends chuckled along with him.

"Tell me half breed. How badly do you want your nigger lover free?" the man who held Lily asked. Snaking his arm around her neck, he squeezed his hand over her throat. "Answer me when I talk to ya! I asked you a question! Do you want this man free?"

Lily nodded her head.

"Then tell me, how far you willin' to go to make that happen?" The man moved his hand to her breasts and rubbed them. "Would you be willin' to show a few lonely boys a good time?"

"Get your hands off me you contemptible barbarian!" Lily hissed indignantly.

The man who had put the rope over the tree branch motioned to the man who spoke.

The man who held Lily removed his hand from her breast and cleared his throat. "You not opposed to giving money are ya?"

Lily did not answer.

"Looks like you don't understand. This bucks gonna hang unless you can convince us not to let him," the man said.

"Hey! Ain't she that Frasier girl?" the hooded man who had dragged Brock to the horse blurted out.

The man who held Lily took a long moment to stare at her then let out an elated snort. "You is that Frasier girl! You Syrus Frasier's sister!" he wrenched out. "This is gonna be easy! You gonna give us some money and you gonna get it from Syrus! After we get our money, we'll release your buck and you can go on to have young buck babies," the man chuckled.

"How much money we talkin'?" one of the hooded man who stood beside Brock queried.

"Five thousand should be enough," Lily's captor said. "You got that half breed? Five thousand. That's all it's gonna take to free yo man. Go straight to Paradise Plantation. Go to Syrus Frasier. Tell him to bring five thousand dollars to the old Stephan's farm...you know the one up the road that's abandoned. You go straight to Syrus. Don't tell anyone else. Tell him to come and if either of you tells anyone or brings anyone with you, your boy is

159

dead. You hear me? I said, do you hear me?" the man hollered in Lily's ear.

A sob caught in Lily's throat as she nodded her head.

"Then the matter is settled," the boisterous man beside Brock said.

"Just keep your end of the bargain and we will keep ours," came the command in Lily's ear. "Do we have an agreement?"

Lily nodded her head.

"Are you sure?"

Lily nodded her head again.

"Good. Then you have exactly two hours to get Syrus to bring the five thousand dollars to the Stephan's farm," the man blustered and gestured toward Brock.

The third man who had remained silent pulled the rope from the tree.

Brock fell from the horse and landed on the ground.

The man holding Lily slackened his grip.

She pushed from his clutches and ran to were Brock lay.

"Oh my God! Brock sweetie!" she cried and hugged him as he gulped for air.

"Tie him to the back of a horse!" the man who once held Lily ordered.

A second later, Brock was ripped from Lily's embrace and dragged to his feet. The excess rope that hung from Brock's bound hands was looped around the horn on one of the saddles.

Lily watched in horror as the man who remained silent climbed on the horse and spurred the animal into a slow trot. She whimpered when she saw Brock get jerked forward and stumble slightly. She watched as he began to run to keep from falling on the ground behind the horse.

The remaining two men climbed on their horses.

"You got two hours! I suggest you get going!" one of them yelled while the other began to laugh.

§

Lily ran up the steps of Paradise Plantation and burst through the front door.

"Lily, ya all right? Ya lookin' foe Miss Marla? She down at the slave quarters," one of the slave girls announced informatively when she saw Lily.

"Is Father here?" Lily questioned.

"He not here," the slave revealed.

"Where is he?"

"He been called to town. Seems some sort of unexpected business came up and he needs to take care of it tonight."

"When will he be back?"

"Not sure."

"Where is Syrus?" Lily questioned.

"He went out. Said he'd be right back."

As she finished speaking, the front door opened and Syrus walked inside.

"What happened to you?" Lily questioned when she saw a bright red bruise on his cheek.

"It's nothing," he said running his fingers through his ruffled hair.

"I need to talk to you, it's important," Lily said.

"You look upset. What's this about?"

"It's private."

"We can talk in my room. Go on up, I will be there in a second," Syrus instructed.

Lily rushed up the stairs and scurried to Syrus' room.

When she stepped into the dimly lit room an ominous feeling engulfed her. Suddenly, she remembered the illicit kisses he had stolen from her and the indecent proposition he had made.

"What can I do for you?"

Syrus' voice interrupted her thoughts.

Turning sharply, Lily saw him standing beside her.

"I'm here because something horrible has happened and I need your help!"

"What happened? You look upset," Syrus placed his hand on her shoulder.

Lily wrung her hands nervously.

"Have a seat," Syrus instructed gently and nodded to his bed.

Lily walked to the edge of his bed and sat on it. "It's my husband! I need help! The Klansmen... Some Klansmen came upon us tonight after we left the Morgan farm! There was a scuffle! They've got Brock! They're threatening to hang him!"

"The Klan has Brock?" Syrus sat down next to her.

"Yes!" Lily nodded her head.

"Why would they have Brock? How is that possible?"

"Somehow they know I'm half black. They went after Brock for being with me. They want money and then they say they'll free him."

"Money? How much money?"

"Five thousand dollars."

"Five thousand dollars? That's outrageous!"

"I know! But, we have to pay them! They've given me two hours to get the money to the Stephan's old farmhouse," Lily explained.

"Have you told anyone else about this?" Syrus asked.

Lily shook her head negatively. "No. They told me not to."

"And they asked you to bring the money?"

"They told me to come to you, ask you for the money then have you take the money to the Stephan's farm."

Syrus stood up and walked to a nearby table that held a flagon and a small glass. He picked up the flagon and poured an amber colored liquid from the flagon into the glass.

"The Klan. Now that's serious stuff," he said after he took a sip. "You must be terrified knowing that Brock is in the same predicament as his father and his father was killed by The Klan."

A sob caught in Lily's throat.

"You were separated from Brock for three years. It would be very sad if Brock were hung. Then, you'd be separated from him for a whole lot longer."

Lily rose to her feet. "Father will know what to do."

"You can't tell him!" Syrus snapped. An instant later, he softened his tone and said, "You told me you couldn't tell anyone."

"But Father will know what to do."

"Something unexpected came up and Father had to go to town. He won't be back anytime soon."

"I wish Brock had the money. But, as I told you, he spent his savings to buy me. So, you're my only hope. You've got to get the money."

Syrus gulped from his glass then remarked, "Honestly Lily, I don't know if I can do that."

Lily walked to where he stood. "You can get the money, can't you?" she questioned.

"Of course, I can get the money, Lily. But, what I want to know is, can I get you?"

Lily took a step back. "What are you saying?"

"I'm saying you don't have the money to save Brock and you can't go to anyone else to get it or Brock will be harmed. You want five thousand dollars and you want it from me. Well, my dear, I want you." Syrus sat on the edge of the table. "I've gone a long time without getting what I want. I think it's time that changes."

Lily stared at him in determined disbelief.

Syrus shrugged his shoulders in response to her expression. "What can I say? I guess I'm like my mother after all. That selfish whore didn't let anyone get in the way of her getting what she wanted. The bitch was only concerned with herself and her own happiness. Alas, I find, I follow in her footsteps."

"You can't be serious," Lily stated.

Syrus took another gulp from his glass then he locked his gaze with Lily's. "You tell Father or Marla what takes place in this room tonight and I will be the first to sing the secret of your birth from the mountain tops."

"How dare you threaten me with my birth!"

"I am well aware of how important it is to you and your mother to hide your secret. It's important to Brock too. That's why he made Sylvia keep her mouth shut. If you tell Father or Marla and they confront me about this, your sweet reunion with your precious Brock will be over because I will tell the world you're a Nig. And, once I do, Brock will be shunned for being with you and the unanimous glory he gets from everyone will disappear."

Lily shook her head. "Syrus, I don't understand why you are talking this way."

"Oh yes you do, pretty one." He let his gaze roam over her body. "You knew this day would come. I told you there would be a reckoning if you spurned me."

"Syrus! No!" Lily backed away from him.

"From the day I spied you in your room and realized you were no longer a scrawny girl, I've wanted to possess you. It's kept me awake at night. It's been true torture. Thinking about you with Brock...his hands on you...touching you..."

Suddenly, the glass in Syrus' hand crushed under the pressure of his fist. Its delicate pieces shattered and clanked onto the floor.

"Syrus!" Lily gasped. "My God! What's come over you?"

"Lust my dear. Indescribable, undeniable lust."

"Don't talk like that! I owe it to my marriage—"

"Damn it woman! You owe Brock nothing!" Syrus slammed his hand on the top of the table. When he lifted it, red droplets of blood began to appear on his palm.

Lily screamed.

"You can scream all you want. After I sent you up here to my room, I sent the servants away. They won't be returning to the house tonight."

Lily tried to walk past Syrus.

He seized her arm. "What is so good about Brock? Do you think he's better than me because I'm adopted? Is it because you think me a bastard since I wouldn't know my own father if he passed me on the street?"

Lily pulled against Syrus' grip.

"Come here," he breathed and drew her against his chest. "You should be grateful I still want you, you nig. Besides, I have all the money you need. I will give it to you if you give me what I want."

"Syrus No!"

He leaned down and catching her off guard pressed his cold wet lips on her mouth.

164

"Oh my God! No! No!" Lily shrieked and struggled to pull away from him.

"Lily, I've wanted this for so long... I've wanted you," Syrus whispered in her ear. "Ever since that night I saw you undressing in front of the mirror all those years ago. Your skin was so lovely. Your breasts—"

"Let me go! Let me go!"

"This can't be a surprise to you, just be honest with yourself. You want this just as much as I do. I know you do."

"No Syrus! You're my brother!"

"Your brother? Huh! I'm far from it my dear. I want you in my bed. I want to make love to you."

"No! Noooo!"

"Damn it Lily! You're so beautiful! Just let me touch you. I want to touch you and kiss you..." His hands moved to her breasts.

"God no!" Lily slapped his hands from her body.

"Lily, I will give you the money if you do it," he promised gently.

"Why are you saying these things again? When I returned home you apologized for behaving this way in the past."

"I just said what I had to say. Now, I will do what I have to do to get what I want," Syrus revealed.

Lily reared from him. "Brock was right about you! He told me you couldn't be trusted!"

Syrus pressed his lips hard against hers cutting off her breath.

When she could no longer stand it, Lily opened her mouth and gasped for air. Syrus' tongue wiggled between her lips then slithered out. She closed her mouth and jerked from his touch. He clinched her firmly against him and smashed his mouth to hers once more. Lily bit down on his lip.

Syrus pushed her from him. "Bitch!" he spat.

Lily stumbled backward barely able to remain on her feet.

"You bastard!" Lily screeched and rushed toward the door.

As her hand touched the door, Syrus called out, "You leave this room and Brock dies!"

Lily came to a screeching halt.

"You can't get the money anywhere else. There's no time. So, I'm going to tell you what you are going to do and you're going to do it," Syrus' tone was low.

Lily remained still.

"You're going to turn around and walk back to me. Then, you're going to persuade me to give you the money. If you don't, Brock will pay for your refusal with his life."

Lily remained motionless for many moments as she contemplated her fate. With her back toward Syrus, she thought of Brock and her heart ached. She knew he would not want her to consider for one second Syrus' offer. However, she knew she would not see her husband dead. She loved him more than her own life and knew she must do what she could to save him.

Squaring her shoulders, Lily whispered a prayer for strength then turned to face her foe.

Chapter Fourteen

As Lily slowly walked to Syrus, she thought about how ominous Syrus looked with his gaze fixed on her as if he were a vulture eyeing his prey.

"Syrus, I can't. We can't... It's not right. Let me see the money."

An impish smile enveloped Syrus' face. He stood from the table, walked to his chest of drawers and rummaged through a drawer. After a moment, he pulled out a wad of bills. "Five thousand dollars. That's what you want, isn't it?" Quickly, he counted the bills which totaled five thousand dollars exactly. Then, he came back to where Lily stood and tossed the stack on the edge of the table.

Lily stared at the money that would free Brock. She did not move when Syrus placed his finger under her chin and lifted it upward.

"Kiss me," he whispered.

Lily stared at him as if she could see through him.

Ignoring her stare, he repeated his command. "Kiss me like you kiss Brock."

Lily did not move.

"I am not going to force you to make love to me. You'll do it willingly or you don't get the money."

At his words, Lily lowered her eyes, leaned her head forward and placed her mouth on Syrus' mouth.

Syrus responded by pulling her against him and running his lips over hers. "Don't look so distressed, Lily. You will enjoy this too," he rasped when their lips parted. Casting a glance at his bed, he said, "Let's move to the bed."

Lily took the few steps to stand next to the bed.

Syrus came to a stop in front of her and slowly began to unbutton the buttons on her dress. After all of her buttons were unclasped, he opened her dress and pushed it off her shoulders. A groan rumbled from his throat as he gazed at her breasts. He gripped the dress then tugged until it fell in a heap around her ankles.

167

Lily closed her eyes and willed herself to stand still under the heat of his bold stare. *I love you Brock*, she thought.

Syrus clasped her hand in his. "Finally, I get the benefit of what Brock enjoys," he said ruggedly then touched his lips to her neck.

A shutter of disgust coursed through Lily and she recoiled in revulsion.

Suddenly, anger flashed in Syrus' eyes. Clutching her wrist, he spat, "I am willing to over look the fact you're a no good darkie with inferior blood contaminating you. Yet, you cringe when I touch you! Even the darkies in the fields of this plantation know better than to do that! Those black wenches from the fields who grace my bed know to treat me with respect! It's time you learn to act like them! It's time you learn your place!"

Defiantly, Syrus unbuttoned his shirt and threw it to the floor. After which, he stripped himself of his trousers.

Abhorrence filled Lily's eyes and she looked away from the sight of his nude body.

Incensed by her response, Syrus pushed her backward onto his bed. A second later, he fell over her pinning her down on it. In the next instant, he pried her legs apart and sank between her thighs.

Lily tried to raise herself.

Syrus coiled his huge fingers in her hair and jerked her head back. "What's it going to be? Are you going to fight me and lose the money? Or are you going to let this happen?" he inquired.

Lily's answer was to fall back on the bed and lay motionless underneath him.

Syrus flexed his hips once then plunged his pulsating member inside of her. Lily inhaled sharply when Syrus began to move within her sheath. He groaned and her stomach turned in disgust. She wanted to push him off of her. But she did not. She remained motionless, closed her eyes and thought of Brock. Her heart filled with sadness as she thought about the anguish he was going through at the hands of The Klan. She prayed Syrus would be done soon so he could take the money to the Klansmen and free Brock.

"Oh... oh... You're so good! Just like I imagined!" Syrus grunted as he fondled her breasts.

Lily opened her eyes to look at the shadows splayed along the wood paneling and paintings that outlined the bedroom walls. Syrus quickened his pace. Several moments later, he let out a loud moan and his body convulsed slightly.

Suddenly, he fell on top of her.

"That was fantastic! Brock is a lucky son of a bitch," Syrus panted and pulling himself out of her moved to lay on the bed.

Refusing to look at him, Lily turned her back to him.

Syrus reached out and rubbed her shoulder. "It wasn't all bad now was it, pretty one?"

Lily wrenched away from his touch and covered herself with the bed sheet.

"You kept your end of the bargain. So, I'll keep mine. You'll have your precious Brock back in a short while," Syrus muttered then climbed out of the bed.

Without further words, he picked up his shirt and trousers and pulled them back into place. He walked to the table, scooped up the stack of bills then walked to the door. Once there, he turned to look at her.

"I suggest you enjoy your time in Brock's arms. Something tells me it won't last," he stated then made his exit.

§

Lily sat in the tub and scrubbed her skin in an effort to erase the feel of Syrus' touch. She wondered if Brock would know what she had done when he saw her. She hoped he would not because she knew how angry he'd be if he found out.

The sound of the front door opening echoed through the cabin interrupting Lily's thoughts. She straightened herself in the tub and held her breath as heavy footsteps advanced in her direction. In the next moment, Brock appeared in the doorway. Her heart leapt for joy. He was safe!

Without a word, Brock walked to her and scooped her out of the tin tub. He smelled of sweat and musk. However, Lily ignored it and buried her face in his neck as tears stung her eyes.

"I just want things to go back the way they used to be," she whimpered.

Brock didn't speak. Instead, he carried her to their bedroom and lay her on their bed. Gazing down at her, he said, "I'm sorry for the way I've treated you. I've been such a fool."

Lily reached up and captured his lips silencing him.

He responded by kissing her passionately.

When their lips parted, Brock said, "Having a noose around one's neck makes one think. From the moment I saw you on that auction block I knew it. But, I was so full of anger and mistrust I didn't want to admit it. But, I can admit it now. I'm still in love with you, Lily. I don't want Angela. I just want you. Only you. That's all I've ever wanted. I want to start being the husband you need and deserve, if you still want me."

"Oh, Brock."

"I want to forget about all of the hurt I've felt in the past and spend the rest of my life loving you. I love you, Lily. God help me. I love you. I'm so glad we have a second chance to be together. I'm sorry for the hell I've put you through, sweetheart. I've been such a fool. I do want to stay married to you, if you still want to stay married to me."

"I want to stay married to you, of course."

Brock rubbed her arm. "We'll pick up right where we left off. Just like you want. There'll be no more secrets between us. Whatever comes our way we'll face it together."

Their lips met again.

A second later, Brock's lips left Lily's and trailed across her cheek then down her neck to the mounds of her breasts. His tongue circled her right nipple as his hands slid over her hip. When his hands slid between her thighs, Lily let out a blissful sigh as she thought how this was the moment she had dreamt of...the moment she had hoped for. For three long years, she had wanted more than anything to be in Brock's arms...to be in this bed...to have him tell her he loved her and have him make love to her. Now she was. Now he was. Her dream was finally coming true. Unable to contain her happiness, she widened her legs apart.

In response to her beckoning, Brock peeled off his shirt while she pushed down his pants. Kicking his pants to the floor, Brock let out a contented sigh and took a long pleasurable look at her naked body. Her tiny breasts. Her delicate arms. The shapely curve of her hips. The dark patch of curly hair above her feminine place. This was what he wanted. She was what he wanted.

"You're beautiful," he whispered and swept her into his embrace.

Careful to balance his weight with his arms, Brock stretched over Lily's body and with gentle deliberation began to enter her.

Forgetting about her encounter with Syrus, Lily responded with a playful squeeze and arched her hips to him.

Throwing caution to the wind, Brock began a smooth rhythmic motion with his hip.

Lily moaned a little.

Brock smiled at the sound which was music to his ears. As he continued to move his hips, he thought of his love for Lily. He knew he would always love her in his heart. But now, it was time to worship her with his body.

§

A smile eased across Lily's face. She was happier than she ever thought possible. After the encounter with the Klansmen and Brock's return to the cabin, they had spent many hours making love. In the weeks that followed, they spent hours entwined in each others arms and hours talking as they reconnected with each other. To Lily, it seemed as if the time they spent together almost erased the years they had spent apart.

171

But, despite her happiness, there was one thing that weighed heavily on her mind. Her indiscretion with Syrus. She imagined Syrus confronting Brock and telling him about the events that led to his release. Lily thought about Sylvia and knew she had planted suspicions in Brock's mind about her relationship with Syrus. Because of those suspicions, she was sure Brock would never understand why she did what she did.

Sensing something was wrong, Brock asked her to tell him what was bothering her. But Lily refused to confide in him. Instead, she tried to forget about her night with Syrus. Upon finding she couldn't erase the memory, she confided the truth to her mother.

"That godforsaken scoundrel!" Marla yelled and threatened to confront Syrus.

Hastily, Lily revealed Syrus' threat to expose her as half black if he were confronted.

Marla clutched her fists together. "I'm not gonna let him get away with this!" she vowed.

A few days later, Lily was working in the garden when her mother arrived at the ranch.

"I have some news to tell you."

"What is it, Mama?" she asked after her mother knelt beside her.

"Syrus won't be botherin' you anymore," Marla declared cheerfully.

"What do you mean?"

"After you told me what he did to you, I knew I couldn't just sit by and let him get away with what he did. So, I figured out a way to get him out of our lives at least 'til I can think of a permanent solution."

"What did you come up with?" Lily questioned.

"Believe you me, I wanted to tell your father what happened so he could deal with Syrus properly. But, I know Syrus wouldn't hesitate to tell the world our secret and that can't happen. So, I talked your father into sendin' Syrus to Europe. Your father agreed to send Syrus there to expand the number of merchants who sell our tobacco. Syrus left yesterday and he'll be gone indefinitely."

"Oh thank God!" Lily sighed.

172

"Now, at least for a while, you can stop worryin' that Brock will find out 'bout what Syrus made you do. No one else knows 'bout that night and with Syrus gone no one will find out."

As Marla finished speaking, the squeak of a wheel met the women's ears. Marla and Lily looked up to see Sylvia's buggy advancing over the field.

"What does she want?" Marla questioned as the buggy came to a stop near the cabin.

The buggy's door swung opened and Angela Allen stepped out of the buggy.

"Hello, Marla Jane. Hello, Lily," Angela uttered sweetly as Sylvia exited the buggy.

Taking Sylvia's arm, Angela led her up the steps of the porch.

Lily and Marla made their way to the porch.

"I've come to see my son," Sylvia announced loudly when the women came to stand beside her.

"Brock's not here," Lily said.

"Well, where is he?" Sylvia demanded peevishly.

"He's at the Morrison ranch looking at their sick horse," Lily answered.

Sylvia folded her arms and glared at Lily for several moments. "Angela told me the truth," she finally proclaimed.

Lily looked at Brock's mother perplexed. "The truth?"

"Angela confirmed what I've suspected all along," Sylvia remarked harshly.

"You thought you could get away with hiding the truth, didn't you?" Angela challenged.

"The truth about what?" Marla asked.

"I was wondering how long it would be before Brock found out and left you, Lily. Then, I heard Philip sent Syrus to Europe. I know you had him do it to keep Brock in the dark," Angela uttered.

"What are you talking about?" Lily demanded.

"She told me you slept with Syrus," Sylvia bit out.

Horror filled Lily's eyes and all of the blood drained from her face.

"So it is true!" Sylvia declared upon seeing the look on Lily's face.

Lily lowered her eyes.

"How did you find out?" Marla questioned Angela.

"When it comes to Brock, I find a way to know."

"I knew you could never be faithful to my son! I knew you'd been carrying on with Syrus! You've been doing it for years!" Sylvia accused.

"No! That's not true! You don't understand!" Lily screeched.

"Oh, I understand! I understand perfectly! You're a whore just like your mother!"

"Watch it lady!" Marla snarled and took a menacing step toward Sylvia.

With a haughty air, Sylvia lifted her chin. "Brock has to know about this!" she said matter-of-factly and stomped down the steps.

"No! No! No!" Terror reverberated in Lily's voice as she raced down the steps after her mother-in-law. "Please, don't tell Brock! Please!" she pleaded as she traipsed beside the stately woman.

"No more hiding secrets, Lily! Brock has to be told you were with Syrus!" Sylvia exclaimed and pushed past Lily.

"Sylvia Cunningham, you stay outta this!" Marla shouted belligerently and rushed to block Sylvia's path.

Sylvia halted her steps and let out an aggravated sigh. "You two scheming wenches want to hide yet another secret. I've kept your first secret because my son demanded it and I wanted to protect his reputation. But, I won't keep this one! My son is a good man. He deserves to know that he's married to a whore!"

Lily grabbed her mother-in-law's arm. "Don't you dare tell him! He'll never understand! He'll never forgive me! Sylvia! I only did what I had to do!" Lily shouted.

Sylvia rolled her eyes.

"Sylvia Cunningham, what kinda mother are you? How could you be happy hurtin' your son! Brock loves Lily. Yet, you insisted on fillin' his mind with suspicion! You've made him think there's a possibility Lily's been carryin' on with Syrus! But, that ain't true! After all Brock and Lily have been through, instead of lettin' them be happy, you're intent on destroyin' their relationship!" Marla shouted angrily.

"So you propose Sylvia keep Brock in the dark?" Angela hedged.

Marla nodded her head.

"There is not a chance in hell I'm going to let that happen," Sylvia assured and jerking her arms from Lily took a step forward.

Lily lunged at her mother-in-law and grabbed her arm again. "Do you really hate me that much? Are you so blinded by hate that you can't see that I love your son?" she questioned.

"It's too late for lies, Lily," Sylvia remarked then shoving passed Lily marched to her buggy and climbed inside.

"Well, well, looks like I was right. You should have listened to me when I told you I could make your life a living hell." Angela smiled brightly. Then, flicking her hair from her shoulders, she turned gracefully and sauntered after Sylvia.

§

Lily trembled uncontrollably. She couldn't sit still yet she didn't want to move. Pacing in front of the stove, she tried to convince herself Brock would listen to her explanation and not be angry enough to leave her. She stopped pacing and pressed the palm of her hands against her forehead which pounded painfully.

Brock's buggy sounded in the yard.

Lily lowered her hand and shot a look at her mother who sat at the table nervously wringing her hands.

Her mother opened her mouth as if she wanted to speak. Then, the sound of Brock's heavy footsteps started on the steps and she didn't say a word.

A fire roared warmly under the pots. The smell of roasting meat filled the air. But, Lily didn't notice any of it as Brock's footsteps sounded on the porch. Her breath caught in her throat and she stared at the front door.

The door opened and Brock stepped inside.

Forgetting all else, Lily rushed to him. "Brock!" she exclaimed.

Without warning, Brock's hand came across her face stinging her cheek. A second later, the back of his hand hit

175

her cheek in a follow through so forceful she was almost knocked off her feet.

Marla let out a scream then ran to Brock and placed her arms around his shoulders.

Brock pushed her away effortlessly.

"Brock, I can explain!" Lily shrieked.

Brock grabbed her shoulders. "You treacherous wench!" he yelled.

Lily began to cry.

Immediately, Brock seemed to gain some of his composure. He released her and stomped to their bedroom.

Marla rushed to Lily and taking her daughter into an embrace began to wail loudly.

Lily pushed her mother from her and followed Brock into the bedroom.

"You fucked him!" Brock roared as he pushed items off of the dresser.

The sound of shattering glass filled her ears.

"You fucked him!" he roared again.

"Brock, I'm sorry!" Lily cried ruefully and covered her face.

"Sorry?" Brock closed the distance between them. "Sorry? You're sorry! You think that can begin to be good enough!"

"Brock!"

"How could you, Lily? How could you do this to me? To us?"

"Brock, let me explain!"

"Explain? You think that will make it all better? Do you think your explanation will wipe away the pleasure my mother received from telling me that you screwed that bastard? Do you think your explanation will erase the thrill she got confirming what she thinks about you is true? Well, do you? If so, go ahead and explain how you…my own wife spread her legs for a man that's supposed to be her brother!"

"I did what I had to do for you!"

"Let me get this straight. You did this for me?"

"I had to do it or—"

"Or what? Or what, Lily?" Brock yelled, his voice echoed through the house. "We've spent hours talking over these past few days. Yet, you conveniently left out the fact you spread your legs for your brother!"

"He's not my brother! And it's not like you think!" Lily insisted.

"How long has this been going on? Have you been screwing that bastard for years just like my mother says?"

"No! That's disgusting!"

"Just think, that piece of filth scum knows what it's like to do my wife! My cheap, cheating whore of a wife!"

"Hold your tongue!" Lily yelled irately. "I only did it once! Once! I would not have done it at all if I didn't have to! But, I did it for you!"

"What do you mean you did it for me? If I know you, you didn't do it for me! There's some selfish reason that benefits you regardless of how it affects my feelings or our marriage!"

Lily gasped. "How can you say such hurtful things to me? I should have let them hang you except I love you!"

"Love? You don't know the first thing about love! If you did, you wouldn't have kept this from me! After all this time, we're right back where we started! You have yet another secret you're hiding from me! I knew you were hiding something! I knew it! I just didn't know it was something so vile, so—"

"I wanted to tell you! I wanted to tell you a million times!"

"Just like you wanted to tell me you were black? I had to find that out from my mother too. You just don't get it do you, Lily? You take me so for granted. You think you can treat me any way you want. You thought you could walk out of my life and I'd just be sitting around waiting for you. Now, you sleep with another man and keep it a secret from me and I'm just supposed to say it's okay?

"Lily over and over again you take my heart and slam it on the floor. You take my love for you and stomp on it! I forgave you once for keeping a secret and not trusting me. But this...this I can never forgive!"

Brock clutched his hand into a fist and let out a painful roar. He shook his head and hissed, "If I had known you were easy, I wouldn't have bothered to marry you."

Lily gasped. "How dare you say that to me!"

"You know...one of the reasons my mother didn't want me to marry you was because of your mother."

"You leave my mother out of this you...you brute!"

Ignoring her words, Brock continued, "My mother knew your mother was Philip's mistress. She was worried that you learned some unseemly things from her. If my mother could see the way you seduced me over and over again when we were on the trail, she'd know she was right. The apple doesn't fall far from the tree."

For a moment, Lily was too flabbergasted to say a word. Then, she found her voice, "I cannot believe you said that!"

"Of course you can't! You think you have me so cuckold you can get me to do whatever you want when you want! And, hell, you have been able to do it! All you've had to do was tempt me with that body of yours and it always ended up with me all over you! Well, not this time, Lily! I will never touch you again!"

"Please! Brock! Just let me tell you how it was! I was with Syrus to get money—"

"Money? Uh! I don't want to hear this!" he roared with disgust and waving his hand dismissively grumbled, "That day you were on that auction block, I bought and paid for you because I thought I was getting my wife back. Little did I know, I was paying for a whore!"

Lily gasped.

Brock turned his back to her and stomped to the bedroom door. Once there, he turned back to face her. Through clenched teeth, he said, "You say Syrus gave you money to sleep with him. Sorry I can't be as generous as I'm sure he's been. But, I want to pay you all the same."

Reaching into his pocket, Brock pulled out a coin. He flicked the coin toward Lily and it landed at her feet.

"For your services," he remarked icily.

Lily let out a horrified shriek. Bending down, she snatched up the coin and with an incensed growl, threw it at Brock.

"I hate you!" she screeched as the coin hit the door with a loud clink then fell to the floor.

"You hate me?" Brock chuckled lightly. "Sweetie, you don't have to tell me because I just figured that out."

Then, turning his back to her, he stepped from the room and slammed the door behind him.

Chapter Fifteen

An endless stream of tears soaked Lily's pillow as she lay across the bed that night. Brock did not return home and she wondered where he was spending the night. She imagined him entwined in Angela's arms and cried a fresh batch of tears.

The next morning when the sun came up, she looked out of the window and saw him busily attending his horses. She rushed out to talk to him. But, when he saw her coming, he walked to a nearby horse, climbed on the steed and rode away.

Disheartened, Lily returned to the house.

That evening, after Brock finished his work, Lily watched him head in the direction of his mother's cabin. Her heart sank as she thought about the things Sylvia would surely say about her.

The next day, when Brock arrived to begin his day's work, Lily once again ran out to talk to him. But, as before, when he saw her approaching him, he walked away before she could reach him. The third morning when Brock began his work, Lily did not go out to see him. For the rest of the week, she stayed in the house.

As one week turned into two, Lily found she spent countless hours crying because she could not explain to Brock why she did what she did. What hurt the most was the fact that he had vowed to never touch her again. The thought of never feeling his hands on her body caused an ache deep within her which she could not vanquish.

As Lily lay in bed one night, she buried her face in Brock's pillow and wondered if things were ever going to be as they had been before they were separated. She thought about Brock's statement that their love could overcome any obstacle. Now, it seemed they would never find their way back to each other.

Lily shook her head to banish the thought and realized she felt nauseous. She clutched her stomach and leapt from the bed. She was barely able to make it to the basin before the contents of her stomach came up. When she could breathe again, she fell on the bed and once again began to cry.

§

As another week went by, instead of Lily's nausea getting better, it persisted.

Finally, Lily decided to go see the doctor.

When she made it to town, she realized it was the day for the town's annual picnic. She told herself she would stop by the picnic after her doctor's visit.

When she entered the doctor's office, he asked her to describe her symptoms. Lily told him. Then, he led her to the examination room. After the exam, the doctor looked at her and said, "Mrs. Cunningham, you are going to have a baby."

"A baby!" Lily exclaimed.

"It's hard to say exactly when your baby is due. But, I'd say you're around six weeks along," the doctor announced.

Lily let out a squeal of joy as a wave of excitement and elation engulfed her. She realized she was overjoyed at the idea of having Brock's baby and knew she had to tell him right away. Realizing he was probably at the picnic with his mother, she left the doctor's office and headed for the picnic.

As Lily walked down the boarded walkway, she thought about the last time she had been at the picnic. She and Brock had snuck away from the others to be alone. She hoped that happened again. This time, when they were alone, she would tell him he was going to be a father.

Lily smiled. With any luck, their baby would be what brought them back together.

§

Brock sighed as he lowered himself onto the blanket and looked out at the river. It had been three years since he and Lily had snuck away from the others and come to this very spot. He wasn't sure why he returned to the spot that

181

day except for the fact he needed to be alone to deal with the pain he felt.

Brock lay back on the blanket and closed his eyes. A frown encased his lips as he thought about Lily. She firmly denied being Syrus' lover and insisted she had only been with him once. But why once? Whatever the reason, one thing was for sure, she couldn't be trusted. Brock wished he could confront Syrus. But, thanks to Angela, he knew Syrus had left the country. If Syrus was in town, Brock knew he wouldn't do the accepted thing and challenge him to a duel. Instead, he would dole out his own brand of retribution upon Syrus.

A shadow blotted the sun's rays from his face a moment before soft lips touched his mouth. Brock opened his eyes to find a pair of green eyes gazing at him.

"Hi there suga," Angela's soft voice sounded.

"How did you find me?" Brock asked.

"I'll always find you no matter where you try to hide," she replied gently and stretched out beside him. "It's all right I don't bite," she said when he started to rise on his elbows.

Brock lay back on the blanket.

"I'm here if you want to talk about the problems you're having," Angela revealed.

Brock remained silent.

"I knew she would hurt you. I told you she would. I told you she wasn't good enough for you," Angela uttered staunchly.

"I don't want to talk about it." Brock turned from Angela.

Angela put her hands on his shoulder. "I am not trying to be insensitive. You should know I wouldn't have hurt you. I would never be unfaithful to you. You could have saved yourself a lot of heartache if you had stayed with me."

"Angela, this is a private issue. I just need to deal with it myself," Brock replied stiffly.

"Deal with it? How? By isolating yourself from those who love you? I won't let you do that." Angela moved her hand to his chest and gently nudged him down so he was once again lying on his back. "Even though you keep going to Lily, my heart still belongs to you, Brock. I'm here for you just like I have always been." She rubbed the back of her hand against his cheek.

"Angela…" Brock tilted his face from her touch.

"You've tried to make it work with Lily. But, every time you try, it always ends the same." She ran her fingers over the outline of his lips then replaced her finger with her lips, "I want you back," she whispered and began to unbutton his shirt.

After his shirt was unbuttoned, Angela ran her hands over his muscle carved chest. "Let me take care of you like I used to," she pleaded. Then taking his hands in hers, she pressed them against the soft mound of her breasts.

"Angela…" Her name left his lips when he felt her nipples grow rigid under his palm.

She pressed her lips against his cutting off his protest.

The feel of Angela's body against his caused a heady cloud of pleasure to saturate Brock's mind. Unable to stop his hands, Brock's fingers ran through the silky strands of her hair then rubbed along her arm. As if it had a mind of its own, his arm found its way around her waist.

Angela moaned and moved to straddle him.

Brock shook his head to clear it. Then, with much effort, he placed his hands on her shoulders and nudged her back a little.

"What is it?" Angela questioned with a frown.

"This isn't right," he said solemnly and tried to sit up.

Angela pushed him back to the ground. "I know Lily was with Syrus. There's no reason for you to be faithful to her. I know you still want me. I can feel it," Angela proclaimed then moved her bottom seductively over the bulge covered by the material of his pants.

Brock groaned.

Angela smiled and lowered her lips to his once again.

§

When Lily arrived at the picnic, the sun was high in the sky. She scanned the crowd for a glimpse of Brock but did not see him. Instead, she saw children scampering close to

183

a group of women sitting in lounge chairs conversing with each other. Next to the women, a horde of men stood over fledgling flames that roasted delicious smelling meat. A man with a fiddle sat a short distance from the group playing a merry melody while several couples danced to the tune.

"Lily, you decided to come."

Lily turned to see her father walking to her. She smiled and hugged him.

"I'm looking for Brock. Have you seen him?" she asked.

"Something is going on between you and Brock. I can tell. If you ever need to talk about it, I'm here," her father said.

"Thank you for saying that, Father. But, this is something Brock and I have to work through together," she replied.

"All right, dear child, I won't pry. I saw your husband disappear into those trees a little while ago," Philip pointed to a cluster of trees.

Lily smiled. "Thanks Father," she said then headed in the direction her father indicated.

With quick strides, Lily entered the knot of trees and toward the spot she and Brock had visited three years earlier. As she neared the river, she saw a couple in the distance lying on a blanket entwined in an embrace. For a moment, Lily managed to convince herself she did not know who the people were. But as she neared the couple, their forms crystallized and there was no mistaking the woman with the golden blonde curls and the muscular male.

Lily's heart broke into a thousand tiny pieces as she watched Angela straddle Brock. She contemplated retreating when she saw Angela lean down and kiss him. However, in the next instant, anger erupted in her and she darted to the spot where Brock and Angela lay. Reaching out, she entangled her hand in Angela's hair and yanked on Angela's tresses. Angela let out a shriek as she was dragged off of Brock and to her feet. Once she was on her feet, Lily slapped Angela's cheek.

Angela howled as her hand flew to her cheek.

184

Brock shot off of the blanket. "Lily!" he called out when she turned to walk away.

"Let her go! It's not like this is the first time she's abandoned you," Angela said to Brock.

Upon hearing Angela's words, Lily whirled around and letting out a growl shoved Angela hard.

Angela screamed boisterously as she fell to the ground. She looked up at Lily through hate filled eyes. "Damn you Lily!" she hissed then scrambling to her feet lunged at Lily.

When Angela's hands met Lily's arms, the women fell to the ground.

The small clearing suddenly filled with the participants of the picnic who heard Angela's loud shriek. Upon seeing the two women rolling around and Brock trying to separate them, chaotic shouts erupted from the onlookers.

Philip rushed to Brock and the men managed to separate the women and pull them to their feet. Sylvia emerged from the crowd and scuttled to Angela. She held Angela back when Angela cursed brashly and lashed out to strike Lily.

Lily screamed and lurched toward Angela.

Brock grabbed Lily's arms preventing her from hitting her mark.

"Oh my God! Brock take her home! You can use my carriage!" Philip shouted to his son-in-law.

Brock moved his hands to Lily's waist, lifted her off her feet and tossed her over his shoulder as if she were a sack of potatoes. Lily began to kick her legs and scream. Laughter erupted from the crowd at her antics. Inhaling sharply, Brock trekked to Philip's carriage as small children gleeful of the commotion scampered after him.

Upon hearing the tumultuous commotion approach, the coachman sprinted from the group of men he was talking to and headed to the carriage. Once there, the man opened the door for Brock and Brock shoved Lily inside.

"Get your hands off me!" Lily shrieked when Brock climbed in the carriage behind her.

The carriage jerked forward causing her to fall against him.

185

Lily pushed away from Brock and settled on the seat across from him.

"You made a spectacle of yourself!" Brock fumed.

"You were with Angela to punish me!" Lily accused as she smoothed her ruffled skirt.

"Don't you think I'm allowed revenge after what you've done?" Brock inquired hotly.

"You want to be with Angela? Fine! Be with her! See if I care! You've made it perfectly clear that she's who you want!" Lily yelled.

"Why is it okay for you to have your hands all over Syrus but it's not okay for me to have my hands on Angela?" Brock questioned in an infuriated tone.

"I never had my hands on Syrus!" Lily protested.

"No? That's not what I remember. I remember seeing your hands all over him when you were dancing with him at The River Room. How could I have been so blind even then? How could I have not seen you've had your hands all over him many times before? My mother could see it. She could see what was going on between you two. She knew you and Syrus were lovers."

Lily shook her head. "Your mother can't see a damn thing!"

"I didn't see it because I didn't want to see it. I wanted to think you were innocent and trustworthy." Brock tilted his head to one side. "So tell me Lily, why did you marry me? It's still not clear. Was it because you wanted to use me to hide the fact you're part black? Or did you think by marrying me you could change your wanton ways and not be with him? Did you try hard to control your lust once you got back to town? But, in the end, did you find you had to give in to Syrus again?"

"No! Of course not!" Lily objected.

"It was foolish of me to think there would be no secrets between us. It's obvious to me you've always had something to hide!"

"Damn you! That's not true!" Lily seethed.

"You've been fucking Syrus long before I met you!"

"That's not true! Syrus was nothing but a brother to me! Until that one night!"

186

"You actually expect me to believe that you've only been with Syrus once? Well, I don't believe it! When we got married, we made a vow before God to be faithful to one another! But you've broken that vow! You betrayed me the first chance you got without a second thought! I, on the other hand, stayed faithful to you even when you weren't here! Even when Angela was throwing herself at me, I kept my end of the bargain! I told her no! You want to know why? I did it because I loved you enough to say no! I hoped beyond hope and prayed that you'd come back to me! But you...you're unbelievable! After a short time of being back in town, you return to Syrus' bed! You managed to make a fool of me once again!"

"Brock, I told you I'm sorry about what happened." Lily covered her face with her hands.

"Sorry! Sorry?" He looked at her with a terrifying glare. "That's not good enough!"

"Just let me tell you everything!"

"I've already heard all I want to hear!" Brock thundered.

"Just listen to me! It wasn't like what you think! There was a reason I was with Syrus and that reason is I was terrified of losing you!"

"You always have an excuse as to why you do what you do! You always have a reason why you have to keep secrets from me!" Brock shook his head.

"Please believe me!"

"Why should I believe you? I believed you loved me and I believed you wanted to continue our marriage! But none of that was true! If you really wanted this marriage to work, you wouldn't have gone back to being a whore for a man who doesn't love you as much as I do! There's no way he can! But, it doesn't matter! I believed your lies before. I won't believe them again!"

In one swift motion, Brock leaned forward and shoved her shoulders. Lily gasped as she fell backward onto the cushioned seat. She tried to raise herself. As quick as lightning, Brock lowered himself on her and clutching her shoulders pinned them against the soft cushion.

"Get your hands off me!" Lily fumed twisting against him.

Brock responded by wrapping his fingers around her wrist and unceremoniously pinning her arms over her head.

"Release me you brute!" Lily panted.

Brock shook his head.

"Let me up!" She flailed about struggling to free herself. "You bastard! Bastard I say!"

"You shouldn't have left me." The words were out of his mouth before he could stop them.

"I thought I had to!"

"You are my wife! You didn't have to leave!" The words gushed forth uncontrollably. "But, listening to your mother was more important than trusting me! It was more important than our marriage!"

"That's not true!" Lily protested.

"Not true? You only care about yourself! You don't give a damn about how your actions affect me!"

"That's a lie!"

"The day you were on that auction block should not have been a problem for you, Lily. Let's face it. You've always been for sale to the highest bidder."

Lily stared up at Brock paralyzed by the venom in his words. After a moment, she managed to find the strength to pull her hand free and slap his face hard.

The afternoon sunlight that filtered through the carriage window seemed to singe Brock's eyes as he gritted his teeth against the unexpected sting.

Brock speared her with an inquisitive glare then asked, "Is it that you just can't control yourself? Is it in your blood like my mother suggests?"

Lily shook her head.

Suddenly, he began to loosen his belt.

"What...what are you doing?" Lily sputtered suddenly aware that his swollen member nudged against her thigh.

"What does it look like I'm doing?" he asked.

"You can't mean you want to..."

"That's exactly what I want."

"You expect me to..."

"Yes. I expect you to do it."

Lily shook her head negatively.

"If you don't want Angela to have the job, you should take care of me yourself," Brock stated then with one sharp yank he stripped his belt from around his waist.

Lily gulped the protest that rose in her throat. A second later, Brock reached out and yanked her blouse apart causing the buttons to scatter about the carriage.

Lily gasped and moved her hands to cover her breasts.

"Don't act so shy, sweetheart. I've seen them before. After all, I do remember your grand performance. You remember the performance? The one you gave the night you bathed in the stream. I remember it. I remember it well," Brock said as he tossed the hem of her dress to her waist. Then, in one crude motion, he moved his knee between her legs, pushed them apart and sank between her thighs.

"You wouldn't dare!" Lily shrieked.

"I bought and paid for you. I will get my monies worth if it's the last thing I do," he said.

Lily pushed her hands against his shoulder, raised her knee and lifted her body upward causing Brock to lose his balance.

They were a delirious stir of energy for a few moments as Lily writhed underneath him. However, Brock managed to pin her back against the seat cushion. Clutching her wrists once again, he lifted her arms above her head and watched her breasts flatten and spread.

Lily tried to raise her shoulders in an effort to escape. "Why are you doing this?" she wanted to know.

Suddenly, Brock didn't trust his voice to speak. How could he explain the pain he felt when she left? How could he explain he didn't want to be angry at her...hadn't intended to be so hurt... so irrational... so god damned turned on.

"It's what you want, right? Don't deny you want it. You begged me for it. You've been begging me for it since I got you off of that block."

"I...I don't know what you're talking about."

Brock's eyes glowed defiantly. "What do you mean you don't know what I'm talking about? Well, let's see... you wanted me to make love to you so you lathered soap

189

here…" Brock traced his finger over her shoulder and arm. "And here…" He slid his finger across her belly. "…And here…" His finger circled her breast. "You asked me once if having you in my arms brought back memories. I must admit, touching you like this is bringing back memories…delicious memories… Do you recall what it's like to have my finger here?" His fingers slid between her thighs. A wicked smile spread across his lips as his finger slipped along her wet folds.

"Some things never change," he taunted.

Lily's eyes narrowed in to thin slits. "Get off me you brute!" she rasped.

"No!" Brock snapped curtly.

Lily flailed about. Unable to free herself, she blurted out, "You're a… bastard! Bastard I say!"

"And also your new owner," he sneered.

Lily inhaled sharply. "You don't own me!" she spat.

Brock slipped his finger into her moistened sheath. "Feels like I do," he replied.

Lily let out an outraged gasp.

"Let's see if the teasing temptress is worth the price," he whispered in a low husky voice as he lowered his head and curled his lips around her nipple.

Lily inhaled and fruitlessly tried to raise herself even as tentacles of hot liquid warmth crept through her body.

Brock raised his head, brought his mouth to hers and gluttonously drank from her lips.

"Not like this!" Lily breathed as she turned her face from him.

Brock placed his fingers on her chin and turned her face to his. "This is what you want, remember? You want me to make love to you, remember?"

Lily shook her head. "But, you said you'd never touch me again."

"I lied," he said and pushed down his pants. A second later, his throbbing member grazed the entrance of her treasure.

At that moment, the carriage came to a stop.

With a frantic wail, Lily shoved Brock off of her.

"Get off me!" she ordered and rose to a sitting position.

190

Brushing down her skirt, Lily clutched her blouse together and opened the carriage door. In a flash, she leapt out of the carriage and ran to the cabin. With Brock close on her heels, she rushed to their bedroom and slammed the door shut then locked it from the inside.

The door shook as Brock tried to open it. A moment later, he pounded on the door.

"Open the door Lily!" he shouted.

"No!" Lily called out and took a step backwards.

Brock let out a boorish curse. A second later, his foot rammed through the door causing it to burst open.

A startled scream left Lily's lips.

Brock strode into the room then came to a halt. Piercing her with a devilish stare, he roared, "Come here!"

Lily shook her head and took a step back.

Brock stepped toward her.

Lily shook her head and took a few additional steps backwards until the back of her legs bumped against the bed.

Brock advanced on her and came to a stop in front of her. Without speaking, he yanked the blouse off her frame and tossed it across the room. Remaining silent, he pushed her shoulders back causing her to fall onto the bed. He watched as again her breasts flattened then expanded. Then, he placed his hands around her waist and stripped her skirt down her legs before throwing it across the room as well. Quickly, he shed himself of his shirt and pants. A second later, he fell on top of her.

"I'm going to give you what you want wife," he rasped.

Lily shook her head. "This isn't what I want," she managed to say.

"Really? Then why'd you drag Angela off of me?" he asked as he slid his hand between her thighs.

"Brock—" Her words melted into a gurgle as his fingers slid along her moistened folds.

"You want it badly," he said as his finger once again slipped easily in her.

Lily shook her head. "No! I don't!"

"That's not how you've been acting or what you've been telling me. You've been telling me you want to be my wife. Well, my dear, this is what a wife does for her husband."

Lily shook her head in disagreement.

"So all of your teasing was just a game? Is love just a game to you? A game you play whenever it suits you. Well, is it? You're good at playing games...at being a tease."

Lily attempted to squirm away from him.

Reacting quickly, Brock grabbed her waist and held her still.

"Tell me, do you like playing the part of the whore? Do you like performing for me? Or do you like performing for Syrus better? Tell me, who do you like better?"

Lily let out a sigh of disgust and turned her face from him.

Suddenly, Brock thrust himself into her silken surface. Lily gasped as he pulled his hips back slightly then lunged into her warm sheath again.

Then again.

"You like it like this, don't you?" Brock asked grinding his hips against hers.

Lily opened her mouth to protest. But, her words evaporated into an uncontrolled moan of pleasure.

"Let me hear you say you like it. Let me hear you say you like it with me more than you like it with Syrus," Brock commanded.

Lily, angry with Brock for his domination of her and her body's wanton submission, shook her head, fighting to hold on to a shred of resistance.

Brock delved in her again. She moved her hips as a prick of pleasure oozed through her.

"That's right, my love. Tease me like only you can," Brock whispered then kissed her cheek.

Lily turned her face from him once more.

"Come on, my love! Let me hear you say you want me more than you want Syrus," Brock prodded and rammed into her again. And again.

Lily shook her head fighting to resist the blissful feelings the onslaught his shaft created within her.

Suddenly, Brock fell still.

Lily bit her lip and turned to look at him. She wiggled her hips underneath him then looked at him inquisitively.

"Say you want me," Brock demanded.

Lily let out a frustrated breath and moved her hips.

"Say it!"

She shook her head refusing to say the words.

"Say you want me or this ends right now."

Lily remained silent for one second relishing the feel of him swollen within her. Suddenly, she blurted out, "I want you! All of you! Now give it to me! Give it to me! Please!"

She wrapped her arms around his neck.

With a smirk, Brock granted her wish and plunged his enslaved member in her. Over and over again, he greedily took what she freely offered.

"I want this! I want you!" she admitted breathlessly.

"Of course you do, my little whore," Brock muttered in a voice hoarse with desire.

"I hate you," Lily replied moving her hips frantically.

"I hate you too," Brock whispered. "I hate you so much, I'm going to kiss you," he said and pressed his lips to hers.

His hands found her breasts adding fuel to the exquisite sensation that mounted between her legs. As her insides exploded into a deluge of sublime torment, Lily tilted her head back and let out a lusty cry. Brock covered her mouth with his muffling the sound of his own euphoric moan.

A moment later, he shuttered in release.

They lay in silence for many moments.

"Look at me," Brock said to Lily after he caught his breath.

Lily raised her eyes to look at her husband. When she did, she saw a sorrowful expression on his face.

"You've hurt me very deeply. You've kept secrets from me. You walked out on me years ago because you had a secret. That led to us being separated for years which ripped my heart apart. And, now, after we got back together and after promising you wouldn't keep secrets from me again, you not only kept another secret, you betrayed me. The pain I feel is so deep some days I feel I will collapse from the weight of it. I don't like the man it's made me

193

become. As much as I want to be with you, I can't. I don't feel I can trust you and loving you just hurts too much. I can't be with you…not anymore," Brock said and rolled off of her.

"But… But we just made love," Lily pointed out.

"That changes nothing," Brock explained and started to get out of the bed.

Acting quick, Lily wrapped her arms around his waist halting his exit. "You wouldn't leave the mother of your child would you?" she asked.

Brock's brow wrinkled. "What?"

"I'm going to have your baby. The doctor says I'm about six weeks along," Lily revealed.

"Oh, Lily," Brock moaned and buried his face against her neck.

"Please, don't leave me," she whispered.

"Lily, sweetheart. I love you so much I ache from it. I wish all of the issues between us would disappear," Brock murmured sadly.

"They will. As long as we stay together we can overcome all of the problems that face us. You told me that a long time ago and I believe it."

Brock raised his head to look at her. Somberly, he asked, "Can you look me in the eye and tell me the child you are carrying is mine and not Syrus'?"

Horror flooded Lily's eyes as the gravity of Brock's question sank in. She lowered her eyes unable to hold his gaze.

Brock groaned raggedly and rose to a sitting position. "Even if I could forget your past with Syrus, I know I can't raise his child."

Lily sat up. "This is your baby! Not Syrus'!" she insisted even as her heart thumped in her chest.

"And if it's not. What if the baby comes out with gray eyes and red hair? What then?"

"Brock, please let me explain what happened the night I was with Syrus. It was the night you were attacked by those Klansmen. They said they were going to kill you if I didn't get the five thousand dollars they wanted. You heard them! Can't you see, what I did, I did for you? I had to do

194

it." Lily's voice caught in a sob as tears began to run down her cheek. "I know you hate me because of that night. It's just that Syrus said it was the only way he'd give me the money. You spent all you had to purchase me and there was no one else I could ask. My father was not at home. I would not have done it if I felt I had a choice. But, I love you and there was no way I was going to let you die."

"Syrus said you had to..."

Lily nodded her head.

"In exchange for the money?"

Lily nodded her head again and began to cry.

"Oh, Lily, I've been such a fool," Brock groaned and pulled her into his arms.

"I am carrying your baby, Brock. I can feel it. Please don't walk away from me and our marriage. I want us to be together like we were before all of this mess happened. I want you to stop hating me and I want to stop hurting you. I want our marriage to work. I want us to be a family," she sobbed.

"That's all I want too," Brock admitted tenderly. Then, tilting her face to his, he brushed away the tears that stained her cheeks. "Listen Lily, we will be a family. What happened in the past doesn't matter. None of it matters. I should have listened to you. If I had, I could have realized a lot sooner that you really did do what you did for me. Because you love me."

"But, if this baby isn't yours—"

"Ssshh. Don't say it." Brock placed his fingers over her lips silencing her words. In a voice filled with love, he whispered, "This baby is mine. We've got to believe that."

Chapter Sixteen

The next morning, when Brock and Lily woke up it was raining. Lily urged Brock to stay inside the house with her. But he insisted he had to tend to the horses. So, after they ate breakfast, he left the house and ran to the barn.

As she cleaned the dishes, Lily thought about the baby but refused to think about the possibility that the child she carried could be Syrus'.

A rapid knock sounded on the door.

Lily walked to the door and opened it.

Without speaking a greeting, Sylvia stepped into the cabin.

"Brock left the picnic with you and he didn't come home last night. Did he sleep here?" Sylvia asked as she took off her wet coat.

Lily nodded her head.

"Where is he?"

"In the barn."

"What did you say to get him to stay with you? I know he wants nothing to do with you now that he knows how it is between you and Syrus."

"Sylvia, you've tried your best to break up my relationship with your son. But, you can't do it. I'm Brock's wife, he loves me and we are going to work things out."

"You should be ashamed of yourself and what you've done," Sylvia said ignoring Lily's words.

Lily sighed pensively as thunder rumbled in the sky.

"How could you do this to my son?" Sylvia persisted when Lily made no attempt to defend herself. When Lily still did not respond, she hissed, "I knew you would do this. I predicted it because that's the way you grew up. That's all you know."

"You've got it all wrong," Lily said then walked to the window, pushed back the curtain and looked outside at the rain.

"My precious son. When I think about all of the hurt you put him through by sleeping with that rake." Sylvia frowned.

196

"I had no other choice," Lily rebutted.

"No other choice?" Sylvia rolled her eyes.

"Listen to me, Sylvia! I had to. It was that or the Klan would have hung Brock!"

At the mere mention of the Klan, Sylvia shuttered. "What are you talking about?" she questioned.

"The Klan attacked Brock for being with me. They said they knew I was black and they threatened to hang him. Didn't he tell you about The Klan?"

"Oh God! No!" Sylvia exclaimed, fear showing in her eyes.

"Those Klansmen threatened to kill Brock unless they got money. I was told to go to Syrus to get the money. I went to Syrus. But, Syrus said he would only give me the money if I..."

"Oh dear God! But what about your father? He has money."

"He was not at home. Those Klansmen gave me two hours to get the money. I was told I couldn't tell anyone but Syrus. They recognized me as Syrus' sister. So, I went to Syrus. There was no time to figure out anything else."

"Why didn't anyone tell me this before?"

"You didn't wait to hear it. You were so eager to ruin my marriage to your son, you didn't let me explain. So, I'm telling you now. I didn't want to do it. I didn't want to be with Syrus. I swear."

"I could have lost my son," Sylvia groaned then clutching her stomach she doubled over as if she were in pain.

Unable to stand any longer, Lily sank into a nearby chair.

Sylvia walked to her and placed her hand on her shoulders.

"You saved my son's life," Sylvia said and encircled her arms around Lily.

When Sylvia's arms circled her, all of the hurt, pain, fear and humiliation of the past flooded over Lily like a tidal wave. Unable to hold back the torrid emotions inside her, she began to cry.

Sylvia held Lily as sorrowful sobs wrenched her body.

"You poor dear. What you've been through," Sylvia whispered softly and rubbed Lily's back.

The sound of rain pounding the side of the house grew louder then slackened as Lily cried.

When Lily finally gained her composure, she said, "I never meant to hurt Brock."

"I can see that now. You did what most women would not have done. I can see just how much you really do care for my son. I didn't want to see it before. But I see it now. I'm sorry for the horrible way I have treated you. Thank you for saving my son's life."

"I'm going to have a baby," Lily blurted out.

"A baby!"

"Because of that night, there is a chance this child may not be Brock's," Lily revealed sadly.

Sylvia was silent for several moments. Finally, she said, "The child you are carrying will be Brock's."

A new batch of tears started to roll down Lily's face.

Lily thought of the time she was a slave. When she had been away from Brock, she had prayed for a miracle. She wanted the miracle to be the two of them finding their way back to each other. That miracle had happened. Now it seemed another miracle was happening. Was it possible that she and Sylvia could find a way to forgive each other? Lily hoped that it was possible. For if they could, it would be a new beginning for all of them.

§

As winter arrived, Lily's heart filled with hope. The wall of ice that had once been erected between she and Brock seemed to have thawed. The tender way he touched her and the gentle way he grazed at her breasts when they made love was all the evidence she needed to feel reassured that things would be as they had been.

For Lily, the winter months ticked by slowly. She found she couldn't wait for spring when her baby would arrive. She spent hours imagining life after the baby was born. She prayed the baby was a child created out of love between she and Brock.

198

Finally, balmy weather announced the arrival of spring. As spring settled in, Lily spent every day with her mother talking about and preparing for the baby. One day, a planter who heard of Brock's horse ranch, sent a notice that he wanted to purchase several quarter horses. The planter sent a partial payment with a note asking Brock to deliver the horses to his plantation in Richmond. Upon his arrival, the note explained, he would receive the rest of the payment.

"I'm not sure how long I will be gone. Are you sure you'll be all right?" Brock asked Lily before he left.

"The baby is not due for another month. I will be fine," Lily assured him.

Brock kissed her then headed on his journey.

However, that night as Lily prepared for bed, a gush of water rushed down her legs. A short time later, she began to feel the discomfort of mild contractions. Knowing the baby was not due for another month, she hoped the contractions would stop during the night.

However, by the time the sun came up the next morning, the pain from the contractions were very intense.

"Lily, what is it?" Marla asked when she walked through the door of the cabin and saw the ashen look on Lily's face.

"I think it's..." Lily paused as a contraction gripped her. "...the baby," she breathed after the contraction passed.

"How far 'part are the pains?"

"A couple of minutes. I need to see the doctor."

"There's no time, honey child! You are havin' your baby now!" Marla proclaimed.

"But it's too soon! The baby isn't due for another month," Lily protested.

"Well, if the baby ain't due for another four weeks someone forgot to tell the baby. Your baby is comin' and he's comin' now! Go lay down!" Marla instructed as she busied herself collecting what she needed to assist her daughter with the birth.

Lily draped her hand across her heavy stomach and managed to make it to her bed just before another contraction gripped her.

After several minutes, Marla entered the room.

Marla rushed to Lily's bed and prepared her for the delivery.

"Push! Push!" Marla instructed when it was time.

Lily pushed and cried out as pain overpowered her.

She whimpered when the pain subsided.

"It won't be long now," her mother assured.

Encouraged by her mother's words, Lily raised herself upon her elbows in preparation for the next contraction.

It came. As did several more.

Tears of happiness flowed unchecked down Lily's face and she fell exhaustedly on the bed when the baby was finally pulled out of her.

"It's a girl!" Marla exclaimed.

"A girl," Lily managed to whisper.

Lily looked toward the foot of the bed and saw her mother hold the baby in the air by her feet then slapped her back.

A tiny wail erupted from the baby.

Lily closed her eyes and laughed with joy at the sound that was music to her ears. "She came early," Lily mused.

"No darlin'. I seen babies that come early and this child ain't one of them," Marla informed her daughter.

"Really? Let me see my daughter," Lily breathed.

Marla quickly wiped the birthing fluid from the baby's body then walked to the side of the bed and placed the baby girl in Lily's arms.

Tears streamed down Lily's face as she took in the sight of her new daughter. A sob caught in her throat as she viewed the thick patch of golden blonde hair atop her baby's head. Tenderly, Lily touched her baby's fingers and toes and placed a sweet kiss on her cheek.

"She's beautiful," Lily whispered.

"There can be no doubt that Brock is her father," Marla noted.

Lily thought about her mother's words and wondered when the baby was conceived. Since the baby was not premature that meant her daughter was conceived while she and Brock were on the trail traveling home. Lily wondered if it had happened the night after her performance in the stream. Her cheeks redden as she recalled her attempts at seduction. The result was the baby she held in her arms. As she thought of it, Lily pressed her cheek against her daughter's cheek and began to laugh.

§

Marla summoned the doctor a short time later. When the doctor arrived, he woke Lily and checked her. After checking the baby, he confirmed that he had been mistaken about the baby's due date and assured Lily the baby had not arrived early. Lily let out a relieved sigh. Due to the timing, it was impossible for Syrus to have sired her child. With a joy filled heart, she pulled the covers to her chin and fell into an exhausted sleep.

§

Sunlight was shining brightly in the room when Lily opened her eyes. She smiled as she thought about the days that had past since she had given birth. When she climbed out of bed and walked into the kitchen, she saw her mother holding the baby.

"I'm glad you're awake. The little one's hungry," Marla said and placed the baby in Lily's arms.

Lily looked into her baby daughter's amber colored eyes and smiled. "I can't wait for Brock to see her," she remarked.

"He's gonna take one look at his daughter and fall in love," Marla predicted.

Lily kissed her daughter's forehead after she sat in a nearby chair then began to nurse her child.

As she nursed her baby, she and her mother talked about the joys she would face in motherhood.

The sound of a buggy approaching interrupted their conversation.

Marla ran to the window.

"It's your father!" she exclaimed and ran out to meet him.

Marla returned minutes later with Philip in tow. Philip took one look at his granddaughter and tears smarted in his eyes.

"She's beautiful, daughter," he said after Lily placed the baby in his arms. "I'm not leaving my girls here another night. Lily, pack your things. I'm taking you, your mother and my grandbaby back to Paradise. You can stay there until Brock returns," Philip said.

Needing no further encouragement, Lily quickly packed a bag for herself and two bags for the baby. She wrote a note to Brock letting him know where she was then rushed to join her parents and child already waiting in the carriage.

"It's going to be wonderful having our daughter and granddaughter staying with us at Paradise," Philip said to Marla once they had started on the road back to the plantation.

Marla shook her head in agreement.

Lily smiled at her parents then settled back in the seat.

As her parents talked about the baby, she said a quick prayer for Brock and hoped he would return soon.

After a while, Philip looked at Lily and said, "We can be one big family just like we used to be now that Syrus is back home."

Lily straightened herself in her seat and exchanged an unsettled glance with her mother.

"Syrus is home? When did he return?" Marla questioned.

"He arrived last night. I'm sure he'll be glad to see his new niece," Philip said happily.

The carriage slowed.

Lily stretched out her arm and pulled back the white curtain that covered the window. "I don't think..." her words died in her throat as the carriage rolled between the iron gates of Paradise Plantation.

Lily pressed her nose against the window and looked at the mansion. Its windows looked smoky and gray in the wake of the early morning sun. Suddenly, panic filled her. She couldn't be at Paradise. Not with Syrus there. If Brock found out...

The carriage rolled to a stop in front of the mansion.

"We're here!" Philip announced and holding the baby securely, exited the carriage.

"Mama, Syrus is here! I can't go in there!" Lily whispered under her breath.

"You two coming?" Philip poked his head back into the carriage.

Marla touched Lily's hand. "It'll be all right. I'll think of somethin'," she promised and exited the carriage.

Lily scooted to the edge of the seat and stared at the mansion. "I...I can't," she stammered.

"Lily, what's wrong?" Philip questioned concern evident in his voice.

"I...I..." Words refused to form on Lily's lips.

"Here let me help you," her father said. Handing the baby to Marla, he held out his hand to Lily. "Come on, be careful," he coaxed.

Lily found she couldn't move.

Her head began to pound.

Philip reached out and clutched her elbow before nudging her out of the carriage. Once she was on her feet, he guided her up the stone steps and through the front door.

When they stepped into the foyer, Lily looked at the grand staircase leading to the bedrooms on the second level and a wave of nausea passed over her.

"I need to sit down. I don't feel well," she mumbled.

"Lily?" Philip's face clouded with concern.

"I'll be in my room," Lily stated and taking her baby from her mother, scurried up the stairs to her old room.

Once in her room, Lily closed the door behind her and sat on the bed to catch her breath. Breathing deeply, she thought of Brock. If he returned that night and found Syrus there... God! She didn't want to contemplate what he would do. She did not want to see Syrus let alone stay at the mansion with him in the next room. Leaving the house would be her only option.

Lily rose to her feet just as her mother walked in the room.

"I can't stay here. I have to go," she said anxiously.

"Syrus ain't here. Your father said he will be out 'til later tonight. Just stay in your room tonight. Syrus won't know you're here. I'll think of somethin'. I'll have a solution for you in the mornin'," Marla promised.

Lily clutched her baby to her chest.

"Close the door to the veranda," Lily told her mother, suddenly remembering Syrus' numerous appearances in that doorway.

Marla walked to the door and shut it.

Lily inhaled deeply. If she could just get through the night, hopefully, everything would turn out all right.

§

Lily opened her eyes slowly and stared into the darkened room. She wondered what had awakened her and let her eyes scan the shadows. She noticed the curtains on the windows had not been drawn which allowed a bright slice of moonlight to stream into the room. The sound of her baby's whimper in the midst of a restless sleep met her ears. Sitting up, she looked at her baby who lay in a crib next to the bed. Suddenly, she felt a cool breeze waft over her. Immediately, she shifted her gaze to the door that led to the veranda.

Her eyes widened when she saw a dark figure standing in the doorway. Lily's eyes traveled up the darkened form. Though a noxious shadow dimmed one side of his face, Lily recognized Syrus. The feral expression plastered on his face sent chills up her spine. Anxiously, she pulled the bed sheet to her throat.

Syrus shifted on his feet and straightened himself to stand in an upright position. Without a word, he took a step toward her. When he stepped forward, he stepped into the stream of moonlight and a crop of his crimson colored hair caught a glint of the silver light.

Suddenly, recognition flooded Lily's remembrance. She blinked at Syrus as if she were seeing a ghost. Managing to find her voice, she screeched, "It was you! It was you in the alley that night!"

Syrus began to clap his hands. "Bravo! You finally figured it out!" he exclaimed as he walked to her bed.

"You kidnapped me!" Lily shrieked.

"Well, actually, the slaver kidnapped you. I was just there to watch."

"How could you?"

"I warned you there would be a price to pay for rejecting me. But, you didn't listen."

"Damn you!" Lily hissed then rose to her knees as if she were going to pounce on him.

"Angela came by the cabin after you left. She wanted to find a way to get you out of Brock's life. Yep. She planned everything down to the last detail. Like telling you to leave out of the back door of the hotel. She wanted you to do that so no one would see you leaving at that time of night. She did not want you to raise suspicion."

"What?"

"Brock never got the letter you left for him. Angela took it. The unsigned note you received at the hotel telling you to go to the warehouse…that note was concocted by Angela."

"But why would she do such a thing?"

"After Angela read the note and found out you were black, she wanted to stop you. I went along with her because I wanted to find a way to stop you from telling Father about my proposal. I love Father and I couldn't risk you turning him against me. And, I wanted to make you pay for rejecting me. She convinced me she would make sure you got everything you had coming to you."

"You beast!" Lily screamed and lunged at Syrus.

The wild punches of her fists made contact with his face and chest.

After several attempts, Syrus managed to catch her flailing wrists.

"Settle down now!" he commanded and pinned her against his frame. When he did, the whip on his belt burrowed into her side.

"How could you do that to me you son of a bitch!" Lily screeched.

"I am a son of a bitch. That's precisely why I could do it. My bitch of a mother rejected me. My father, whoever the bastard is, rejected me. I will be damned if a black bitch like you is going to reject me too," Syrus hissed and twisted her arm behind her back.

Lily winced in pain.

"Philip is the only person who ever cared about me. He treated me like a son. He even promised this plantation to me. Then, Marla came along. That black bitch ruined everything! She took Philip away from me. Then, you came along. I was willing to share the inheritance with you because I thought you were Philip's legitimate heir. Then, I saw you undressing... I didn't see why I couldn't have you for myself. When, I found out, you were the spawn of an illicit affair, you aren't really white and you rejected me...you had to pay. Angela made me see you are not Philips' legitimate heir. She said I should not be forced to share the inheritance with you."

"But when I returned home you seemed sorry for the way you acted. Why did you act that way if you hate me so?"

"I was surprised to see you. In my amazement, I felt a bit of remorse. That was until Angela made me see I could have what I really wanted."

"Why would you listen to Angela?"

"We are partners. After we sold you to that slaver, she was sure Brock would come to her. But, he didn't because he respected his wedding vows too much. For years, he kept thinking you would return home one day. Angela tried to wait. But, she's a woman with needs. She came to me to fill those needs since Brock wouldn't. I was happy to do it. After the darkies in the field, it was nice to have a white woman grace my bed for a change.

"Angela almost succeeded in getting back in Brock's bed. But, when he came back with you well... When we were at The River Room and Brock dragged you out of my arms, she could see he was still in love with you. That's when she came up with the so called Klan attack."

"What?!" Lily screeched in outrage.

"After Brock let you move back into the cabin, Angela couldn't stand the thought of you taking him from her again. She wanted to come up with an idea to break up your marriage to Brock for good. I remembered what you told me that evening before I took you to The River Room. You reminded me that Brock's father was killed by The Klan. You told me how frightened you were when you and Brock ran into Klansmen on the trail. I remember you saying you didn't know what you would do if you ever ran into members of The Klan again. I told Angela what you told me. She decided the rest."

Lily fidgeted against Syrus.

"I assure you, Brock was never in any real danger. Angela saw to that. She found those men and I told them what to say. They were great actors. Don't you think? I did some acting too for you see…" Syrus shifted her slightly and patted the whip hanging at his side. "I was the Klansman with the whip. I was the one who came up with the idea to ask you to get five thousand dollars. I thought it was only fitting since you told me that was the amount Brock paid for you. I knew you'd have to come to me because I remembered you told me Brock was out of money because he'd spent his savings when he bought you.

"I must say, you followed the plan nicely. Too nicely. I was barely able to get back to the mansion in time."

Lily thought back to the night of The Klan attack and remembered Syrus rushing into the house with a bruise on his face. She growled and attempted to break from his grasp.

He laughed and tightened his grip.

"I made sure Father was out of the house so we could be alone. After you granted me your treasure, I left and met the men to deliver their cut of the cash. It was an outrageous scheme, I know. But, I wanted to partake of your wondrous delights. I couldn't let Brock have you all to himself. I thought it only fair that I get you too. I still want you," he whispered and leaned down to kiss her.

Lily jerked away from him. "Help!" she screamed loudly.

Immediately, Syrus cupped his hand over her mouth muffling the sound.

"Ssshh, pretty one," he whispered and he ran his fingers through her hair. "I'm not going to hurt you. I'll be real nice to you just like before," he said.

At that moment, the baby whimpered.

Syrus turned to look at the source of the sound.

"Stay away from her you sadistic snake!" Lily spat.

Syrus turned back to Lily. "You hurt me with such words. I'm not that horrible. If I were, I would have told the world you are black a long time ago. I've made Angela keep your secret in exchange for Brock never finding out about her involvement in any of this.

"Angela suspected you would tell Brock what happened between you and I. But, I know you didn't tell Brock because he never came to confront me. If he had, keeping your secret was to be leverage against any threat he might have made. But, he didn't find out. Now, I want to know just how far you will go to keep that night a secret from him."

"Brock knows what you made me do that night! If you had been in town when he found out, he would have made you pay for what you've done! When he finds out you're back, he's going to do a whole lot more than threaten you!"

Syrus chuckled harshly. "Brock has no power over me. Not if he wants to keep your secret safe."

"Brock doesn't care that I'm half black. He loves me! The fact I am half black doesn't matter!"

"Your mother would disagree. Marla would say it does matter and now more than ever. For you see, if people find out you have black blood running through your veins, your baby will be tainted. Think of her and her future. She will be shunned and forced to live as an outcast. Is that what you want?"

Lily whimpered.

"I can keep your secret. Think about it Lily. It could work. We could work out some arrangement that is beneficial to both of us."

"If you think I will ever be with you again you're crazy, you worthless worm! I love my husband and I will not betray him! You're trying to blackmail me because you know you can never be as good as Brock!"

208

Syrus' eyes lit with ire and he let out a furious growl. "I am just as good as Brock!"

Lily shook her head. "You can never measure up to Brock! Never!"

With a snarl, Syrus pushed Lily on to the bed and fell on top of her.

Lily opened her mouth to scream.

The scream died in her throat when she saw a shadow rise behind Syrus. In the next moment, a tenebrous roar reverberated in the room and in the next instant Syrus was plucked off of her.

Lily rose to a sitting position and when she saw Brock standing over her, she screamed, "Oh my God!"

Chapter Seventeen

Lily stared in astonishment as Brock lifted Syrus over his head and tossed him across the room.

Syrus let out a yelp of pain as he hit the wall on the other side of the room.

A picture fell to the ground with a loud clank.

"Brock!" Lily screamed in astonishment.

A second later, both Philip and Marla rushed into the room.

"What the hell!" Philip exclaimed.

Ignoring Philip and Marla's entrance, Brock took two long strides to Syrus. Reaching out, he clutched Syrus by the shoulders and threw him across the room once again.

Syrus hit the wall near the door and the baby began to wail.

Brock walked to Syrus and punched him across the face.

Syrus stumbled backward and out of the door of the bedroom and into the hallway.

Brock stalked out of the room after him.

Lily shot to her feet and ran after Brock.

When she stepped into the hallway, she saw Syrus reach out and swing his fist at Brock. Brock moved his head to avoid contact with Syrus' fist. He clutched Syrus' arms and gave him a brutal push.

Syrus stumbled backwards but managed to stay on his feet. Straightening himself he began to laugh. Taking a menacing stance, he clutched his hands into fists. "Is that all you got?" he taunted.

Lily screamed as she watched Syrus rush Brock and ram his shoulder into Brock's chest.

Brock stumbled back slightly. Recovering quickly, he belted Syrus in the stomach.

"Dear God!" Marla's voice sounded.

"What the hell is going on here?" Philip asked as Syrus stumbled backward and clutched his stomach.

Seemingly unaware of Philip's presence, Brock was upon Syrus again and released a potent punch.

Syrus' head snapped to the side. He lifted his hand and swung his arm. His fist made contact with Brock's face.

Lily and Marla screamed in unison.

Brock growled and threw Syrus against the railing of the staircase. In a flash, Brock was upon Syrus and holding him precariously over the railing, he tightened his hand around Syrus' throat.

"You goddamned bastard!" Brock hissed and tightened his grip.

Undistinguishable sounds erupted from Syrus' throat. His face turned red and his eyes bulged grotesquely.

"Brock! No!" Philip yelled in horror and clutched Brock's arms.

Several slaves appeared and joined Philip in trying to pull Brock away from Syrus.

With much effort, they managed to loosen Brock's grip.

Coughing violently, Syrus slid to the ground and wiped his bloodied nose.

"What the hell is wrong with you?" Philip demanded of Brock as he knelt beside Syrus.

"Syrus forced himself on Lily! That bastard's got to pay for what he's done!" Brock yelled.

Philip grabbed Brock's arms when he reached for Syrus. "What are you talking about?" he questioned. "Syrus? What the hell is he talking about?"

"He's mad!" Syrus coughed.

"What Brock says is true! Syrus blackmailed me into sleeping with him! He and Angela paid some men to dress as members of The Klan and attack me and Brock! They threaten to hang Brock unless they got money! They told me to get the money from Syrus. Syrus was there with the whip. But, we didn't know it was him because his face was covered. He beat Brock. I didn't know it was him and when I came back to the plantation to see him, he said he wouldn't give me the money unless I gave myself to him!"

Brock flailed against the grip of the slaves that held him.

"But that's impossible!" Philip protested.

"No! It's not impossible!" Lily insisted.

"I didn't do anything she didn't want," Syrus managed to wheeze after another cough.

"You liar!" Brock bellowed and once again bucked against the grasp of the slaves who held him back.

"It's because of Syrus I was kidnapped. He told me he and Angela sold me to that slaver. He said Angela came up with the plan to keep me away from Brock. Syrus told me he went along with Angela because I refused to be with him when he wanted it. He felt justified because he found out I'm half black. He wanted to punish me and he didn't want to share the inheritance of the plantation with me."

Philip looked at Syrus in disbelief. Slowly, his expression turned from one of confusion to disgust.

"Father! I can explain!" Syrus said and rose to his feet.

Philip shook his head. "This can't be."

"It is true!" Marla cut in. Stepping next to Lily, she glowered at Syrus.

Philip looked at Syrus as if he were seeing him for the first time.

Syrus shook his head. "No, Father! Don't listen to them! They are trying to turn you against me! You need me and I need you! This plantation is ours! You made me your son! I worked by your side to build it into what it is today!"

Philip shook his head in disbelief. "How could you do this, Syrus?" he questioned bewilderedly. "I loved you as my own son!"

"I love you too, Father. You and me we were a team. Remember when it was just the two of us. We use to work side-by-side in the fields. We were happy until *she* came between us." Syrus turned hate filled eyes on Marla. "Your black whore! How could you do it, Father? How could you let a nigger come between us and change things? I finally found a place that I could call my own. I finally found a father who wanted me. Then she came and brought her bastard whelp to masquerade as your legitimate heir. I was not going to let some black wench's baby take that from me. It's not like Lily can hope to be your legitimate heir because she's a no good black."

Philip laid a punch across Syrus' jaw.

Syrus raised his hand to his cheek in astonishment.

"You vicious demon!" Philip roared. "I take you into my home! I love you as a son! I open my heart to you! I give you everything! Everything I had was yours! You need but ask! And this is how you repay me? You disrespect me by defiling my daughter! You force yourself on her! You have her kidnapped!

"For three long years you watched me and her mother suffer not knowing where she'd gone or what happened to her! Now, on top of it all, when it all comes to light, you try to disrespect her mother! The woman I love! You disgrace yourself and defile this house! You are no longer my son! You will leave this house the way you came! With only the clothes on your back! Get your feet moving! Get out of this house! I never want to see your face again!" Philip shouted.

Syrus stared at Philip a moment as he wiped blood from his lip. Suddenly, he leaned his head back and began to laugh. When he composed himself, he bit out, "You can't banish me. You're stuck with me, Father. You banish me and I will tell the whole world Lily is black. You don't want that to happen. Do you Father?" Syrus turned a spiteful gaze on Marla. "Tell Father he doesn't want that to happened, Marla."

When Marla remained silent, Syrus turned to look at Brock. "And you. There's nothing you can do to stop me. If you try, I will tell everyone you're married to a nigger and you can watch your place and your daughter's position in this town disappear. So you see? Do you all see? There is nothing you can do to threaten me. Nothing you can do about what happened between me and Lily and nothing you can do to stop it from happening again."

Upon hearing Syrus' words, Brock let out a rancorous roar and broke free of the slaves' clasp. Reaching out, he yanked the whip from Syrus' belt. With a curse, he reared back then thrust the whip forward and cracked it.

Instantly, the whip uncoiled and its fangs reached out and lacerated Syrus' face.

Syrus let out a surprised yelp.

A twist of his wrist and Brock sent the whip sailing toward Syrus again.

This time, the whip landed across Syrus' chest. Red stains materialized through the tears on the front of his white shirt. Syrus staggered back against the on slot of another blow from the whip.

As if marking his prey, Brock advanced on Syrus releasing another punishing blow.

Syrus stumbled back and raised his arms across his face. He let out an agonized scream when the whip sliced into his arms. The whip scrapped across his chest bringing an assault of fire. He stumbled backward as his shirt ripped like paper under the piercing slashes of the rawhide.

Syrus stepped back toward the landing at the top of the stairs. His foot slipped off of the top step. His arms flailed about for a second as he attempted to retain his balance. But, unable to manage it, he fell backward.

A scream left his lips as he tumbled down the massive stairs. Several moments later, he landed head first at the bottom of the staircase.

Lily screamed and buried her face in her mother's neck.

The slaves who had once been holding Brock ran down the stairs.

Brock and Philip followed the slaves to where Syrus lay.

Philip knelt beside Syrus and carefully rolled him over.

Shallow gasps left Syrus' lips. Blood oozed from his mouth. He opened his eyes and stared at Philip through glassy eyes. "Father, don't let them do this. Don't let them come between us," he whispered.

"Peter! Cornelius! Get him to a doctor! Quick!" Philip instructed the slaves.

The slaves grunted and quickly bent to do Philip's bidding. They picked up Syrus' limp body and carried it out of the house.

Philip looked at Brock. Then, he lifted his eyes to look at Marla and Lily who stood at the top of the stairs.

"Come down here!" he called to the women.

Marla and Lily rushed down the stairs.

Marla ran to Philip and Philip wrapped his arms around her.

"If he gets better, he gonna tell everyone the truth 'bout Lily," Marla fretted.

Philip looked at Marla. "Let him tell. It's about time the truth came out."

Philip reached out his free arm to Lily.

Lily walked into her father's embrace.

"My girls. I love you both." Philip raised his eyes to the female slave who appeared in the doorway.

"Come here, girl!" he called to the slave.

The girl, wide-eyed, ran to Philip and came to a stop in front of the small group.

"Everyone in this house has had something to hide. But, starting tonight, there will be no more secrets in this house. We will have nothing to hide. Girl, go to the slave quarters and start spreading the word. Tell everyone you can that Lily is my daughter and Marla Jane is her mother."

"Philip!" Marla screeched.

Philip silenced her with a tender squeeze. "I love you and I'm tired of hiding it. I have a beautiful daughter with you and I'm not ashamed about that fact. Come what may, we will face all of our problems together. You got all that girl?"

"Yes Massa," the slave girl responded before scurrying from the foyer.

The baby's strong wails sounded loudly in the now silent house.

"The baby!" Lily exclaimed and raced up the stairs followed closely by Brock.

The baby's cries grew louder as Brock and Lily neared the room.

Lily stepped into the room then paused at the door allowing Brock to rush past her and walk to the crib. Once he neared the crib, he paused then looked inside.

Brock looked at the baby lying amongst white sheets. The soft glow of the moonlight caressed the baby girl's golden blonde hair, sun-kissed skin and amber colored eyes.

Brock smiled.

As if drawn by an unseen force, he placed his finger against the baby's hand. Instinctively, the baby girl wrapped her tiny hand around his, stopped crying and cooed.

"She's beautiful," Brock whispered as a tear rolled from his eye.

Lily came to a stand beside her husband. "She's your baby, Brock," she said softly.

"Oh, Lily." Brock turned to her and wrapped his arms around her.

"Please tell me you forgive me and we can be a family now."

"Lily, I love you so much. There is nothing to forgive. We will be a family. We will start over and it will be better than it ever was before."

Tears stung Lily's eyes. "I'm so glad to hear you say that."

Brock leaned down and kissed her lips.

"Brock and Lily. You finally found your way back to each other," Philip's voice sounded.

Brock and Lily turned to see Philip and Marla, arms wrapped around each other, standing in the room smiling.

Philip's smile widened. "I want the two of you to know, I will take care of Angela Allen. I will make sure you never have to worry about her again."

Brock smiled at Lily.

"By the way Brock, we never talked about the money you spent to rescue my daughter. I say it's time we do so," Philip stated.

"What do you mean?" Brock asked.

"I heard the money you spent to purchase Lily was your life's savings."

"It was. But—"

"No buts. You must be repaid. Raising tobacco takes a toll on the land. A time will come when the land will be worn and we will have to give it a rest. Before that happens, I think it's best to diversify. I've been thinking about this since you came back to town. Your ranch is growing by the week. It's getting to be too much work for one person to manage. You know that.

"If you were to move your ranch here, you'd have plenty of space. After all, there's plenty of room here at the plantation."

"Move the ranch here?"

"Sure. I'd like to start raising horses here at Paradise Plantation. I'd need a partner who knows all there is to know about horses. There's only one person I know who can fit that bill and it's you, Brock. Actually, I was hoping you'd decide to be more than a partner to me."

"What do you mean?" Brock questioned.

"Well, I've always wanted a son but God didn't bless me with a son of my own. And, since Syrus is no longer my son... I was hoping you wouldn't mind... I was wondering if maybe you'd consider being my son."

"I'd like that," Brock replied.

"Wonderful! Then if that's settled there's only one more issue to discuss," Philip rubbed his chin. "I was also wondering... I'd like to know if you and Lily would consider moving here to Paradise. After all, you'll be spending a lot of time working here. If you lived here you wouldn't have far to travel home after a hard days work."

"Philip! You can't be serious!" Brock exclaimed.

"Oh but I am. We will build up Paradise so that one day you and Lily can take the reins. In the meantime, this huge house has rooms that will be empty unless they are filled with laughter from my granddaughter."

"And the other grandchildren you two have to give us," Marla cut in with a smile.

Brock looked at Lily.

"What do you think? Should we move to Paradise?"

At the same moment, the baby gurgled happily.

Lily and Brock turned to look in the crib.

Marla and Philip came to stand beside the crib as well.

The baby gurgled again and contentedly waved her hands in the air.

"Looks like she thinks moving here is a good idea!" Marla exclaimed and looked at Lily.

Lily smiled and looked at Brock who looked at Philip. Suddenly, they all broke out into cheerful laughter.

Chapter Eighteen

Later that night, as Lily lay in her old bed next to Brock, she smiled as she nestled her head against his arm.

"Are you awake?" Brock asked softly.

"Yes," she answered and opened her eyes to look at him.

Brock looked lovingly at her then said, "I want you to know I love you. I never stopped loving you and I'm glad you are back in my arms. I was laying here thinking about the time we were together before you left. The swims we used to take and our wedding day. The years without you were long and painful. I am so glad we found our way back to each other."

"It hasn't been easy but we found our way back to each other. Our love did overcome all of the obstacles in our path. Despite it all, we're still together. That's all that matters." Lily reached out and gently ran her fingers through Brock's hair.

He smiled.

"Why are you looking at me that way?" she asked.

"I want you to know, you healed my prejudice heart. I want you to know, I don't care what color you are or who your mother is. I don't care what people might say or what they might think. I want you to know I will always love you…and our daughter," Brock promised.

Lily reached out and rubbed his cheek.

"Tell me you forgive me for acting like a fool. I tried to prove I had moved on and prove I could live without you. But, the facts are, my life means nothing without you as part of it," Brock said.

"Brock you don't have to—"

"I have to say this. I acted horribly and I'm truly sorry. I love you. I never stopped loving you. I should have acknowledged my true feelings the moment you walked down off that auction block."

"Brock, it wasn't your fault. I should have trusted your love for me and never left you all those years ago. I shouldn't have hid any secrets. I should have told you what Syrus made me do." Tears began to roll down Lily's face.

Brock gathered her into his arms as she began to sob.

"Sweetheart, it's all right. None of that matters now. The only thing that matters is somehow we've managed to stay together. Oh Lily, I love you. I always have and I always will. More than any other woman on the face of the earth. I want to spend the rest of my life loving you. I want to be your husband no matter what life throws our way."

"Oh, Brock. We will be so happy."

"We're going to start over and this time it will truly be a new start. Tomorrow we'll return to the cabin and pack our things. Then, we'll move in here."

"All right, my love. I will trust you and your love for me. Now and always," Lily whispered.

"That's all I've ever wanted to hear," Brock said as he wiped the tears from her eyes.

The baby cooed from her place by the bed.

Brock picked up the baby and kissed her cheeks before placing her in Lily's arms. Settling next to Lily, he wrapped his arms securely around her and kissed her forehead.

Lily snuggled against Brock's chest and smiled as she gazed at their child. Happily, she thought about the fact her dreams had come true. After everything that happened, she was back home and back in Brock's arms. Just as she wanted things were now as they had been. No, she told herself, things were better than they had been. Things were better than they had been because not only was she back in Brock's arms, she was also the mother of his child.

Yes. Things were just as she wanted them to be. Everything would work out just fine. This time, no matter what obstacles the future brought them, they would face their problems together...as a family...without something to hide.

§ § §

About the Author

Sheniqua Waters is an author who writes unforgettable historical romance novels which transport readers to a spectacular time in the past. Books by Sheniqua Waters have all of the elements needed to make a great romance. From the dazzling character conflicts to the ravishing love scenes, you will love all of this writer's intriguing books.

Find more at the author's website
www.TheWorldsBestBook.com

More Books To Read

Slave Girl in the Harem by Sheniqua Waters is the story of an Egyptian girl, Laila, who is kidnapped and sold into a Turkish harem. When given the chance to return home, will Laila do so? Or does going back to relive the past mean there is no hope for the future?

Seduced by the Pharaoh by Sheniqua Waters is the story of Latifa, the courageous daughter of the King of the Nubians, who takes a vow of chastity to become a fierce female warrior. Latifa swears vengeance upon the handsome Pharaoh of Egypt who she believes killed her father and destroyed her village. When the two sworn enemies encounter each other, will love seize their hearts? Or will Latifa refuse to be seduced by the Pharaoh?